THE
DORDOGNE
DECEPTION

Sherry Joyce

To Barbara
"True love is
always worth
the Risk"

Sherry Joyce

iUniverse LLC
Bloomington

THE DORDOGNE DECEPTION

iUniverse books may be ordered through booksellers or by contacting:

iUniverse
1663 Liberty Drive
Bloomington, IN 47403
www.iuniverse.com
1-800-Authors (1-800-288-4677)

ISBN: 978-1-4759-8777-5 (sc)
ISBN: 978-1-4759-8779-9 (hc)
ISBN: 978-1-4759-8778-2 (e)

Library of Congress Control Number: 2013907554

Printed in the United States of America.

iUniverse rev. date: 7/8/2013

To Jim, my husband of nearly fifty years—
destined at birth for a love of a lifetime.

ACKNOWLEDGMENTS

Eight years in the making, following a fantastic once-in-a-lifetime trip to the Dordogne, a Romantic Suspense novel was born. Not only do I thank my husband Jim for that trip, but for his unending support of all of my creative endeavors. You are my best friend and soul mate.

Lisa Dane, I could not have asked for a more dedicated editor and film producer who willingly and enthusiastically collaborated with me on this novel, helping me grow as an author and sharing my voice with Francophile pleasure. I adore you! Thank you for everything you have done. The journey just begins.

Cindy Sample, you have been the best mentor and successful author who found the time despite your hectic schedule to return an email, have a glass of wine and support my launch of yet a new career. You are a fantastic inspiration.

Joey Cattone, artist extraordinaire, for all her help in designing an artistic cover that perfectly matched the vision in my head and to her equally amazing husband, Dan for creating my website with exceptional technical skills. I am so grateful for your friendship and support.

To Althea, Catherine, Carla, Carol, Dianne, Ethlyn, Evelyn, Lesleigh, Jeannie, Georgia, Lolly, Debbie, Tiffany, Maureen, Kathryn, Linda,

Rick, Elizabeth, Karen, Mikki, Kate, Ginni, Rhonda, Gina, Ginger, Jody, Joey, Jeannie, Jennifer, Jessica, Joyce, Mary Ann, Mary, Paula, Lori, Dodi, Dolores, Sandy, Mary Ethel, Roger, Dan, Nancy, Nora and the entire cheering section of Serrano book club, I appreciate your encouragement and support. Also, I am indebted to an unspoken English professor who challenged me to write, never knowing the enormous influence he had on my life.

Last, but not least, I thank my family and friends. You are everything to me. Thank you for giving me the courage and inspiration to keep writing.

Former Silicon Valley Vice President of Human Resources, author Sherry Joyce enjoyed years of creative and technical writing. Owner of SJ Designs Interiors, and a member of Romance Writers of America and Sisters in Crime, she lives with her husband and their two West Highland terriers in El Dorado Hills, California.

PROLOGUE

Windermere, England 2006

The massive ornate wrought-iron gates opened with a dull grinding sound. He sat in the car, engine idling, until both gates fully flanked each side of the entrance to the estate. Then, with a gentle nudge, he shifted gears. Although the black canvas convertible top was up, he was forced to make peace with the inadequate heater, his breath fogging the cold windshield. He cranked the window down a few inches and braced for the sting of frosty air. Squinting, he crept along without headlights, wiping the inside of the windshield with the back of his right hand to keep his visibility clear.

Deep indigo painted the sky, now nearing dusk, creating a faint crimson hue on the horizon. Relying on the intermittent glow of the waxing moon shining through drifting clouds, he could barely discern the driveway beneath the shadowy cathedral canopy of entwined towering branches of massive sycamore trees on each side of the road. As he grasped the steering wheel of his 1931 *Invicta*, his hands shook. The rare vintage car was one of very few in the world, and he was not about to dent it, even for her.

His controlled, rapid breathing was the only other sound he could hear, as gravel crunched under the tires. He could see the amber glow from the light in her bedroom in the corner turret window of the enormous castle. The light was a signal they had agreed upon. Driving past the porte-cochère, he parked adjacent to the side of the building and shut off the engine. Feeling an adrenaline rush pulsing through his temples, he pulled his leather jacket collar up around his neck and walked to the side entrance door Diana had left ajar after disabling the security alarm system. He met her in the giant vestibule, motioning her not to speak, by putting his index finger to his lips. He crept up the carpeted back staircase to the second story...and waited.

Diana stood in the vestibule at the bottom of stone stairwell, and in her loudest, most contrived and terrifyingly shrill voice, shouted to her husband, *"Raleigh! Help! Help me!"*

Startled, Raleigh backed away from his writing desk, dropping his pen on his memoirs. Glancing toward the dimly lit doorway of his second floor bedroom, he muttered under his breath, "Why is she yelling at me? She knows better than to disturb me when I'm writing."

"Raleigh!" she called out in a loud piercing scream.

He yelled to her, *"Diana, what's wrong?"* Dead silence.

Concerned and annoyed when she did not respond, Raleigh rolled out of his room. The only sound was the excruciating squeaking of the old wheelchair, like a rusty door hinge persistently swinging back and forth. Despite his pain, he deliberately moved his hands on each wheel, propelling the chair forward until he reached the top of the staircase. His voice cracking, he called to her again in the dark hallway, *"Diana?"* Pin-dropping silence.

Raleigh could not see Diana from his vantage point at the top of the staircase. Questions raced through his mind. Why didn't she answer? Had she fallen? Panic paralyzed him as he knew he could not navigate the stairs and it would take him too long to get to the elevator lift at the far end of the hallway. Raleigh shifted his weight forward in an attempt to stand up, but it was useless. A sudden thud cracked the back of his skull. The wheelchair cascaded down the wide stone treads, careened into the walls hurling him into the balustrades, splattering blood and cracking bones, as he tumbled down. The wheelchair flipped, throwing him onto the stone floor, landing in a contorted position, head twisted over his shoulder, eyes wide open, blood drooling out of his mouth. Sir Raleigh Aubrey lay pitifully broken and very, very dead, as planned.

The assailant carefully wiped the granite object in the palm of his leather glove and then replaced it on the console. He cautiously came down the stairs, careful not to step in any of the blood splatters.

Diana stood, her body shaking with her hands over her mouth, aghast at the distorted body, wishing his demise had not been so gruesome. She felt a sense of remorse, but mostly relief it was over. "Are you sure he is dead?"

"Yes, he is dead. I made sure the base of his skull fractured from the blow, a severe blunt force trauma, long before the stone staircase broke most of his bones. With advanced osteoporosis, his brittle bones would have shattered instantaneously. If you stopped giving him his medication several days ago as I'd told you to do, he would have no chance of surviving this fall."

"Yes, of course. I did everything we discussed. Should I call the police now?" she asked, nervously fidgeting with the buttons on her blouse.

"No don't. That could imply a crime. You want this to be a believable accident."

"Who do you want me to call? I'm so nervous, I've forgotten."

"Diana, as soon as I leave, contact the Windermere medical emergency service. Tell them there has been terrible accident but don't tell them he is dead. Instead, advise them your husband fell down the stairs and does not seem to be breathing. Don't say anything more. Ask for immediate medical help and sound hysterical. Can you do that?"

"Yes, but then what do I do when they arrive and discover his body?"

"After checking his pulse, they will take him to the hospital to wait for the coroner. If they want to do an autopsy, agree to it, but don't bring it up yourself. When they question you, reiterate the same story about how he must have fallen. Use your skills and act the role of the disconsolate wife. It should go exactly as we planned. Don't worry," he said, placing a comforting hand on her shoulder. He noticed her skin beginning to pale.

In a barely audible whisper, Diana uttered, "I...don't feel well." Her eyes rolled back, knees buckling as he reached forward to catch her limp body, sending both of them crashing to the stone floor.

Momentarily shaken, he did not plan on her fainting and having her clammy, limp body sprawled across his legs like a sack of wet laundry. He could hardly leave her on the floor, but he had to get out of there. Throwing his head back in frustration, he clenched his fists, looking for an answer. His slap across her face brought her back to consciousness.

"What happened?" she murmured, rubbing her hand across her reddened cheek.

"You fainted. Try to sit up," he glowered at her, wishing he had left minutes ago.

Diana sat up and, catching a glance at her dead husband's ghastly body, let out a stifled gasp. Standing up, he extended his arm to help her back on her feet. The rosy color returned to her face.

"Diana, you will be fine," he said, kissing her lightly on the forehead. "I have to leave.

Don't forget to close the entrance gates after I'm gone, lock the front door and then turn the security alarm back on. There is no evidence of an intruder or a forced entry. Everything will be fine. I'll talk to you tomorrow."

He rushed to the *Invicta*, settled in, shuddering from the cold, and started the engine. The crime, which should have taken only a few minutes, had taken much longer. The delay rattled his calculated composure and his pulse raced.

"Honestly," he muttered under his breath, "women…who else would dare faint during a murder?"

Flipping the wiper switch on so he could see through the mist that had accumulated on the windshield, the car crept along without lights down the long, winding gravel road. Despite his anxiety, he was confident he had orchestrated a flawless crime. It would look like a terrible accident where an old man had lost control of his wheelchair, falling to his tragic death. A death that would greatly benefit him for a long, long time. This was not the first crime he had committed. Money was an addictive, powerful motive and murder was a convenient way of getting it without having to work for a living.

As he drove out of the entrance gate, he did not notice the elderly gardener in a dark gray cap and wool coat, standing behind the tall laurel hedges, watching the car depart. The gardener wondered why someone would be driving without headlights in the dark and leaving the grounds at such a late hour.

The next evening, Diana waited for him to call. He didn't. She paced the floor of her bedroom, her stomach in knots, wondering what had happened. She had so much to tell him. He said he'd call by 7:00 p.m. It was already past 8:00. Why didn't he call her? The strident ring startled her.

"Hello?"

"It's me," he said.

With an enormous sigh of relief she blurted, "I was afraid you weren't going to call. I've been a nervous wreck!"

"I'm sorry," he pleaded. "There was a five-car accident on the toll bridge and traffic was tied up for hours. This is the first chance I've had to call you. I had to buy a prepaid phone so this call could not be traced. So, what happened last night?"

"Well, as you said, the emergency medical team arrived shortly after you left. I was sobbing hysterically when I opened the entrance door. Once they saw Raleigh on the floor, they rushed over to him immediately, checking for a pulse. I could see one EMT shaking his head to the other not to bother with the oxygen. It all happened so fast. They put him on a gurney and I could not see what they were doing. One EMT was making a phone call, possibly to the coroner, and another asked me what had happened. I explained I had come downstairs for glass of milk and the next thing I heard was a horrible crashing sound. By the time I arrived in the vestibule from the kitchen, Raleigh was on the floor, contorted, with blood dripping. They took one look at the crushed wheelchair and spattered blood along the walls, and said he must have gotten too close to the edge of the stairs and lost control. One EMT said, 'Maybe he had a stroke'."

"Good," he said. "Did they believe you?"

"Yes, I'm sure I was completely believable. I put on quite a show. With the stress of the commotion, I had no trouble crying as they hauled him away in the ambulance. The coroner called today to express sympathy for Raleigh's death. The body was taken to the funeral home

I selected. I told them under the circumstances, it should be a closed casket, and they agreed, of course."

He cleared his throat to expel the doubt troubling him before he could call her. "What about the servants?"

"As we previously discussed, I sent them home today. They were in shock, of course, deeply upset and didn't want to work anyway. I told them the funeral would be later this week and I had a lot of people to contact."

"You did really well," he said, rubbing the tension out of his neck with his free hand. "As I said last night, this was a perfect crime."

"I hope so," Diana said, while kicking off her shoes and rubbing her toes in the carpet. Taking a deep breath, she controlled the tone of her voice, dropping the pitch to finalize a business transaction. "Can we please go over the details one more time?"

"Of course." He reminded himself to be gracious. Getting upset with her now might cause her to rescind her agreement to pay him.

"After the funeral, how long do you want me to stay at Brightingham?"

"Wait at least three months before you contact real estate brokers about selling the castle. A property of this size and value will take considerable time to sell. Stay in Windermere until Brightingham is sold and the entire estate is fully settled. There could be nasty allegations that you were after his money—ugly tabloid gossip. Just be prepared. People may speculate about how he died, but they won't be able to prove anything."

"You'd better be right. I don't intend to spend the rest of my life in prison. One thing I need to discuss. I'm worried about Raleigh's attorney."

He heard a knock on the door, which jolted him to the bone.

"Wait," he muffled his voice with a cupped hand over the phone, "There's someone at the door." "Yes, who is it?"

A timid female voice cheerily offered, "Turndown, sir?"

In a contrived, confident tone he said, "No thank you." Expelling a huge sigh of relief, his shoulders began to relax. For a brief moment he half expected the police to be on the other side of the door. He never felt safe until he was out of the country.

"Sorry to keep you on hold. Damn turndown service." He flipped his hair off his forehead, concentrating. "To answer your question, Raleigh's attorney knows you are the sole inheritor of his estate. He might contact the police and they may want to investigate this accident and question you thoroughly. Repeat the story over and over, not adding any new details. Then, go about your normal day-to-day routine. Look distraught around the servants and act the part of the grieving widow. Keep the servants working until the estate is sold."

"This seemed easier when we talked about it. When do you want the money?" Diana asked in a frustrated tone, biting the inside of her mouth.

"After the estate is sold, wire five million pounds to this account in Switzerland. Keep the account number secure. Do not lose it or copy it. After the funds are deposited, I will get in touch with you through a third party courier in London and will arrange for you to live in my home in Switzerland where I'll continue to pay the expenses," he said, pausing to see if she would object. She didn't. "You'll get a stipend to live on for one year and you must pay cash for everything so no one can trace you. I want it to appear that you have simply vanished after you leave England and, as promised, I will provide you with a new identity. When the opportunity arises, I will contact you in Montreux and send for you."

Wiping her clammy hands on her skirt, she stiffened. "Fine, but I'm still very nervous about someone suspecting this was a planned murder."

"Let them speculate, Diana. No one knows we have been seeing each other. We have not been together in public. Even if the police think you pushed him down the stairs, they won't be able to prove it. There were no servants in the house because they had already left. You alone are the only witness to a terrible accident. Trust me; we will get away with this."

"I'm just worried something will go wrong. Maybe someone saw us on the ship?"

"Diana, please stop fretting. No one saw us together."

"I hope you're right," she swallowed and took a deep breath, tension lifting from her chest. "Talking about killing him and actually doing it has made me question everything and whether we will get away with it. I'm the one who would look guilty. What if we missed something?"

As he listened to the panic in her voice, he sighed to himself knowing he'd heard this story before. The crime is committed. The wife feels guilty. She has second thoughts about the money. The risk he wouldn't be paid becomes real. It was necessary now to become aggressive.

"Diana now is not the time for recriminations. Calm down. This is what you wanted. You begged me. I seized the opportunity and the plan was put into place. I did what you asked and you owe me every penny of the five million pounds, as we agreed. Arrange with your broker to get whatever you need to pay the taxes and real estate commission. Since Brightingham was his primary residence, you should not have to pay an inheritance tax, but consult with Raleigh's attorney."

Wiping her forehead, Diana tried to regain her composure. "I know he planned to leave most of his business holdings to others and Raleigh told me he intended to give a great deal of his personal wealth to several charities," Diana pointed out. With her green eyes ablaze, feeling as if an invisible rope had been placed around her neck, coiled like a cobra constricting her breathing, she blurted out in a raspy tone, "I feel considerable regret now about all the money I'm giving up!"

"Yes, Diana, it's a very high price to pay to get out of a marriage. Not having this entire fortune for the rest of your life is what you sacrificed. But some day I will make you a wealthy woman. Remember dear, I am very, very good at this."

She tugged at her earring trying to unfasten the clasp. The clock ticked loudly on her night table, as she realized there was no way out of this.

"I'm exhausted. I have to get some sleep. When Brightingham is sold, I'll contact the courier. You'll get your money. It's not like I have any other choice."

"No you don't," he said firmly with calm, icy certainty.

He hung up, put his arm behind his head on the pillow to get comfortable, and stared absently at the nondescript hotel's watercolor painting on the opposite wall. For a brief moment he permitted himself the memory of the night on the cruise. Diana had been insatiable, her porcelain skin contrasting with her cool green eyes, chestnut hair and her incredible, voluptuous figure. In his mind, he could still imagine how her skin felt to his touch. He knew it would take time, but he would feel her skin and breathe in her essence again.

CHAPTER 1

San Francisco 2006

For Cherise Eden, the idea of running a bed and breakfast chateau in the Dordogne, Perigord region of Southwestern France, was much more than a whimsical fantasy resulting from a recent large divorce settlement. It was a necessary emotional escape from San Francisco. What had been their shared apartment now felt empty and held too many painful memories. It was time to find new surroundings. The apartment was now filled with a pervasive sadness, a deafening silence. Cherise found it depressing to see her ex-husband frequenting many of the same restaurants and bars where she went with friends. She tried not to run into Andrew when he was in the city, but when she did, it re-opened a wound that would not heal.

She heard the keys rattle in the door lock and knew it wasn't Andy, but their housekeeper, Julia. Cherise dreaded seeing anyone and didn't make an attempt to get off the sofa.

"Oh Mrs. Eden, I'm so sorry. I didn't know you were home. Shall I come back at a later time?"

"It's okay, Julia. The place is a mess."

Julia tried to put on a positive face but taking one look at Cherise in her flannel pajamas, she just shook her head from side to side.

"Girl, you gotta get a grip. You can't be sittin' around and mopin' like this, week after week," she said, while putting down her handbag on the dining room table. "Men cheat. Men leave. You're gonna survive. It just takes time."

"You're right, Julia. Men are jerks," (not the word she wanted to utter, knowing a distasteful expletive would have been far more satisfying). "I'm doing the best I can."

Julia tightened the ties on her floral apron with a concerned look on her face. "Can I fix you somethin' to eat? I can't bear to see you wastin' away like this." Reluctantly, Cherise nodded her head in agreement. "You think I like spending my days sitting cross-legged on *this* sofa— what had been *our* sofa? I hate the person I've become. I used to be strong, confident, capable."

"You haven't lost those things," Julia offered, trying her best to be supportive, picking up the vase of dead yellow tulips from the coffee table.

"I know," Cherise said, "but I feel as wilted as those tulips. It's as if someone vacuumed all the energy out of my body. I've been sitting here trying to figure out how this happened to me." She reached for a box of tissues and began dabbing one lightly against her red-rimmed, swollen eyes. Her blotched stuffy nose hurt as if she had a bad head cold, and her hair was uncombed, looking like a matted rat in a windstorm.

Julia hung on to the edge of the sofa, bending her plump frame forward, reaching for the large plastic wastebasket filled to the brim with wet tissues. It was also crammed with empty bags of potato chips and numerous week-old, hastily devoured chocolate ice cream cartons that had tumbled out of the wastebasket, littering the floor.

"You know," she said, "I think it's this place that's makin' you feel worse. Look at it. There ain't no sunshine comin' in most of the time."

Cherise realized Julia was right. The deep gray walls in the apartment felt dreary, as if she were engulfed in a box without windows. What she could see through the glass, was a depressing tendril of fog, rolling in across Alcatraz.

"I'm cold," she said, as she uncrossed her legs and pulled the cream cashmere chenille throw tightly around her shoulders.

Julia studied her for a moment, feeling she had to say something. "Here's what I think Mrs. Eden. I want you to get out. Take a drive down the peninsula to Menlo Park where it's sunny. Get some decent food like salad fixin's and fruit. You gotta stop eatin' this junk." Julia pointed at an empty bag of Cheetos peeking out from under the sofa. "And heaven knows how old these rat-bait empty pizza boxes are, strewn across the dining room table!"

Cherise prepared to defend herself, crossing her arms and curling the side of her mouth into an unattractive smirk.

"Ordering take-out food is such a blessing. I don't have to fix my hair or put on make-up. What's the worst that could happen to me?"

"Honey, if I met you at the door lookin' like you do, I'd be terrified. It ain't right to scare some poor delivery boy into thinkin' you're some crazy lady." Julia meant to make Cherise laugh, but instead she burst into tears. "Honey, you gotta stop wallowin'. You're gonna meet another nice man someday," Julia offered.

"Oh God, no! I don't want to meet another man. I just want the life I had." Cherise sniffled, wiping her irritated red nose.

"Well, girl, you're gonna have to create a new life for yourself. You know, when my husband left me with five kids to raise…"

As Julia's voice trailed off into the kitchen, Cherise tuned out the rest of Julia's words and slipped deep inside the recesses of her mind to the safety of a familiar depressed place—a beckoning abyss pulling her further down, down.

At night when she couldn't sleep, she found herself ruminating over details. Twenty years of marriage shattered. It was unthinkable he would divorce her. Andy was the one who wanted to leave. No warning. No discussion. A simple, "I want a divorce," he had said, one traumatic night, obvious anguish written all over his face. His voice still echoed, forlorn and miserable. The fact his new interest was a young, twenty-something stewardess trained to cater to passengers' needs, made it much worse. Such a cliché, the young flight attendant serving the pilot on their many shared trips together.

Cherise remembered the confrontational conversation. "Do you love her?" "I don't know," Andy had said. "I don't know what I feel anymore," he'd mumbled sheepishly staring at the carpet. She'd cringed and demanded, "Do you still love me?"

He'd paused too long and could not find the words. Exasperated,

Cherise had walked out of the room and slammed the door. She'd yelled through the door, "Dammit Andy! It's simple. You either love me or you don't." He had not answered.

Looking back on it now, she realized the situation wasn't simple. He said it wasn't that he didn't love her. He just did not feel he had a place in her hectic executive life, or so he told her. She considered at the time it was a mid-life crisis for Andy, but it no longer mattered what it was. He wanted to move on without her, so she had to let him go.

"Do you want cheese on your hamburger?" Julia yelled from the kitchen.

"Yes, that'll be fine. Thanks." Cherise pulled the blanket around her shoulders tighter, trying to erase her worst memory at the courthouse, immediately after the divorce was settled. She had sobbed as Andy left with his attorney. The room had begun to tilt, she'd felt blood draining from her face, her knees wobbling. All she could do was cling to her attorney's arm while the world crumbled around her.

She remembered Andy had turned briefly toward her as he left the hallway at the courthouse seeing her standing, crestfallen, on the arm of her attorney. Cherise had wished he would walk over to comfort her, but as Andy started to move in her direction, his attorney grabbed his arm, shaking his head, telling him "No." From the look on his face as he bit his lip, it appeared perhaps Andy dreaded seeing her in so much pain. He had told her the night before he would cease to exist if he remained in the marriage. They had come to an impasse. She'd refused to quit her high-profile job, and he refused to stop flying. It seemed pointless to keep fighting and there was no way to resolve their irreconcilable differences.

"Almost finished," Julia bellowed. "Patties were frozen in the freezer. It will take a little while to cook 'em. Do you want them medium or well-done?"

"Umm...whatever," Cherise said, while squeezing her nostrils together. The smell of freshly fried hamburger made her stomach flip. She sighed and prayed if she could swallow the hamburger, she wouldn't hurl the contents up as quickly as they went down. "I'm makin' some tea," Julia said.

"Make mine herbal," Cherise yelled, straining her voice to reach the kitchen.

Cherise scratched her head in disbelief. Now many months after the divorce, she was annoyed she was still not herself. She hated stumbling through life, distracted and disoriented. Unable to read or watch TV, she found it impossible to concentrate. Sitting on the sofa staring out the window had become her new normal.

Waves of pain and tears overcame her at the most inopportune times—in the grocery store, at church and driving to her job. Cherise cried so often on the way to work, she started carrying an extra packet of eyeliner, mascara and cucumber soaked pads to blot her puffy eyes.

Julia jolted her back to the present, handing Cherise a cup of steaming hot tea with honey and a juicy hamburger on a toasted bun, slathered with butter and mayonnaise.

"Here, eat this. You'll feel better."

"Thanks," Cherise said, taking a cautious sip of herbal tea. "I feel like I'm half dead," she groaned, clutching her stomach and stifling a gag from the smell of the greasy fried meat.

Julia put her hand on her shoulder to offer comfort. "You're sufferin' from grief. That's all. It's normal. It's gonna take time."

"Grief," Cherise grimaced, taking a small bite, "is a crappy unwelcome guest."

"I know," Julia mulled, "Grief from a divorce is not so different than an actual death. Your divorce was the death of a relationship. It's gonna' hurt because you loved him and you were together a long time."

"You know Julia, if Andy had died, I would not have to think about what he is doing now with this new woman. I wouldn't have to avoid going to cafes where I might run into him or worse—both of them."

Julia nodded, listening patiently while lifting the second half of the hamburger bun to Cherise's face. "Eat a few bites. Please eat more. You'll feel better."

Cherise complied, like the dutiful child she had become at the moment. Julia patted her on the knee, and then abruptly stood up with her head tilted in exasperation, her arm resting on her hip. "You ain't got no ma or pa or siblin's, which is a shame, so I'm doin' my best to be your momma and your friend right now. You're gonna' pick yourself up and dust yourself off," Julia continued, "I want to see you gettin' in the car and takin' yourself to work tomorrow with a new attitude. No more sitting around wrung out like a wet mop. You deserve better than you got with Mr. Andy, but life ain't gonna' fix itself. You gotta be the one to fix the rest of your life. Be strong and good things will happen to you. I just know it. Promise me you'll try?"

Cherise hugged Julia and mumbled a weak "I'll try, I promise. I ate the hamburger, didn't I?"

Julia gave her a hearty laugh. "Yes you did, uh huh, yes you sure did." Julia finished cleaning and after she left, for the first time in weeks, Cherise easily drifted off to sleep.

As she drove to work the next day, Cherise didn't cry. She sat in her office, recognizing she needed to contend with the realities of her workplace. Even as she tried to manage her job responsibilities, Cherise realized she could no longer focus and sustain a high-profile executive level Silicon Valley marketing job. Although her boss was somewhat understanding about her divorce, his focus on the bottom line motivated his fear and concern for his own position, making him less tolerant of her inadequate performance.

Cherise muttered to herself, "I wonder if I should resign. I'm making absent-minded, costly mistakes and I'm sure I am going to get fired sooner or later." Human Resources had emphasized that business had no place for a grieving employee beyond what was considered normal, despite the fact there was no 'normal' for getting through grief. If someone close died, the employee received only three days off to attend the funeral and heaven forbid it was necessary to fly to some other location. The company attitude was, *Mend your emotions with a stiff upper lip and be ready for work on the fourth day.*

"What's normal about that?" Cherise asked herself. "Andy left me. Am I supposed to be back to normal in three days?" Right now, *normal* meant floundering at work. "I'm doing everything I can to stay on schedule," she had told a co-worker, with a look in her eyes confirming the terror she was feeling.

When Cherise missed a major critical deadline for launching the company's new product line, her supervisor's patience wore thin as rice paper. Brad Jenkins, her boss, walked into her office, closed the door, and sat in a chair in front of her desk, leaning toward her with a stern look.

"Cherise, it's been months now and I'm getting a lot of pressure from the Board about your performance," he spoke unflinchingly. Silver flecks in his hair matched his steely eyes, now narrowed into slits.

"I know," she stammered, avoiding the drama of begging him for a little more time to adjust to the trauma of her divorce. Brad was a well-respected CEO and Cherise felt she had let him down. They both sat there looking at each other. He did not fire her outright and she did not offer her resignation—at least not yet. There seemed to be no way out of the impasse. Brad rose from the chair, shaking his head at her with a mixture of respect and remorse for the inevitable. As he walked toward her office door, he grasped the doorknob and then turned to her and spoke in a decisive tone, "Cherise, I think you know what you have to do." The door closed so hard, the glass window panels vibrated.

Now rattled, Cherise bit the eraser off her pencil, knowing the gauntlet had been thrown down. She either had to resign or she was going to be fired. Treading water in a calm sea was one thing—staying afloat in a vortex was a totally different challenge.

Life has a way of stabbing, twisting the knife and dumping the unsuspecting victim headfirst into the ocean. You expect to drown. You prepare for it, welcome it. Then fate steps in and tosses a life raft. A few days after her CEO sat in her office, hinting she'd better resign, the life raft appeared. To Cherise's dumbfounded surprise and enormous relief, her company was acquired by a highly successful conglomerate.

She remembered being called to an executive meeting and hearing about the takeover for the first time. As shock registered on her face, her arm jerked, spilling coffee down her light blue suit. Without reservation she'd blurted out, "No shit!" and knew for the first time she had magically floated out of the vortex. Brad Jenkins wasn't going to fire her. There was no more Brad. He was released with a golden parachute severance package, as were several other executives on the top management team. New management provided her the option to either work in a less important, demoted, position or take a large severance package.

With her career at risk, Cherise wisely took the severance money and was able to cash out her vested stock options, as well. She knew it was far better to leave with one's reputation intact than to get fired later. *Besides*, she thought to herself. *I've already been demoted as a wife. I'm not taking a demoted job position. Enough, already. I'm taking all I can get out of this merger.*

In the passing weeks, Cherise felt better, stronger. Julia had been right. She had dusted herself off. Without Andy in her life, it seemed odd her job was no longer as important. How could she have made her job so crucial while he was her husband? She began to think about what to do with the rest of her life and she was grateful she had more than enough money to figure it out.

On a particularly clear evening in the city, she called Cindy, a friend from work who had managed to hang on to her job during the takeover. They agreed to meet at Cherise's favorite diner named after the foggy city offering the best fresh ocean mussels in spicy saffron broth.

Cindy walked into the diner and saw Cherise sitting in a red vinyl-seated corner booth and immediately opened her arms to give her friend a big hug.

"How are you doing?" Cindy asked, carefully folding her beige trench coat, placing it on the seat.

"I'm a walking cliché. I'm the divorced, smarter, but older wife whose mid-life-crisis dopey husband left her for a ditsy younger woman. I guess I am doing as well as can be expected although I didn't think it would be this hard. I'd always thought of myself as a strong, competent woman and now I feel wobbly and unsure of everything," Cherise sighed with embarrassment.

"Given what you have gone through," Cindy offered, "I think you are doing really well. It's natural to feel adrift."

Cherise nodded, noticing the waiter had arrived at their table. "You've got to try the mussels," she prodded Cindy. "They are the best in town."

Although she felt like having a salad, Cindy decided to placate her friend and try something different, even though she disliked the texture of squishy seafood.

"Okay," she said, "I'll be brave and try them, but I can't promise they will stay down." They both laughed and it felt good to Cherise. It had been a long time since any words were funny to her.

They browsed the wine list, ordered Cindy's favorite Napa Valley Chappellet Chardonnay, and waited for the soup to arrive. The waiter brought a basket of fresh sourdough bread and poured Perrier into ice-filled glasses.

"Do you mind if I freshen up a bit? I really didn't have a chance to go to the restroom before I left work," Cindy apologized while grabbing her make-up bag.

"No, of course not," Cherise smiled, tucking her own straggly curls behind her ears.

Scooting out of the bench seat, Cindy headed down the hallway giving Cherise a chance to nibble on the freshly baked bread, heavily slathering on sweet cream butter. As she sat, watching the cars drive by during rush hour, she contemplated the positive aspects of her current situation. No matter how awful life's unexpected setbacks, there was always some silver lining to be found, if one looked hard enough.

Cherise felt she had been blessed with the passage of time. Despite the stress of a recent divorce, her face showed no obvious dark circles from lack of sleep, and she had only a few small crow's feet lining the corners of her eyes when she smiled. She told herself she didn't look forty years old and had the energy of someone much younger. Those were all good things. Her long, light brown, sun-streaked hair had a natural curl at the ends, adding to her youthful appearance. She was lithe and model-thin—not so much from exercise, but from the stress of haggling through the divorce with her attorney, Andy's attorney and the unexpected loss of her job and career. No wonder she could wolf down half-gallons of chocolate ice cream at night and not put on a pound. How many women can say that? It made her smile. Mentally, she checked off another positive thing to be thankful for.

When the divorce was settled, Cherise and Andy had divided

everything, and she had gotten more than she expected, but nothing less than what was due to her in the state of California. With her divorce settlement and the money from her severance package, along with the cashed-out vested stock options, she was now a modestly wealthy woman. That alone was quite a bit to cheer about.

Cindy reappeared from the restroom looking refreshed, golden bangs arranged around her icy blue eyes, surrounded by flatteringly long, black mascaraed eyelashes. She slid back into her seat. Taking a sip of wine, she toasted Cherise with a tactful, "Let's drink to the future. Speaking of the future, what are you planning to do now since you are not working? Are you interviewing for any new jobs?"

"Actually, no. Based on past vacation travels with Andy and my love of France, I decided to shop around on the Internet and look for the right bed and breakfast place for sale."

"You mean you are not going back to work?" Cindy gasped.

"Well, no. Definitely not." Cherise gestured excitedly, "I found the most perfect place. It's exactly what I want."

"I think I'm going to need another bottle of wine," Cindy quipped. "Where is this bed and breakfast exactly? Did you say France?"

"Chateau Roufillay is in the Perigord region of Southwest France, fifteen kilometers from the town of Sarlat, and is priced right at 900,000 Euros. It's on a very high cliff, backed by mountains, with an enormous forest that overlooks the local village nestled along the Dordogne River. Seeing it on the Internet was one thing, but I need to visit it in person. I'm flying over there to meet with the listing agency. I read as much as I could about buying property in France and it is surprisingly easier than I would have thought. So, what do you think?" Cherise asked, taking a big gulp of her wine.

"Are you kidding?" Astonished, Cindy dropped her butter knife with a clank on her plate and took a huge unladylike bite of the sourdough. "Do you think you can just move to another country and start a new life? I mean, movie stars can escape from Hollywood but you are running away from San Francisco! You're going where? Dorwabony something?"

Laughing, Cherise said, "No. Dordogne—like the sounds *door and bone.*

"*Dorbone?*" Cindy wrinkled her brow, confused.

"Close. *'Door-doe-own','*" Cherise reiterated, waving a finger in midair as if to draw it on a blackboard.

Cindy didn't attempt another pronunciation. "Okay. I'll have to look it up on the web. But why leave the country, for heaven's sake?"

"You know, Cindy, I never would have planned my life this way, but now I have enough money and it's exactly what I want to do. I want to get away from San Francisco, but mostly I have to get away from Andy, and of course, his mother, Karen."

"His mother?" Cindy's leaned her swanlike long neck forward, inquiringly.

"Karen disliked me from the beginning. She wanted her son to marry someone who would stay at home, be a housewife, and raise a family to suit her very traditional values. In her mind, I was not supposed to work, much less become an executive. She always acted as if Andy was being neglected."

Cindy shrugged. "When I was married, my husband felt I neglected him, too, but at least I didn't have to deal with his mother-in-law. She was deceased when we met, which was probably a good thing. Did you try to get along with Karen?"

"I was always very courteous to her," Cherise offered, "but I could feel the tension from the time she came to visit until the moment the door hit her backside as she left."

Laughing as she sipped the flavorful saffron-infused soup, Cindy furrowed her brow wondering, "Are you going to tell Andy you are moving out of the country?"

"I don't know yet, Cindy. I probably should tell him, but I've not yet purchased the bed and breakfast property. Maybe when I have, then I will tell him. I'm going to take a trip there and meet with the real estate agent to make sure I get the chateau at a good price. It's been on the market for a year."

The waiter refilled their wine glasses while Cindy raised hers and, with a tilt of her head and a gleam in her eye, smiled. "I envy you. Not everyone can pick up and move to another country, but honestly, I really wish you well. I've never been to France. This is going to be a wonderful adventure for you, and since you speak the language, you'll fit right in. Maybe you will meet a wonderful French guy…"

"Oh please no," Cherise scoffed. "I don't want to meet anyone for a long, long time. It's the furthest thing from my mind."

Treading lightly, Cindy teased. "You might find someone when you least expect to. French men can be very charming."

Cherise smiled, but could not imagine getting involved in another relationship.

"What I want most," Cherise struggled with her words, "is to find myself. I don't have a husband. I don't have a job. I need to discover who Cherise Eden is and find my inner compass again."

"Understood," Cindy nodded, patting her hand comfortingly.

They enjoyed the rest of dinner, catching up on the latest work gossip. At the end of the evening, circling back to the France plan, Cindy asked wistfully, "Will you let me visit?"

"Oh, of course. I would love to see you," Cherise smiled.

"Sorry, I've gotta run," Cindy said as she slid out of the booth, skirt sticking to the vinyl, she tugged at it to keep it from hoisting up around her thighs. "This was a lot of fun," she winked, wrapping her trench coat and tying it tightly. They warmly hugged and Cherise watched Cindy through the restaurant window as she ducked into her black Mercedes CLK coupe. Cherise knew Cindy was one friend she was really going to miss.

That night, Cherise snuggled into the comfort of her king-sized bed. Despite the lack of Andy on the other side of her pillow, she felt both contented and excited for the first time in a long while, knowing she would be leaving in the morning for France.

Cherise flew to Paris, and then on to Bordeaux to meet with her real estate agent. The exploratory castle-hunting trip would be concentrated in the southwestern part of France in the Dordogne region. Her agent showed her several other properties, some in a state of disrepair requiring remodeling, but reasonably priced. Others were updated, with decent plumbing and lighting, but beyond her budget. They continued to look at prospective bed and breakfast hotels, but it was Roufillay she loved the moment she saw it and could not get it out of her mind. This was the castle she would buy. Leap of faith. New life. She could see it happening.

Cherise pictured herself standing at the edge of the terraced cliff of the south promontory of Roufillay, where could see across the horizon for miles, watching the storms coming up the river before they reached the castle. Flowers were abundant with red and pink climbing roses weaving ribbons of color among the rocks. Ivy crept along several levels of tiered, Dordogne yellow-beige stone block walls, where the French history of the chateau could fill a novel. It was a place where time stood still, literally stopping the breath. This was precisely what Cherise needed to start over, to heal and to find herself again. Putting as much distance between California and a new life seemed to be the rational way to avoid painful memories.

She discussed an offer with the agent who immediately called the seller, who was anxious and enthusiastic, having waited a year without one offer. After a modest pricing negotiation, Cherise's offer was accepted. Papers were signed, requisite money deposited in the appropriate accounts. Pending a final inspection of the property, Roufillay would be hers.

Cherise flew back to San Francisco and was fortunate to have a good friend who wanted to live in her apartment building and take over the rent. Able to sublet, she did not get stuck with the remainder of the lease and the apartment was furnished. Having their furniture divided up was something else Andy did not want any part of—he wanted her to keep all of it, his guilt-ridden conscience expunged. Cherise remembered being livid when he wanted to leave so suddenly. Now, in retrospect, she realized it was a blessing to be able to sublet and not worry about selling furniture.

Moving to France for some would be a huge undertaking but,

except for the clothes she wanted to pack, favorite pieces of jewelry, some photos and several conversational French books, Cherise did not feel overwhelmed at the prospect of leaving California. She had studied French in college, could speak fluently and understand the language sufficiently to manage a business. Starting a new life created a sense of apprehension, but also excitement. Enthusiastic as she was about moving to France, Cherise felt a nagging responsibility to call Andy to tell him she was moving. She dialed his number and expected to get his voice mail, but instead he answered the phone.

"Hello?" he said, distracted, watching the end of the baseball game.

"Andy, it's me. I want to talk to you about something really drastic I plan to do."

He hesitated, taking in a deep breath, worrying this was going to be about the divorce settlement…or worse. "Uh, what do you want to talk about?" his voice faltered.

Biting her lip, she gained composure. "Can I come over? I don't want to discuss this over the phone."

Andy hesitated, fearful about where her visit would lead. Guilt surged within as he contemplated her request. The tone in her voice was very upbeat, so he doubted she was thinking about ending her life, but she had used the word *drastic,* concerning him. He did not want them to become enemies and he had always tried to treat her with respect. He owed her that much.

"Okay, can you come over in about forty-five minutes? Let me clean up the place a bit. Will that work for you?"

"Works just fine. Give me the address and I'll be there within an hour. It won't take long, I promise," she said.

As he hung up, Andy stood, his nerves jarred, staring out the window, wondering what just happened. What could be so important she needed to see him in person—something troubling she could not discuss over the phone? It scared him. Maybe his ex-wife was suicidal. He knew sometimes when a woman decided to end her life, it was the decision to do it and actually finalize a plan that made her happy. Andy was worried and perplexed as he started picking up soda cans and day-old Chinese food cartons from the coffee table to put in the trash. He really did not look forward to seeing her.

Cherise walked through his building's lobby entrance. The desk guard asked her to sign in and he informed her of the floor number where Andy lived. She walked to the elevator, pushed the button and took a deep breath. The elevator rose quickly up to the tenth floor and she could feel her palms getting sweaty on the brass support railing. She could see herself, biting her lower lip, in the crackled mirror slits between the dark wall panels. The elevator doors abruptly opened. Her heart began to flutter. "This is silly," she told herself. "I have nothing to be nervous about." Untrue because she was apprehensive about seeing him. Where was apartment twelve? She found it at the corner of the long mahogany, wood-grained hallway carpeted in grayish brown, wool Berber carpeting. Taking a deep breath, she knocked on the door. Cherise could hear his footsteps and her heart thumped unexpectedly.

Andy removed the brass security chain, opening the door cautiously. He stood still, looking at her, offered a calculated "Hello," gesturing with his right arm for her to come inside.

Not knowing what to expect, Cherise moved past him, stealing a fleeting glance at the surroundings, without revealing reaction or emotion. She was surprised her ex-husband's apartment was not only small, but rather clinical and devoid of warmth.

"Can I take your coat?" he offered.

"Uh, yes please," she swallowed, while struggling to untie the belt and pull her arms out of her coat sleeves. He carried her black wool coat to the hall closet and told her to make herself comfortable. Glancing around the room she looked for something sensible to sit on. The sofa was inviting but she preferred a chair so there would be some distance between them if he chose to sit down. How could being married to someone for so long suddenly become so awkward?

"Can I get you anything?" Andy asked.

"Uh, just some water would be fine, if you don't mind," she said, surveying the sterile surroundings as he headed into the kitchen. Beige entry floor tiles. Beige carpet. Beige walls. Black leather sofa. Modern artwork on the wall, encased in glass, with a chrome frame. Cigarette butts in an ashtray and a half-empty bottle of beer on the coffee table. Newspapers piled next to the sofa. Soothing jazz music playing softly on the sound system…rather romantic, if the circumstances had been different. In the corner, Cherise noticed a black nylon gym bag with a woman's pair of pink and white running shoes poking out through the zipper. Her stomach lurched. Of course he was seeing someone, but she had not expected she—whoever *she* was, that nameless, husband-stealing stewardess—might be living there.

"Do you want ice?" he asked from the kitchen.

"Yes, that's fine." Part of her wanted to bolt out of the room, yet she found herself glad she had exciting and shocking news to share with him. Andy sat down on the sofa and handed Cherise a large glass of ice water. "So, what's so important you needed to see me?"

"You certainly get right to the point," she said, face flushing. "Aren't you even going to ask me how I am doing?"

Flustered, he shifted his shoulders as if he were removing a kink from his neck, and muttered, "Of course. I'm sorry. How are you?"

"I'm fine actually," Cherise smiled smugly, knowing she would be surprising, no actually shocking, him with the unexpected news of her life-changing decision.

"That's good," he said, gulping his beer.

Clasping her hands together, she leaned forward in her chair. "Andy, I am going to move to France. I bought a bed and breakfast chateau there and I plan to run it myself with a small staff."

Andy looked at her in disbelief, eyes as large as soccer balls. "You have to be joking. You can't just pick up and move out of the country!"

Disdainfully, she quickly retorted, "Of course I can. I have a right to do whatever I want."

Not sure where this was going, Andy could feel himself getting angry. "You won't be able to take care of yourself in a foreign country. After all, you are a single woman," he barked at her.

"Well, Andy, you've made me single!" she shot back, teeth gritted.

He sat in silence, staring at the carpet. No words making any sense seemed to come to mind, so he got up from the sofa in order to gain dominance. He had not expected her to leave the country. "Why do you have to move to France? Don't you need to get another job? What about money?"

She explained she had received a large severance package from work due to the buyout and she had cashed out her stock options that had become vested after the merger. His expression changed from frustration to sadness. He looked as though he'd been punched in the gut. "Is there nothing I can do to change your mind?"

"No, of course not. I've thought about this for a long time," she said, regaining her composure and self-control.

Andy muttered, "I will really worry about you, Cherise. I wish you would not do this. After the divorce, I just expected you would stay here and be close by."

Shocked, Cherise stood. "Close by? You divorced me and now you want me close by! Honestly, what for?" she asked, the expression on her face changing to utter disbelief.

"I thought we could be friends, maybe have dinner once in a while," he offered.

Astounded, Cherise blurted out words she knew she would regret but spewed out anyway. "Andy, that's just plain stupid. You are sleeping with your girlfriend. I can see her running shoes sticking out of the gym bag and you want to be friends? You are such an asshole! You are the one who ruined our marriage!"

"Oh wait just a minute here," he stammered. "I didn't ruin the marriage by myself!"

Angry, she planted herself a few feet from him and shook her closed fist, "You never offered to go to counseling. You didn't tell me how you felt or that you were miserable."

Red-faced, Andy frowned but calmly said, "You knew I was miserable. You were miserable too. We both knew it."

Cherise raged at him, her voice going up an octave, "I was not miserable. Maybe I was unhappy, dammit, but I was too busy at work to find time to be miserable!"

"Exactly," he mumbled below his breath.

Cherise shouted, "What did you say?" Tears filled her eyes.

Andy paced around the room, searching for an out. "Look, Cherise, we grew apart and the marriage disintegrated. It happens."

She went to the closet and grabbed her coat, tossing it over the arm of her black knit dress in a huff. "No Andy, it does not just happen. *You* had an affair. *You* destroyed our marriage. It was in trouble, but you did nothing to try to save it, either." She had the last word, even as tears streaked black mascara down her face.

"Isn't there anything I can do to talk you out of this ridiculous idea to move out of the country? For heaven's sake, what am I supposed to do?"

Feeling like an actress with a reverse role borrowed from the melodramatic ending in *Gone With the Wind*, Cherise stopped at the door and, holding the edge of the door frame with stiffened shoulders and her chin tilted upward, she announced with resolve, "Andy, quite frankly, I don't give a damn what you do, but I'm moving to France." Cherise slammed the door, leaving with a sense of righteous indignation.

The hallway felt smaller as she left, with the walls closing in on her. Fearful she would sob on the elevator, Cherise opted to take the stairs to the parking garage. She dropped her car keys on the ground, picked them up, and grappled with her purse for something to blow her nose with. The sobs were coming in hiccup waves, making her gasp for her breath. She had not expected the meeting to end in a bitter argument, nor had she anticipated Andy would be so upset by her move out of the country. She was baffled by his ridiculous notion they would remain friends. For her, continuing on, status quo would be much too difficult. It would be ridiculous and impossible. He had a girlfriend. She was the jilted ex-wife. Not a chance in hell she would continue to see him. In fact, not seeing him ever again was the only thing she wanted.

A few days later, departing from San Francisco to Paris, Cherise knew she would have plenty of time during the flight to ponder the future and release the past. Tears for her failed marriage had dried. Distance from her problems would make it easier to forget the pain

Andy had caused. As she curled up with a fuzzy blue blanket next to her window seat, ensuring the buckle was securely fastened, she drifted into a deep sleep, unaware of her fellow passengers en route to Paris. When Cherise arrived in Paris, she would catch the train to the town of Sarlat in the Dordogne, and from there it was a short drive to Roufillay. Being the proprietress of a bed and breakfast chateau would be a huge undertaking, but Cherise wanted to be consumed by her new life, to be very busy and challenged. The Perigord region of the Dordogne would be her new home. But most importantly, this would be the start of her new life.

Cherise woke up to the sound of the captain's voice on the speaker, "We're beginning our descent and should be landing in twenty minutes."

She rubbed her eyes, sat up in her seat and accepted the coffee offered to her by a matronly stewardess, wishing all flight attendants were slightly plump and on the other side of fifty. As the plane started its descent through the clouds, she mentally envisioned her new residence.

Roufillay was over 30,000 square feet—about 2787 meters, on more than fifty hectares of land. It was an original 17th century stone castle, three stories tall with large, imposing turrets, a slate roof and many outbuildings, including a guest and caretaker's cottage, horse stables and large garage which housed a large four-wheeled lawnmower and garden tools.

She recalled the main castle included twelve charming bedrooms, each decorated with tasteful furnishings. Each guestroom had a 'salle de bain' ensuite private bath, a welcome but an uncommon luxury in old castles. Roufillay had been renovated over the years, so no remodeling would be necessary, and Cherise could afford the upkeep. Roufillay, as a bed and breakfast resort, enjoyed a fine reputation and was well-established as a favored place to stay in the Dordogne.

Cherise delighted in remembering the details. The interior configuration was exceptional. Meal preparation would be a joy in the enormous, updated kitchen, complete with modern appliances. An arched herringbone brick, groin-vaulted ceiling covered the kitchen and a large window overlooked the entrance to the castle, with a convenient service door leading to the courtyard. Behind the kitchen there was a modern laundry room and large wine cellar below stairs. Through the main entry on the other side of the kitchen, guests would be graciously greeted in the large reception area that included the office and a comfortable sitting alcove in front of a gigantic fireplace, complete with spit for roasting meat or fish. She recalled her excitement, meeting with the owner, Isabelle, when they shared their walk-through for the first time.

"Oh my God! This is the dining room? It's enormous!" she had exclaimed. On its well-worn black and white inlaid marble patterned floor, there stood an imposing elongated antique wood dining table that could easily expand to seat twenty guests.

Cherise remembered twirling around the room, touching the carved, linen-fold wood panels that encased the walls with a large pre-cast stone fireplace, and stroking the massive hutches encasing stoneware plates and pewter mugs. An entire wall of leaded stained glass windows, embellished with a coat-of-arms design, overlooked stone-carved Romanesque statues set in the formal terraced gardens. Light darted in the room like a child peering into a kaleidoscope, the beautiful stained glass windows creating prisms of rainbow colors flooding the walls and floor.

"Let me show you the living quarters," Isabelle had said with obvious delight, in her French-accented voice, as she paraded ahead of Cherise. She was chic in her white blouse, navy capris, jeweled silver flats and short trendy blonde haircut.

Cherise had followed Isabelle across the original old cobblestone entry, which had been used for carriages and horses in the 17th and 18th centuries, to a splendid grand drawing room furnished with comfortable burgundy sofas and two matching navy and burgundy print fabric wing-back chairs. A burgundy and navy wool needlepoint Aubusson carpet covered much of the wooden plank flooring. Two wood chests, each over seven feet tall with intricately carved ornate woodwork, flanked each side of the entrance. A full suit of armor holding a sword stood at attention.

"Oh, does the piano come with the property?" Cherise had squealed, clasping her hands together, in prayer-like configuration.

"Yes, of course!" Isabelle nodded. "Do you play?"

"Oh, a little," Cherise said. "Not well, but I used to play Chopin when I was a child." Feeling like she was a child again, Cherise touched the small antique piano with aged ivory keys nestled against one wall, a beautiful oil painting of the countryside, hanging on the wall above. She gazed up at the two-storied ceiling. Its massive, consecutive floral-stenciled beams, had reminded her of the Swiss countryside. She turned her head and noticed several pale, amber-seeded glass windows, opened to the gardens below the main floor. The massive stone fireplace's rustic carved wood mantle was well above her head when she stood next to it. Yet, in its grandeur, Roufillay was not the least bit austere or medieval. It felt like a large private residence, lovingly cared for and lived in. Isabelle told Cherise that Roufillay had been her childhood home.

"I can't believe you lived here. It just doesn't seem real," Cherise said.

Isabelle sighed, "It was a wonderful life. My father was a zoologist who taught at the Sorbonne and wrote encyclopedias here at Roufillay. But, it's become too large for me to manage. My children are grown and I want to spend more time with them," she said wistfully. "I plan to move to Barcelona."

"I completely understand," Cherise said, trying to take it all in.

Isabelle looked at Cherise, admiring her enthusiasm for the property that had been in Isabelle's family for so long. Isabelle had hoped it would be sold to an owner who would care for it as lovingly as she had herself. Isabelle mustered her courage and had asked with a gleam in her eye, "You have seen Roufillay, and know it is an exceptional property. It was my home, but now I think you have fallen in love with it?"

"I absolutely do love it," Cherise had said. "It's exactly what I want. I've seen the bedrooms and the out buildings, can you show me the swimming pool?"

"Oh, of course, my dear. Just follow me," Isabelle had said, briskly moving through the castle, leading Cherise out to the courtyard and down the grassy path to the pool grounds. As Cherise turned around from the pool area and looked up at Roufillay, the sheer enormity of the castle had rendered her speechless.

She remembered writing the check for the negotiated final sale price. Except for utilities, and considerable French taxes, which she could afford, Cherise would be able to manage a bed and breakfast operation from April until October, without a shortage of cash.

To her delight, Roufillay's plumbing had been renovated two years before and the sale included all furnishings, including many unique pieces of furniture crafted specifically for the size and scale of the chateau. Seven months of the year, Cherise hoped to have a steady stream of guests to pay the upkeep, which included a maid to help her keep the place clean and who also would provide modest breakfasts of local freshly-made breads, croissants, jams, cheese and juice, coffee—nothing requiring a huge inventory of food.

"How do I keep up the grounds?" Cherise had asked.

"Not to worry," Isabelle said. "There is a groundskeeper who lives nearby who mows the lawn twice a week, prunes the roses and fertilizes the flowers. He is a capable handyman who will be willing to do whatever work you may need."

"Oh, excellent!" Cherise said, feeling another blessing had just been bestowed. A dependable handyman was indispensable in a foreign country, especially when she knew little about plumbing and wiring. The groundskeeper had been working at Roufillay for years and was very reliable. For that, she was grateful.

After the sale, Isabelle, the petite blonde French owner, formally handed the chateau keys to Cherise. As the two of them stood in the massive vaulted kitchen, its honey-colored stone walls three feet thick, Cherise had felt an enormous weight lift off her shoulders. She was no longer tied to her past and, although cautious and a bit apprehensive about such an undertaking, she had also felt tremendous excitement about the prospect of starting a new life.

As her plane was about to land, Cherise had every reason to feel optimistic about her future. Her strength was marketing and she had excellent organizational skills. She also had a natural affinity for speaking French and fearless energy to take on something new. Running a bed and breakfast would be a good match for her skills because she genuinely liked the idea of meeting new guests and making them happy and comfortable. Besides, she needed something to keep her exceptionally busy so she did not have time to wallow in self-pity.

"Are you finished with your coffee?" the stewardess asked.

"Yes, thanks," as Cherise smiled tossing her cup into the plastic trash bag. The landscape was beginning to appear through her window. Soon she'd be landing.

She tried not to think about Andy or the pain caused by their dissolved marriage but disturbing questions kept creeping into her consciousness. Why couldn't he have told her he was so unhappy? Why hadn't she made time to keep the marriage alive and to make him feel valued? Why did he continue to fly transatlantic flights and not arrange his schedule to be home when she was? So many unresolved questions left her raw. The way their last meeting had ended rattled her. She had not expected a fight. Cherise thought he'd be pleased she had planned a new life and that he'd be happy for her. He wasn't.

Self-recriminations were swirling, a maelstrom in her head. Her previous executive-level job with its excessive demands for overseas flights to visit foreign subsidiaries, to deliver speeches and outline marketing strategies to the parent corporation about how to stay ahead of other high-tech competitors in the field, had been exhausting. When she returned to California, there were the lengthy summaries of the trip to review with her boss, monthly reports, and perpetual expense forms. Cherise now realized she didn't have the time to *work* at a marriage as well as her job. But all of this was in the past and ruminating did not do any good, yet she felt lonely and depressed. With a breath, she determined she would not spend her time thinking about something she could not change. The future was hers to create and she banished negative thoughts as the plane made a safe, slightly bumpy landing.

The sun broke early through puffy white cumulus clouds as Cherise gradually awoke at Roufillay. Her first morning in her new surroundings flooded her with gratitude. Sunbeams streamed through the side-latched open leaded window, shining into her third floor beamed ceiling corner bedroom, onto the edge of the bed. A fuzzy bumblebee hovered near the window, darting in and out of the petals of a yellow climbing rose. She luxuriated, resting her head on two sets of fluffy feather pillows in her queen-size bed, covered in a duvet of red and white toile fabric. Adjacent to her bedroom, up three wooden plank steps, nestled in a turret, was a private reading and writing area. The hidden nook was surrounded by windows overlooking the resplendent garden below.

The soft morning breeze drafted damp air upward, as if it had rained during the night and now the sun was calling the humidity back into the atmosphere. Taking a deep breath, she inhaled delicate wafts of jasmine and fragrant roses. Geese, woodpeckers, magpies and starlings sang in delightful cacophony. Frogs croaked in a pond, squatting on lily pads lifting their floral blooms to the sun. "This is heaven," she sighed.

As much as Cherise wanted to linger in bed, she had to get up. With the blessings of a new job and a new life to live, she was full of excitement, as if she'd never had left her painful past in California. Walking across the bedroom to her large bath, patterned with red and white floral-accented modernized tiles, she turned on the shower. "Ahhh," she sighed in delight, reaching for the shampoo. It was a pleasure to enjoy plenty of hot water at exactly the right temperature. As she poured shampoo on her hair, the sudsy water washed over her body and puddled around her small feet. Cherise felt the emotional cleansing of her crumbled marriage finally washing down the drain.

Quickly selecting her clothes for the day from the large golden-brown mirrored armoire, she walked across the rouge, beige and teal green Aubusson floral carpet, happy to be embarking upon an exciting adventure. The further away she was from Andy, the more the gaping wounds were starting to close, leaving her with a sense of numbness which she could finally accept. She knew for the first time without a doubt, she would survive.

Feeling confident, she took a deep breath and went downstairs to meet with Sandrina, the perky petite maid Isabelle had praised highly. Cherise had seen a photo of her, but it was exciting to meet her for the first time.

Sandrina stood, her glossy straight black hair tied in a long braid with bangs just touching her eyebrows, her pale blue eyes looking directly at Cherise. She wore a crisp white blouse and apron over a very short black skirt and walked on impossibly thin, twenty-something legs. "Bonjour. I mean good morning," she said in her charming French accent, extending her hand to Cherise. "I've heard so much about you." "Oh, I hope it's good," Cherise commented, taking Sandrina's hand in hers. "I'm really looking forward to working with you."

"I so enjoyed working for Isabelle, but I'm sure you will do a wonderful job of managing Roufillay," Sandrina flashed a radiant smile, releasing her hand.

"I know we can do this together," Cherise said. "Tell me about everything you generally do here."

In less than twenty minutes, Cherise learned Sandrina's duties were to prepare breakfast for the guests and to keep the castle clean which entailed dusting and cleaning ten bedrooms and bathrooms when they were fully booked. Changing the linens would be no small task. Thankfully, there was a laundry service to deliver fresh linens and towels weekly.

On this day, Cherise had several guests arriving with room reservations. She had just enough time to savor her own cup of coffee and a buttery croissant with raspberry jam before she would be consumed with her duties as gracious hostess. Sandrina had already hurried upstairs to ensure pillows were fluffed and toiletries lined up in the bathrooms. Standing in the kitchen, with its large wood trestle table and double flanking benches with padded seats and slightly worn yellow checked fabric, Cherise was delighted to see the freshly cut, large sunflowers Sandrina had placed in a beige and blue stone pitcher on the yellow-patterned tablecloth. Against the wall stood a sizeable hutch with a hand-carved floral motif, probably from Provence, displaying various patterns of blue and white earthenware plates and large pewter mugs.

As much as Cherise wanted to stand there, absorbing her surroundings, she could hear guests coming up the driveway and was delighted to be the first to greet them. She would have Sandrina show them where breakfast would be served the next morning, take them up to their expansive rooms and then later offer to help them for the day if they wished to see the many sights in the Dordogne. Nerves rumbled in her stomach as the door-knocker banged against the wood. With a deep breath, Cherise mumbled, "I can do this, I can do this."

CHAPTER 2

Chippenham, England 2007

Brett Maxfield was not a man who made close friends easily, but when he did, he selected them carefully. An only child, he was intelligent but introverted, preferring to keep his feelings to himself. An avid reader, he enjoyed spy novels and solving crimes before the book ended. After graduating second in his class at Oxford, it was not surprising he had chosen a life of crime-solving. Having spent years at Scotland Yard, Brett was more interested in the details of cases he worked, rather than sustaining relationships, but he did value those friendships he had fostered. Nothing rattled him more than unnecessary small talk. Deep discussions on the merits of creationism versus evolution were more to his liking. Brett liked delving into logic as much as speculating about various theories when solving a difficult case…but that was all behind him. His life had changed.

Most evenings now, he would sit on his deep hunter-green velvet sofa, tortoise-rimmed glasses on the tip of his nose, his old hole-toed slippers on his feet. At the close of this particular day, his tweed jacket lay unceremoniously on the floor, while he poured through piles of new and old newspapers, novels and biographies, sipping a cognac. Brett Maxfield liked clutter. It made him feel comfortable. Cotswold's cottages looked better cluttered anyway, at least that was his excuse for not being tidy. His wife, Vivian, had died unexpectedly of a heart attack two years before, his second reason for leaving things messy. Surrounded by their possessions, his life felt less empty.

Before his retirement, while working on a case, Brett had devoted vigorous energy toward solving crimes, often working long hours into the night. Some cases were particularly difficult for the department and his peers depended on Brett to be a Pit Bull Terrier when needed. His successful record was a source of satisfaction but it was the hunt and final solving of a crime that made his blood rush, pulsing through his veins.

Now retired after Vivian's death, Brett Maxfield relished the peace and quiet that came with doing whatever he wanted to do, whenever he wanted to it, with no one to answer to. At fifty-five, he was slim and tall, with sandy blonde hair mixed with strands of gray. His intense hazel eyes bore into the soul, so captivating a person never noticed his age. His skin was lightly tanned and weathered from gardening long hours on rare sunny days in the English countryside. Brett Maxfield appeared serious, but when he smiled, his charm made him irresistibly handsome, in a rugged sort of way.

As he poured through the dusty pile of magazines and newspapers he frequently tossed in a corner in the living room to read when he was bored, Brett came across a year-old newspaper and gasped, recognizing the photo and article. He was astonished to read about Sir Raleigh Aubrey's death.

"Dammit!" he blurted out loud. "How the hell could this have happened?" He gasped in disbelief, setting the newspaper on his lap.

Brett had known Raleigh for years, through friends, and had stayed at Castle Brightingham in the Lake District in England while on business. Now Raleigh was dead.

They had gone fishing many times enjoying a shared solitude of quietly sitting in a boat holding baited poles. They did not talk much while floating aimlessly across the lake. The boat bobbing on the water in silence and, except for the occasional chatter of loons and egrets, provided an easy sense of peace and contentment. There was pleasure in saying nothing at all while drifting through the grey mist rising above the deep, blue-green lake. Sometimes they just dozed on comfortable deck chairs, the sound system playing arias, muffled by the slapping of the waves against the side of Raleigh's sloop.

Raleigh reminded Brett of his own father, who had died when Brett was a child. His mother died shortly thereafter of congestive heart failure, but Brett was sure she had died of a broken heart. Raleigh's companionship compelled him to remember his parents with great affection and love. Perhaps this was the reason why he enjoyed Raleigh's company. The time spent with his older friend lessened Brett's occasional longing for his father. Sometimes after fishing all day, they would get slightly drunk together, Raleigh recounting stories about the invasion of Normandy and Brett would share the cases he had worked on in the past. They enjoyed one another's company.

Uncovering the article about Raleigh's death made Brett realize Vivian's death had taken more of a toll on him than he'd wanted to admit. In his own grief he realized he had shut out many of his dearest friends.

What shocked Brett was the appalling nature of Raleigh Aubrey's death, a horrific fall from a second-story staircase landing, resulting in a skull fracture with several broken bones. He furrowed his brow and rubbed his temple with his hand, thinking about the pain his friend must have endured during his terrible fall. Brett shuddered.

"Crap. I should have stayed in touch and yes, I feel guilty as hell," he groused into the musty air. Talking to walls was a bad habit he had picked up because he lived alone. "I need a drink—preferably a stiff drink." He poured himself a large single malt whiskey on the rocks, and sat back down on the sofa, stunned as if someone had sucked all the air out of his lungs like a deflated tire. The whiskey went down smoothly, calming him while he sat, thinking about his friend's demise.

He knew Raleigh had quietly married but Brett had never met his wife, Diana Aubrey. Losing touch with good friends was something that should not happen, and Brett had let it happen. Business and his wife's illness had gotten in the way of keeping up with his friendships. Raleigh was someone who had been very special to Brett. How could such a tragedy take place? Brett Maxfield had to know.

After chastising himself, to the point of wallowing in guilt like a pig rolling in a mud sty, Brett poured another drink to numb the disdain he could not shake. He decided tomorrow he would drive to the Lake

District and visit the estate. Brett liked driving through the English countryside, especially on a pleasant day, when he could put the top down and let the wind blow in his hair. It gave him time to clear his head and also filled space in his empty life. Maybe Raleigh's wife Diana was still there and could explain what had happened.

CHAPTER 3

Château Roufillay, Dordogne France 2007

François Delacroix appeared to be the epitome of a classy, middle-aged well-bred, educated French man. His thick, dark wavy black hair was streaked slightly white at the temples. Porcelain blue eyes, well-trained to focus intently and purposely, made a person a bit uneasy. When François spoke, his voice carried a lyrical lilt of English tinged with a French accent. When he stared, a woman could lose her equilibrium, feeling unsteady, as if the floor might disappear below her feet. With his striking facial features and impeccable tailoring, François Delacroix emanated sophistication. Slightly over six feet tall, he walked with a sense of purpose and confidence. Seeing him in a crowded room, eyes were drawn to François Delacroix as if some magnetic force pulled his unwary victim into his aura. All of these things about himself, he knew, and had practiced well.

As François Delacroix walked to the front desk to check in at Chateau Roufillay, Cherise turned to greet him, and immediately blushed, dropping her guest book onto the floor. Embarrassed, she bent over to pick it up, feeling clumsy. He made her uncomfortable and she momentarily felt thunderstruck, wanting to say or do silly things in his presence. Gaining composure, Cherise quickly stood up and wiped the dust off the guest book.

"Hello, I'm Cherise Eden…ah, welcome to Chateau Roufillay," she managed to babble, feeling like she was sixteen years old. He extended his hand as she extended hers. He purposely held on to her hand too long, and she felt self-conscious, so she slowly pulled her hand away and opened the guest book. She noticed his perfectly manicured fingernails and handsome onyx ring.

"François Delacroix. I'm checking in. I believe I have a reservation."

"Oh yes, you do. I have been expecting you. *Enchanté*," she blurted in French. Feeling flustered, she asked, "How long will you be staying?"

He looked at her intensely, standing too close for someone she did not know and replied, "I am not entirely certain. I would like to write and paint during my stay but am not sure for how long. Perhaps a month or so. Would that be possible?"

Blushing, she said, "Oh great, wonderful, I mean, fine, of course." Cherise wished she said it over again, less enthusiastically, and less like a school girl with a crush on a boy she just met. "I will have Sandrina, our maid, show you to your room, which will be on the third floor, if that is satisfactory? We are solidly booked right now, and don't have any rooms on the second floor. It's a walk-up with a somewhat narrow, winding staircase. Oh, and watch out for the slanted low ceiling with the large beams. Please be careful. You will need to duck your head," she said apologetically, knowing she was blithering.

François smiled charmingly, presented her his credit card and watched her carefully process it before handing it back to him.

"Thank you," she managed, clearing her throat.

"The pleasure is all mine," he smiled and walked out the main door back to his car, thinking to himself it was worth the time he'd spent on the Internet searching resort and hotel websites, to find exactly the right location and ideal situation. He had read in the French newspapers Cherise Eden had purchased Roufillay, which made headlines in the real-estate section—something especially noteworthy when a French castle was sold to an American—and a very attractive one from California.

From the open front door, Cherise watched François remove his luggage from the car. The body of the car was certainly unique, with a gleaming black frame and considerable chrome, unusual additional wheels mounted on the side and a convertible top. Rather vintage, she thought, and probably very expensive. How exciting the car looked to her and how well it fit his personality. She told him to leave his luggage, a single black leather bag, in the entrance and Sandrina would show him up to his room. Cherise provided a brief explanation about the various restaurants in the nearest town of Sarlat, and told him what time breakfast was served each day at the chateau. If the weather was nice, breakfast would be served in the courtyard surrounded by stone walls and climbing roses.

As he followed Sandrina, toting his small luggage bag, Cherise gazed at François as if he might be a movie star. He stopped, just before he took the first step on the stairwell, and turned toward Cherise and said in perfect French, *"A bientôt."* She blushed again, embarrassed by her flustered behavior. "Yes, *bonsoir."*

That night Cherise lay in her bed, on the opposite end of the third floor, unable to sleep, thinking about him. The last thing she wanted was someone new in her life, but she could not deny the physical attraction she felt. She stared at the ceiling, wondering what to wear tomorrow, how to fix her hair, and whether she was too thin to be attractive.

CHAPTER 4

Windermere, England 2007

Brett Maxfield felt apprehensive as he drove along the long winding roads in the Lake District in Windermere, en route to Brightingham Castle, hoping he would not have to stop at the gate and explain who he was and what he wanted. Sheep dotted the hillsides between rows of painstakingly built-by-hand rock walls. He loved the countryside and the emerald green hills bursting with wild flowers in shades of lavender and pale blue. With a bug-spattered windshield, Brett arrived at the entrance to the estate. What excuse could he give for coming to visit, so long after his friend's death? He was not particularly good at making up sentimental stories.

To Brett's amazement, the entrance gates were open. He drove several kilometers down the driveway, past rows of sycamores laced together in an arch, forming a shady green canopy like a church cathedral. He drove along the gravel road, noting it was a pleasant day in England, with a hazy blue-grey sky blanketing the muggy warm air. Brightingham looked much as he remembered it—an Edwardian baroque estate of classic architectural beauty, numerous mullioned windows, stone edifices and abundant chimney spires. He stopped at the *porte-cochère* and was greeted by an elderly petite woman, dressed in a light blue cardigan, tan tweed skirt and sturdy walking flats, holding a woven basket of freshly picked flowers.

"Hello. I'm Brett Maxfield, a close friend, uh…well, a formerly close friend of Sir Raleigh Aubrey. I had lost touch with him over the past years," he uttered with a stab of guilt, his hands shoved in his jacket pockets.

"Oh, I'm Miriam Weatherly. I'm Carl Weatherly's mother."

Brett frowned, seemingly confused, "Oh, who is Carl Weatherly?"

"Carl and his wife Anna are the present owners of Brightingham."

Brett looked even more flummoxed and shuffled in place, looking down at the ground, kicking pebbles with his brown loafer. He decided to tell the truth, as his conscience was getting the best of him.

"Um…Mrs. Weatherly, I used to know Raleigh very well. He was like a father to me. We used to go fishing together and I always looked up to him. I just read about his tragic death, but I am afraid I'm so behind in my reading that I understand this accident took place over a year ago."

"Yes. Mr. Maxwell, is it?"

"Maxfield," he corrected her, without sounding annoyed.

"Do you know what happened to him?"

"Actually I don't Mr. Maxfield—just what I read and heard about his falling down the stairs in his wheelchair. When Carl bought Brightingham, it was about a year after the accident. His wife, Diana Aubrey, sold the house through a real estate broker. I think it was Sotheby's. The worst of it was cleaning up the walls and the staircase covered in blood. It was dreadful. Darned hard to scrub blood off porous stone stairs and so many balustrades. Took a team of cleaning crews and some of the damaged balustrades had to be replaced."

"God, that must have been awful. I can't imagine…"

"Yes, it was a really tragic accident."

"Mrs. Weatherly, are you living here now?"

"No, Mr. Maxfield," she chuckled, tilting her head, "I am only castle-sitting while Anna and Carl are on holiday in Spain."

"Oh…I know this may sound odd, but do you think I could see where the accident happened?"

"Well, I don't know…"

"Please Mrs. Weatherly. I was with Scotland Yard before I retired a few years ago. I am sure it was an accident, but would just like to take a look. It won't take me long, I promise. It would settle my mind."

"Well, I suppose. Let me show you in. You've been here before, right?"

"Yes, a long time ago."

"Well, let's go in through the vestibule in the grand hall."

Mrs. Weatherly placed the woven flower basket on a table and led Brett across an enormous entry, with a vast, twelve-tiered chandelier hanging over a wide cascading stone staircase, leading up to the second story. Beige limestone and various patterns of granite and marble lined the walls and floors. Large chips were missing out of the stone and there were cracks in the balustrades. Brett wondered if the damage had been caused by wear and tear over time, or if the wheelchair had come crashing down, chipping away pieces of stone as the fall crushed his friend's bones. Brett pictured it in his mind—a horrid thought making his stomach churn. He tried to focus on his surroundings.

Walking up to the top of the staircase he glanced around. Nothing looked unusual. A closet with a closed door flanked the right side of the stair landing and a long hallway was lined with bedrooms. He walked along the oxblood woven wool carpeting leading to the bedroom he remembered had belonged to Raleigh. The furnishings looked oddly different except for the heavily carved four-poster bed and writing desk. Seeing the desk and imagining how Raleigh must have sat writing made Brett shiver. He turned and glanced around the room.

Brightingham must have been sold furnished. Several pieces looked familiar; however the new owners had also brought in their own furnishings and mingled them with Raleigh's antiques. Brett did remember the heavy, deep-red velvet window coverings, the splendid coffered ceiling with gilded rosettes, and the oppressive dark, English musty atmosphere especially when the windows remained closed for too long. The familiar furnishings reminded Brett of Raleigh, evoking a sense of sadness, as if his friend's presence was still in the room.

Thinking he had wasted his time, and feeling more guilt-stricken than he should, Brett decided to go back to the stairs and leave. Perhaps it was instinct, or perhaps it was his professional training, but Brett's eyes were drawn to the long console at the top of the stairs next to the closet. It was a heavy piece of furniture, probably from Spain, constructed of old wood, with ornately carved marquetry and black iron hinges. On the top of the console stood two granite speckled obelisks symmetrically placed on each end.

Brett picked up the obelisk on the right. It was not very large, but it was quite heavy. He studied it, thinking it an interesting object. He put it down. A large ornate mirror nearly seven feet tall stood between the obelisks and he saw himself, squinted, and winced. He had aged. What on earth was he doing there? What was he looking for? Without thinking, he picked up the obelisk on the left, which was equally heavy. He held it in his hand, and experienced a sudden insight as to what might have happened. Brett wondered whether Raleigh Aubrey lost control of his wheelchair...or maybe...worse.

Brett turned over the obelisk. Although it looked clean and polished and had probably sat in that spot for more than a year, unmistakably he saw under a tiny crevice in the base, splats of something red. The general composition of granite was full of considerable black flecks and deep red Juparana colored markings, making it hard to tell exactly what he was looking at...or for.

Without thinking or reasoning, the former inspector cached the obelisk into his inside jacket pocket, and zipped it up. He knew he should have asked Mrs. Weatherly for permission to take it, but he did not want to alarm her, or get into a discussion about why he wanted the object. A bit unethical, he thought, but Brett planned to return it, if his suspicions proved inaccurate.

"Mr. Maxfield, are you doing all right up there?" Mrs. Weatherly's voice pierced the air like an arrow released from a bow.

Startled, he shifted in place, clutching his jacket. "Yes, I'll be right down. I need just a few more minutes." Brett quickly went into Raleigh's former bathroom, knowing he was not likely to find what he needed. He checked the drawers of the bathroom vanity and found nothing but unwrapped toiletries set up for a guest, toothbrushes, shaving lotion and other items. Another cabinet door yielded an assortment of washcloths and towels. He was about to stop looking when he knelt down on the floor and looked in the back vanity drawer, and found an old electric shaver, somewhat rusty. Brett's pulse raced and he slipped the shaver in his other pocket, and started down the stairs.

"Thank you Mrs. Weatherly. I have seen what I came to see. I am sorry to have disturbed you."

"Oh, not a problem. It's nice to see a friendly face in this large place when Anna and Carl are gone. Other than the gardener, I rarely see anyone unless I go to town."

"Did your son hire a new gardener?"

"Well, no, actually. Carl kept on the same gardener as Sir Raleigh had for years. It was much easier to have someone who knew the species of flowers, trees, watering system and fertilizer mixes, than to get someone new to learn about all these complicated gardening duties."

"Is he still on the property?" Brett asked.

"Yes, I think you will find him over by the fishpond located at the back of the estate. You can drive over there if you wish."

"Thanks, Mrs. Weatherly. You've been very kind—more than kind. Please give your son and daughter-in-law my regards. I hope they will take good care of Brightingham. Oh…one more thing, do you know where Diana Aubrey went after Raleigh died or how I can reach her?"

"No, I'm sorry. I have no idea. No one seems to know what happened to her after she sold the property. It was assumed she went somewhere overseas, perhaps."

"Did you ever meet Diana?" Brett asked, hoping he could obtain some idea of what she looked like.

"No, I'm sorry, I never met her and from what I know, neither did Carl and Anna, since they bought the property through the broker."

Brett sighed, his face contorted in disappointment. He had not really expected he would still find Diana living there, much less anyone else who would know where she was. "Thanks again and goodbye Mrs. Weatherly. It was nice to meet you," he said, clutching the objects surreptitiously hidden in his jacket, his arm slightly curled toward his chest while extending his free hand.

"Same here, Mr. Maxfield. Have a pleasant day," she waved to him as he got into his car.

Brett drove along the road leading to the rear of the castle and was struck by the imposing formal clipped topiary gardens, the well-shaped boxwood hedges, and the hundreds of tulips, a parade of pink, red and yellow blooms. He admired the manicured lawns and numerous species of trees. His eye caught the movement of an old man, hovering around the fishpond, sporting a natty gray cap and somewhat tattered wool jacket. The old man clutched a bag of fish food in one hand and plant fertilizer in another. Most likely, Brett thought to himself, here was the gardener Mrs. Weatherly had mentioned.

"Hello, excuse me…" Brett rolled down the car window.

"Yes, what can I do for you?" the gardener stammered, spreading fertilizer on the ground. The old man wondered who it was who had approached him by car.

"Are you Raleigh Aubrey's gardener?"

"Yes, I am. Been here for over twenty-five years. Don't live here, but might as well, given all the time I spend here. Got nothin' better to do."

"I'm Brett Maxfield—an old friend of Raleigh's. As terrible as this sounds, I only just read about his accident. My wife had been ill and I didn't get around to reading the obituaries. When I read about how Sir Aubrey died, I was terribly shaken. I really would like to know what happened."

The gardener stared at him, rubbing his whiskered chin. "What do you want to know?" he asked cautiously, arms drooping to set the fish food and fertilizer bags on the ground.

"Were you here, by any chance, on the night he died?" Brett asked, not expecting he'd have any luck, but it was worth asking the question anyway. He stepped out of his car, leaving the door ajar, and walked over to the gardener, careful to avoid stepping in blooming tulip beds.

"Well, I was, actually. I was on the grounds working late that particular night. So much cleanin' up to do. I'm always goin' around picking up tools, rakes, you name it. Hate to have them ruined by the rain. Usually forget where I left them."

"Did you hear anything unusual that evening?"

"No, not really. With those thick walls and closed lead windows, you could not hear anything if you wanted to. It's well constructed. You'd have to be inside to hear anything I suppose and then given the size of the place, a cannon could go off inside and you wouldn't hear it."

"How did you find out what happened to Raleigh?" Brett asked, rubbing the skin just above his lip.

"Well, as I recall, I was told the next day by one of the maids, Sir Raleigh had a horrible accident—fell out of his wheelchair down them stairs. Diana was terribly hysterical when the ambulance came much later. Door was open. I could hear her crying, even though I'm a bit hard of hearing."

"Much later than what?" Brett asked inquisitively, confused by the gardener's statement.

"Well, there was this car, and I always wondered what that car was doing, leaving the property late that night."

"What car?" Brett's pulse started to race again. "Did you see who was driving?"

"Well, sir, this odd model car, a long dark convertible, wheel on the side and big chrome lights—expensive looking thing—I could hardly make it out, it was beyond dusk. I could not really see the driver clearly. He seemed to have gray or dark hair, but it was night, so I'm not sure."

"Had you seen this car or this person before?"

"No. But people come and go. I don't pay too much attention. Don't want to be a busybody. The grounds are so large and I'm not always in the front of the property."

"Yes, I am sure. Was there anything else unusual you can recall?"

The gardener frowned, looking pensive. "Well I suppose not unusual, unless you consider the car was movin' slow, without headlights. You'd have to know where you were goin' in the dark, or you'd hit one of them sycamores for sure. It's a long way to the main road."

Brett held tightly to his jacket, protecting the obelisk and the shaver and extended his hand to the gardener, praying he would not drop either item.

"Thank you for your help, Mr.? Ah…"

"I'm Henry. Henry Tabbits. Sorry I couldn't be of more help."

"Henry, you've been a big help in more ways than you can imagine."

"Like caring for plants and helpin' people. Makes me feel useful at my age."

"Henry, did the police question you after Raleigh's accident?"

"No sir. No one thought to ask. I'm usually off the property before sunset. That particular night though, I knew rain was comin' in and I just wanted to pick up all my tools—ain't no use in buyin' new stuff."

Brett nodded and smiled at the old man, agreeing with him, thinking about the slim likelihood anyone would have witnessed a car leaving the property on the night Raleigh died. He extended his hand to thank Henry and bid him goodbye.

With an emotional rush pounding his temples, Brett felt like he was no longer retired. His mind was racing backwards, like a spinning Rolodex file, awaking his instinctive detective skills. He now knew there had been someone else on the property the night Raleigh died. He was anxious to get the obelisk to the lab the next morning to have the spatters, tucked into the tiny holes in the granite, sampled. If the specks were blood, it was a good chance it was Raleigh's. Although he could contact the local coroner and get the files pulled on Raleigh Aubrey, it did not seem like a good idea. Brett did not want Windermere's coroner to suspect there was something wrong with the original investigation or that Raleigh's death possibly was not an accident. Instead, he decided he would contact Kent Olson, a good friend at Scotland Yard who owed him a favor.

Brett wondered if an obelisk weighing only a few pounds, when gripped tightly by the sphere, could be a weapon. The size of the base could crack a man's skull if hit with force behind his head. Giving the wheelchair a little push with one's foot would have been the easy part... and down the stairs his friend would have tumbled. Brett weighed these possibilities in his mind. Finding out who committed this crime, if it was murder, was going to be the hard part. Brett had adapted to a comfortable life without stress and he really did not miss working at Scotland Yard. Yet he felt he owed it to Raleigh and himself to find out what had happened. Retirement was not all it was cracked up to be, anyway. Brett Maxfield's mental juices were flowing and he suddenly felt ten years younger.

CHAPTER 5

Chateau Roufillay, Dordogne, France

Without giving conscious rationale to her dressing the next morning, Cherise put on a pale blue, clinging blouse and flowing, deeper blue cotton skirt. She brushed her hair up into a French twist, and then took it down, deciding she looked younger with her hair loose. *What was she doing*, she wondered to herself as she put on her lipstick and a touch of perfume, Cherise intuitively knew, but did not want to acknowledge her behavior, which seemed flirty and foolish. As she went down the flight of stairs to the kitchen, careful not to hit her head on the slanted beams in the hallway of the castle, Cherise arranged the dried flowers in the blue porcelain pitcher, to look attractive for guests.

"Good morning, Cherise." She was startled by his voice, and turned on one foot like a ballet dancer, doing a partial pirouette. His English was flawless, and he seemed to switch from French to English with little effort.

"Oh, Good morning, François. Did you sleep well?"

"Yes, very well thank you. I was tired from the long drive."

Gaining her balance, she struggled to come up with another question to keep the conversation going. Usually Cherise was not at a loss for words, but staring into his eyes made her forget the simplest form of conversation.

"Uh, how was your room?" For an intelligent woman, she was flustered she could not come up with a more eloquent question to ask him.

Moving slightly closer to her, he responded with a pleasant smile, "The room is delightful, as is the view over the river, but I'm enjoying this view even more."

"I'm pleased…I mean about your room," she said, feeling her face flush. "Did you have your breakfast already?"

"Yes. Sandrina set everything out in the courtyard. The croissants were freshly baked, quite delicious and the local raspberry and blueberry jam was exceptional. I can see why you enjoy running a bed and breakfast. This location is stunning, and the views down the Dordogne River, magnificent. This will be the perfect place to write and paint."

Cherise started twirling her long hair—a nervous habit—wondering what to say next and suddenly felt very self-conscious.

"So, what is a lovely woman like you doing way out here in the Dordogne, running a place like this, if I may ask?"

Hesitant to sound flippant, Cherise fought back her original impulse to tell him too much too soon. She was embarrassed about being divorced and it hurt to talk about it. Gathering her thoughts, she suggested they sit down in the lobby. François chose a sturdy needlepoint fabric high-backed wing chair, and Cherise settled herself on a cushioned bench in front of the fireplace, feeling a bit more composed.

"I used to live in the United States. I'm originally from California. I was married for a long time but it did not work out. So I came here to start a new life. Not a very original story, I'm afraid."

"On the contrary," he offered, "your move to France took a great deal of courage. You seem to be doing very well. Not many women would uproot from friends and the life they had, to move to a different country without knowing anyone. It's not easy to run a business, not to mention having to adapt to a new culture."

Thankful that François seemed to understand her motives, Cherise felt she could adequately explain her decision to move to France without sounding defensive. "Yes, I am very lucky. I worked as an executive for a high-tech firm in Silicon Valley, and with my business background and ability to speak basic French, I felt I could take on a new venture."

"Oh, I see," he said, crossing one leg over the other. "Where do you think most of your guests will come from?"

Confident she had researched the market with the previous owner, Cherise explained, "I should have a steady stream of guests who visit annually or seasonally and we get a lot of referrals from our Internet site. I don't have to advertise much. Other than the groundskeeper and maid service, it's not a lot of expense. Just a lot to keep clean, but it's worth it."

"Are you open year-round?" He studied her face as she talked, trying to keep his glance from shifting from her eyes to her blue, clinging blouse. Purposefully, he lifted his gaze and attention back to her face, enjoying her animated gestures and charming smile.

"No, we're only open from April until October. I will live in one of the cottages on the property during the winter, as it will be far easier to heat, and will close up Roufillay."

"Ah, then I came at a very good time. May is a beautiful month here, don't you agree?"

"Yes, the weather is warm and not too humid. If you are adventuresome and brave, you can swim in the river if you like or try the pool on the grounds here. Unfortunately, both are terribly cold. The pool is not heated, perhaps the one downside of buying this castle. The previous owner did not install a pool heater."

"Well, I'm not much of a swimmer anyway. What else do you recommend?" he asked, not taking his gaze off of her eyes.

The intensity of François's eyes looking at her so directly, made Cherise very uncomfortable, yet she had to admit she enjoyed it at the same time.

"Well, we have many other things to do besides sightseeing in the local towns along the river. It can take days to explore everything. There are wonderful restaurants and shops along the river and the countryside roads, en route to the towns, are charming to drive through," she rambled, barely taking a breath. "We also have horses boarded here. My favorite is a black stallion, Dartanian, who is feisty, but disciplined. His nature reminds me of the famous musketeer, but the previous owner changed the spelling of his name. I also like La Femme, a white mare who can be spooked, but is dependable, very gentle and enjoys a good run. Do you ride?"

"I do. I grew up on horses and I prefer English saddles."

"Well I am afraid we only have French and Italian saddles. They are quite well-crafted, however. I'm sorry we don't have the saddle you prefer."

"I'm sure what you have will do just fine. Please do not worry about it."

Without realizing it, the conversation had slipped into genuine ease and comfort and, as Cherise leaned forward on the bench she propped her head up on her arm braced on her knee, unaware her blouse was gaping a bit in the front.

"What are you writing about? Are you a novelist?"

"Not really. I journal on a laptop and sometimes I write poetry. I like words and expressing feelings. It's kind of a hobby."

"And you said you paint too?"

"Well, sketching is my passion. It's more self-expression than talent. Sometimes I work in chalk, other times in oil or pastels. I do it because it pleases me. Actually, much of what I do in life, I do because it pleases me."

Again, she blushed. Not knowing why, but his words and conversation conjured sensual images although Cherise was sure that was not what François had intended.

"How nice. It's wonderful to do something you love," she stammered nervously, and thought it best she get up and get on with attending to other guests. Straightening her rumpled skirt, Cherise stood up and, with courteous propriety, extended her hand to him. "I enjoyed talking with you. There is so much to do, I'm afraid I have to see if Sandrina needs my help."

François rose from his chair and took her hand, holding it too long for Cherise's comfort, but she could not pull it away. "I enjoyed talking with you as well."

The pleasant moment had turned awkward. Cherise felt flushed, hoping he would not see the color of her cheeks beginning to resemble ripe apples. Not knowing what to do or say, or how to break the tension, she carefully slipped her hand away from his, her knees slightly shaking and managed a polite, "I hope you have a pleasant day whatever you decide to do."

"I will," he said, still fixated on her eyes. "You've given the day an enchanting beginning." Cherise's heart pounded hard in her chest. She was sure he could hear it and sense the uneasiness—something she was desperate to conceal.

François watched Cherise turn and walk away, stepping over the cobblestone floor, on the way back to the entrance to the kitchen. He mused she had a gorgeous face with high, well-formed cheekbones and an enticing lithe body, lightly-tanned sensual legs, rising to firm slim hips, creating a graceful line up to her small waistline and ample breasts. Sensing her nervousness while they talked and knowing she was a recent divorcee, François could sense her palpable fragility. There was a good chance she was in denial about her real feelings. It was something he had counted on. This was going to be even easier than he'd originally thought. For François Delacroix, finding vulnerable women as prospective financial targets was something he did exceptionally well. Cherise was a perfect choice. Trusting. Alone. Vulnerable. And most important of all—she was rich enough to own a castle.

As François pondered how easy it would be to make Cherise fall in love with him, he thought about his own childhood with a sense of detachment. Raised in the wealthy Ile de France area outside of Paris, Delacroix was adept at blotting out unwanted memories. His mother, Olivia, was an exceptionally self-absorbed, beautiful pianist who had married Delaine, a seasoned investment banker, when she was very young. Olivia resented Delaine's domineering, detached personality and she began spending more of her free time with her younger friends. It irritated Delaine and they had fought constantly. François could remember his parents' screaming fights when he was forced to put his fingers in his ears to mute the yelling. He would run into the sanctuary of his bedroom closet, humming to himself to muffle the shouting.

Olivia started with pills for sleeping, then pills to stay awake during the day, and ultimately developed an addictive dependence on drugs at a time when it was unfashionable to discuss addiction in social circles.

Eventually, her unhappiness drove her to heroin, and Delaine could not bring himself to understand or cope with her addiction. He was acutely embarrassed by her weakness and felt it devalued him in the eyes of his banker friends.

When François was four, he could remember his mother lying on the sofa, eyes rolled back in her head, needles and a rubber tourniquet on the floor, marks tracking up her arms. Delaine came home one night and found her unconscious. An ambulance rushed Olivia to the hospital. François recalled this event happening again and again. Each time he went through this experience, his increasing sense of helplessness caused panic attacks making his head throb from crying so hard. It was as if someone had taken a hammer and pounded nails with incessant disregard. Too painful for a child to accept, François eventually shut a door in his mind, refusing to cry, stifling his emotions to protect himself from the horror of what each new day might bring.

François stopped bringing his childhood friends home to play because he was ashamed and afraid he would find his mother in a stupor, or worse yet, dead. He could not help her, and he watched in numb horror, as she slipped away from him to become a person he did not know. Eventually, the drugs obliterated her mind and Delaine institutionalized Olivia. He sent François to boarding school when he was eight years old and he was never again allowed to see his mother. François hated his father for taking away his mother, and he hated his mother for being an addict.

After Olivia died, alone and insane, François received a shocking revelation, learning Delaine was not his birth father. Delaine had stopped visiting François at school but he sent him money regularly. Delaine did not write or send cards on François' birthday. His father could not bring himself to love a child who was not his own. Delaine never recovered from his wife's illness and unfortunate death. As far as Delaine was concerned, when François was out of his sight, he simply did not exist.

François was twenty-one when Delaine died of a stroke. He'd refused to attend the funeral, unable to feel anything but anger and relief. He hated his mother for abandoning him and despised his father even more for institutionalizing her. When François learned he was not really his father's natural son, he realized he was illegitimate. This final wound collapsed his fragile emotional world. François never forgave either one for their cruelty. Never loved, François detached himself from people and his emotions.

François had expected to inherit his father's estate, which included several financial companies, but Delaine's investments had done poorly. Funds had been mismanaged and Delaine Delacroix was bankrupt. By the time the estate was settled, François had many debts to pay off, including years of hospital bills for his mother's care, leaving him barely enough to live on for more than few years.

François Delacroix realized by the time he was twenty-two he would have to use his education to work hard for a living which did not appeal to him, or find some other way to survive that required less effort and commitment. The summer after his father's death, he took his money and his car and headed for the beach in Cannes with a well-crafted plan for survival.

CHAPTER 6

London, England 2007

Kent Olsen sat at his desk on the seventeenth floor in the well-known new building, the 'Norman Shaw,' located at 10 Broadway and Victoria Street in Westminster, London. He absently fondled his computer mouse, poring over a vast caseload on his monitor. Kent was single, attractive, and several years younger than Brett, with the same sandy blonde hair, similar height, and medium build. Kent was often taken for Brett's brother, which amused him enormously; especially as he was a Brit and Brett was an American educated in England.

Kent and Brett had worked together for years and were close friends who enjoyed poking jabs at each other. Kent was smart, but sometimes got excessively caught up in the excitement of finding a new clue. He was known around the office as an "eager-beaver," easily distracted by the next most interesting case to come across his desk, often forgetting to do the necessary paperwork to finish up the cases he had resolved. The ringing of the phone startled Kent from his deep-in-thought concentration and he nearly knocked over his coffee cup.

"Hello, Kent Olsen, Homicide."

"Kent, it's me, Brett."

"Hey–bloody good to hear from you! What brings you back to the world of dead body investigation?" he asked, extending his arm to close his door. Kent thought better of putting his feet up on his desk to relax, as he watched several associates huddled in animated conversation outside his office, but did so anyway.

"Well, retirement is damn boring some days, I guess, when you can sleep till noon, sit around reading all day while drinking a good bottle of Bordeaux, playing golf whenever you want, watching the telly…" Brett said, mocking the realities of the working world.

"You're a pain the 'arse. I'm jealous. Seriously, what's up, Brett?" Kent Olsen asked, rattling a pencil on files piled up on his desk, his credenza, and floor. His office always looked like he was about to move in or out.

"Actually, Kent, I need help. And a favor."

"I'm getting knotted," he said, looking up at the ceiling and rolling his eyes. Favors already? Bloke, you don't miss a beat. How about, 'How are you Kent?' 'What's going on in your life, Kent?' 'Got a girlfriend, Kent'?"

"You can tell me that stuff later, buddy. Besides, your love life's a mess," Brett teased.

"Remember my old friend Raleigh Aubrey?" Brett asked, remorse creeping into his voice.

"My current love life is not a mess! I've only been divorced twice. I'm single, attractive, sexy, fun and great shag," Kent said, chuckling and goading Brett.

"Could we focus on the question here?" asked Brett.

Olsen responded, "Okay, Raleigh Aubrey, the dude who owned Brightingham Castle in the Lake District?"

"Yeah. Probably more accurate to call him a Duke than a dude, but that's the guy. He was a good friend."

"It's coming back to me. Something about his having a terrible accident, as I recall. But wasn't that a long time ago?" Kent asked, distractedly looking thorough his office door's glass window pane at a very attractive redhead hurrying down the hall.

"Yeah, well I know now," Brett said, flinching with guilt like a Catholic boy just gone to confession. "I read about it a few weeks ago. I can't believe it happened a year ago."

"Well, blimey with all the time on your hands with golf, of course you are just now getting to current events that happened a year ago."

"I know. Not a justifiable excuse. After Vivian's death, I was in an unrelenting English bog-fog. Didn't care what day it was or what was going on in the world, sorry."

"Well, you were never one to keep up on your current events paper reading, even when you worked here, unless it involved a case you were working on," Kent said with affection. "Seriously, how is living alone in the Cotswolds?"

"It's easier now than it was when she first died," Brett sighed. "It's a friendly town. The people are nice enough and everyone knows who you are, but people don't pry. And you know I don't like to pry either, so we kind of go our own ways. I guess that's one of my faults...and also not keeping up with people."

"That's an understatement," Kent commented, wishing he had not sounded quite so adamant.

Brett continued, "I really liked Raleigh. He was like a second dad to me and a great fishing buddy. Sounds corny, but we enjoyed time together doing the simplest things," Brett mused. Becoming serious he said, "By the way, Kent, was his death investigated by anyone at the Yard since Raleigh lived in London for so long and was such a prominent figure there in the city?"

"Yes, Brett, from what I remember, the original investigation started in Windermere, but some of Raleigh's friends at his club in London suspected foul play—something about the younger woman he'd married. Because of Raleigh's reputation, they insisted Scotland Yard get involved. There was a lot of tension between the local police and our office. I don't recall what came of the investigation," Kent remarked.

"I have a hunch and I really need your help," Brett said.

"So what do you want from me?" Kent hoped this favor was not going to entail boatloads of extra work.

"I need you to pull all his files," Brett said, insistence bordering on pleading in his voice.

"Have you gone barmy? That case is long closed. All that rubbish is in boxes filed away in the bowels of this organization. You know how much red tape it's going to take to get any of that reopened?" Kent took his feet off his desk and stood up in his office, rubbing his forehead, feeling a headache coming on, acutely aware there was no way he would have time now to find out if the pretty new redhead in the office was single.

"Yep. Less than one ounce of the red tape you owe me," Brett said humorously.

"Bollocks. I hate people who remember favors owed to them. Which case did I cock up anyway? Are you thinkin' of the shopkeeper's wife's murder?"

"Of course! You never would have solved the tangled messy case without me, Kent."

"True. Maybe you're right, Brett. I'm a bright bloke—not in your league, of course. I'd have figured it out in another month."

Brett started laughing, "Yeah, a month that lasted a lifetime."

"Right-o, don't remind me," Kent groaned. "It was repulsive at the time and I'd rather not remember the dismembering Hannibal you-know-who copy-cat serial killer. That was the worst case you ever put me on! Crikey, I could not sleep for months!"

"So, you'll get the files?" Brett could sense Kent's reluctant compliance creeping into their conversation for a favor owed him.

"Yeah, I'll get crackin' on the files one way or another."

"Good. Don't tell anyone I am working on this. It's unofficial."

"It better be, Brett. You don't work here anymore, remember?"

"I know, Kent. But I have to do this and you are the only person I can trust at the Met who works in the serious homicide crime directorate. You can do this better than anyone I know, besides myself that is, of course, but I don't work there anymore."

"Okay. Flattery noted. What specifically do you want?"

"Blood type and DNA. Meet me in the parking lot tomorrow. I'll give you a small obelisk I took from the estate."

"You stole something?" Kent exclaimed, reaching in his desk drawer for a bottle of aspirin. "Are you daft?"

"No, didn't steal it…borrowed it while I stopped in for a brief visit to see if I could talk to anyone who was there to talk to about what happened to him. I want the base of the obelisk tested for blood. Just tell me if it matches Raleigh's blood type. I have a gut feeling it does and I don't believe he fell from the stairs. I think he was bludgeoned, probably at the back of the skull, which sent him tumbling down the stairs. I took an old electric shaver I found at the back of Raleigh's bathroom vanity. It may belong to him. Have the hairs in the shaver tested. It's a wing and a prayer, but I have a strong feeling he was murdered."

"No shit!"

"He probably didn't have time," he muffled a snicker.

"You have a terrible sense of humor, Brett. Do you have a suspect?"

"Sort of. Henry the gardener saw an unusual rare vintage car leaving the property late that night without the headlights on."

"Did he see who was driving the car?" Kent asked with interest.

"No. Not really. It was too dark. The gardener thought he saw a man with dark hair, but he's not sure."

"That's a start, isn't it?" Kent tried to sound hopeful.

"Sort of," Brett said, trying not to be vague.

"Waddaya mean sort of?"

"I have no friggin' idea how I am going to find a guy with dark hair and some odd classic car with no idea of the make or model."

"Right. That description fits a lot of the vintage car collectors in England." Kent's forehead furrowed, "Is this going to be a wild goose chase?"

"Maybe. Gets harder," Brett insisted. "No one knows where Raleigh's wife, Diana Aubrey, went after he died. She sold Brightingham about a year after his death. See what she would have inherited."

"Okay. I'll dig around and see what people remember."

"At least look through the papers and files and tell me what she looked like, where she was from, any siblings, clues—I need clues."

"Ok, clueless one. I'll help you on this and do all the forensic work myself. I can get into the lab late at night without anyone suspecting why I'm there. I always pay my debts owed to friends with perfect memories. How do I reach you?"

"Call me on my mobile. It vibrates in my pocket. It's the most fun in my life these days."

"Brett, you really need to get a life!"

"You're being snarky!"

"Aha! I've hit your humor bone. A bright bloke like you would make a lousy curmudgeon," he cajoled with a guttural laugh.

"Tell me something I don't already know. I'll meet you at 8:00 p.m. tomorrow. It will be dark by then. You know my car. I'll be in the parking space where you usually park. Don't be late."

"I won't. Don't want you cheesed off."

CHAPTER 7

Chateau Roufillay, Dordogne, France

François stayed for weeks, plotting unobtrusively. He found an art supply store in Sarlat with Cherise's help and indicated his intension to purchase supplies. She tried not to fixate on what he was doing too much of the time. Besides, she was extremely busy with other guests.

At her suggestion, François saddled up Dartanian for a ride. Impressed, Cherise watched him from a distance as he trotted down the dirt path. François rode extremely well with the discipline Dartanian required.

There were some wonderful riding paths through the forest, past smaller maisons on other properties, with a delightful blend of countryside hills cutting a broad swath through wide-open, grassy fields. Other trails were narrower paths, winding adjacent to rocky Dordogne cliff walls, covered with thick shrubs and clingy moss. A rider could experience an exhilarating gallop with hooves thundering or enjoy a leisurely cantor through the woods, all the while embracing the beauty and magic of this corner of southwestern France.

Summer was a season of exceptional natural beauty. Fields were resplendent with lavender and heather. Lupine flowers grew wild, vivid shades of pink, purple, and lilac as if dipped by a paintbrush. Emerging from the forest, a rider crossed through open fields in the countryside and could glimpse the façades of other castles, many in ruin but picturesque in the distance. A guest could opt to ride to the village, past small stone farmhouses, entering the life of quaint local hamlets. Watching François ride off, Cherise wistfully sighed. Riding was one of her favorite passions, but attending to guests and the duties of a proprietress left little time to spend on the back of a horse.

During of the day, François kept to himself. Cherise spent time talking to him when she was not too busy with other guests. She learned he was involved with investments, mostly technology companies, and apparently he had made most of his money through stocks or seed money for start-up firms having gone public. When his room was being cleaned, while he was not there and Sandrina on another floor getting fresh towels and sheets, sometimes Cherise would sneak into François' room, curious to see what he was working on. There were several high-tech magazines, and a myriad of prospectuses lying about, representing high-tech and biotechnology firms. There was also an art easel, a painting stool, and numerous canvases stacked against the wall on each side of the fireplace. It appeared François did not have to work for a living and was enjoying life and his interests. Cherise tried not to pry or ask too many questions.

Most of the guests had left for the week and no new arrivals were due for a couple of weeks. It would be good to have a break from the daily routine of getting up early, coordinating details with Sandrina, running to the market in Sarlat to purchase fresh vegetables from the local farmers, and of course the chore of endless dusting. Castles collected dust motes and spiders multiplied overnight. There were no screens on the windows and although flying bugs did come in at night, there were not as many as a person would expect. Insects flew in, and then right back out again, preferring nature's warm blessings to the cooler temperature inside the castle.

Cherise was exhausted with the numerous details that included keeping the income and expenses on track. She found herself wishing she had taken more accounting classes, and some advanced computer courses, too. Noting every transaction into a ledger by hand was time-consuming, however she was not fond of spreadsheets or computers which she used now mostly for emails or to occasionally browse the Internet, connecting her with the outside world. She needed more help to run the castle, but was too busy to think about it.

Late one evening heading up to her room, distractedly thinking about the numerous feather pillows to be fluffed and linens to be turned down or washed, Cherise heard the heavy wooden door creak open at the end of the hall, sounding like a ghost rising out of a coffin. She cupped her hand to her forehead and peered out of the doorway trying to discern in the dim lighting what was making the sound.

"Oh, François! It's you. You startled me!"

He came toward her slowly, smiling, his enticing eyes surrounded by thick black eyelashes. His sultry walk and piercing gaze awoke in her sensuality, long-forgotten.

"Cherise, I need a favor, if you would consider it and not be offended."

"Of course. What can I do for you?" she questioned curiously.

"I have been sketching the female figure. I cannot get the muscles of the back quite right. Could you, please, if you would not mind, pose for me?"

"Oh! Well, I don't think that would be appropriate…and…"

He interrupted her. "The guests who were staying here this week have already left. It would not take very long to do the sketch to get the curve from the neck past the shoulders to the center of the lower back. It is very important for me to get it right. These lines are the most beautiful part of a woman's body. As an artist, it would mean a great deal to me. Your back is quite exquisite and I would not ask you to pose nude. You could drape yourself in a sheet."

"Well, I don't know…I suppose I could." The words tumbled out of her mouth without hesitation. She was both startled and flattered by his request.

"Excellent! Then it is settled. You will come by tomorrow night around 6 p.m. just at dusk, when the lighting is soft and luminous?"

"All right," she laughed lightly, a twinkle in her eye. "This will be providing the height of service to a guest!"

"It will be my pleasure. I will see you tomorrow."

With unsettling certainty, Cherise knew she would not sleep that night. She paced around her bedroom, wandering over to sit on the window seat cushion. Perched, holding her knees to her breasts, she watched the sun starting its descent in the distance, casting an amber tint on the landscape like an old sepia photograph. Cherise sat, looking over the Dordogne River and small village below, with dubious apprehension. What was she doing? Was she really just accommodating a guest so he could paint? Her thoughts were in conflict with her heart, as if she were about to touch the flame of a candle, knowing all the while, it would burn her flesh. Cherise rationalized 'art was art' and who knows, maybe he was truly serious about painting. Part of her wanted to believe that. Part of her wanted to believe it was something more.

Wondering what François would be like in bed, Cherise was shocked to find she was having these thoughts. He was a perfect male fantasy. His striking good looks, especially the way he carried himself, and the small cleft in his chin were all so enticing. Mostly, it was the way he stared at her. In his presence, Cherise felt aroused, sensual. She envisioned posing for him and hoped it might result in something more.

Realizing she had repressed her sexuality for a long while, Cherise thought of her marriage. As the years went by, she and Andy had lost intimacy. When they did have sex before the divorce, it had been infrequent and purely physical. Often it was over with quickly, without emotional satisfaction. Sadly, she had convinced herself this was normal for married couples when they had been together for a long time. It was hard to remember what lust and passion felt like.

Toward the end of her crumbling marriage, sex with Andy made Cherise feel empty, so she had focused on her job success to fill the void. She told herself that her executive title, the prestige of her position, the salary, large quarterly bonuses and lucrative stock options, were worth the distance she felt in her marriage with Andy. She had fooled herself, conceiving her job as her identity. In her mind, her worth was determined by her success as an executive, acquisition of new clients and revenue for the firm.

With a briefcase full of contracts, Cherise would often get home too late to eat dinner. Exhausted from board meetings, she did not feel like talking. Even when she did attempt conversation, Andy would be packing to fly to Europe. He would kiss her on the cheek and they would pass in the doorway, each going their separate directions. It was a routine she had settled into without thinking of the consequences of not focusing on her marriage. She did realize Andy was unhappy and, even if he was distant, she had no idea he would consider divorce. Cherise had imagined naively that someday they would sit down and talk about their marriage and their feelings when their lives were less hectic. Andy had never given her the chance.

Alone in a foreign country with a sexy handsome man staying at her chateau, Cherise longed to be kissed, held and touched. She imagined François ravishing her. Shocked and ashamed, she put these feelings out of her mind and attended the week's guests checking out of Roufillay. Her primary goal was the success of her bed and breakfast business and Cherise refused to accept any more failures in her life. Spending several precious hours evaluating new possibilities, Cherise realized time had slipped by and it was late. She pushed the window open even further and took one last look at the millions of stars in the sky, awed by the vast universe and her small place on the planet. She crawled into the comfort of her bed to cuddle into the softness of her pillow.

The next day went by quickly and twilight began to settle. A strong breeze danced in the tree tops, like a ballerina's arms, swaying from side to side. The setting sun created a pinkish golden glow, casting rays into the clouds like giant ribbons stretched across the horizon, along the river.

Cherise contemplated dressing appropriately for the modeling pose requested by François. She changed clothes several times. First she tried on a blue print jersey dress, which hugged her frame, then took it off, deciding it was too formal. She considered a favorite pullover sweater but it was too warm and would be awkward to remove. Selecting an outfit for a sketching pose was worse than going on a first date.

She did not know exactly why she left her bra off, a bold move for her. François was only sketching her back. Telling herself that bra-straps would be too visible and in the way, Cherise reminded herself that desperate women are good at giving themselves ridiculous excuses for their behaviors as she smiled and dabbed her favorite perfume. She considered not wearing panties, but stopped short of being shamefully obvious. Instead, she chose a loose-fitting white silk shirt, threw on a pair of tan capris, copper-colored sandals and, finally satisfied with her choice, walked tentatively down the hall.

Common sense tapped Cherise's shoulder, imploring her to turn around. But before she could change her mind or knock, François opened the door and welcomed her into his room. "Please come in," he said, gesturing her toward the light. The scent of his masculine aftershave made it impossible for her to think clearly.

As she walked into the center of his room, Cherise managed a faint smile, noting her underarms had begun to dampen. François momentarily turned away to close the door, flipping the lock. She glanced at him, sexy in his fitted black tee shirt and black slacks, and sighed deeply. She wanted to run past him, out through the door, but a voice inside whispered, *stay.*

"Would you like a glass of wine?" François asked thoughtfully. Cherise nodded, "Oh, yes please. That would be nice." As he turned to open a bottle, she quickly scanned his room, breathing a sigh of relief. François was serious about his art, as evidenced by the canvases on the floor, others leaning against the ochre-colored walls. Several oil paintings appeared to have been recently completed. Perched on chairs, Cherise noted several graphite sketches of women's bodies. Some drawings were of larger figures, others petite, all in various poses. Obviously he was quite talented. She tried to relax. A fresh canvas was set up on an easel. François really intended to draw the lines of her back, or so Cherise reassured herself silently, the tension in her body subsiding.

"Why don't you sit here, in front of the window? No actually, sit closer to this wall, so the light will shine on you directly, instead of behind you. I will light some candles, to create a soft lighting glow when I sketch," François said calmly, handing Cherise a glass of wine. Her throat felt like the Sahara and Cherise quickly swallowed half the glass of wine, grateful to have something to hold in her shaky hands.

François sat her down on some large cushions, and asked her to unfasten a button or two on her blouse so it would drop it off her shoulders. Cherise set the glass of wine on the floor. Her heart began to flutter, slight beads of perspiration forming on her upper lip. As François touched her shoulders with his fingers, her nipples began to harden and she was very aware she was aroused. Cherise was more anticipatory than apprehensive, and she felt more than a little bit daring. She could have stopped this, but she did not want to. Not at all.

Holding the canvas steady with his right hand, he sketched the curve of her shoulders with his left hand, deftly making broad sweeping strokes. She felt relaxed and enjoyed posing, wondering what her back actually looked like to him.

François asked her to turn this way and that, telling Cherise her body was very beautiful. As he traced the outline of her back, she could also tell he was also mentally tracing the outline of her breasts. She watched him trace her body while he was drawing her frame and it was as if his pen was on her flesh. Cherise could imagine François touching her skin, kissing her nipples, her mouth.

He moved close to her and she unbuttoned another button on her blouse, revealing more of her back. He stood closer, brushing up against her nipples. She nearly stopped breathing while, clutching her blouse to her breasts, he lightly stroked her neck. Cherise was uncertain what to do. François moved yet closer and Cherise could sense his arousal. François' eyes met hers, her mouth quivered as she met his gaze. The desire in his eyes was unmistakable.

"Do you want me to stop?" he asked softly. She shook her head. He lifted her slightly, raising her arms above her head, as her blouse dropped to the floor. He turned her around facing the wall, placing her hands equidistant from her shoulders to steady her. She did not resist. Standing behind her, breathing intensely, he kissed her ear and shoulders, his hands caressing her breasts. Cherise could not breathe. Her passion moistly warmed the apex between her legs in a way long forgotten. François lowered his pants and, bending her slightly forward, removed her capris and panties one leg at a time. He entered her, slowly at first, and then increased the intensity. Cherise's hands pushed into the wall as she moaned with ecstasy. He gripped her breasts as he came into her. She felt faint, but did not want him to stop.

When François was spent he turned her around, picked her up, and gently placed her on his bed. Cherise's head was spinning. She was too weak to think, and her body was both tingling and limp. François kissed her stomach, tracing it with his tongue, moving lower down, down. He parted her legs and moved his lips and tongue between her legs bringing her to a climax and then another like she had never experienced before. Clutching the sheets and grasping his head as she cried out, Cherise was unable to stop herself and prayed the groundskeeper was nowhere nearby and that no one could hear her. Throughout the night of passionate kisses, his tongue discovering every part of her mouth and her breasts, she responded to him over and over. With the flickering candlelight long extinguished, Cherise remained in François' arms, nodding off to a deep sleep until daylight.

When the sun woke her, Cherise felt François's arms around her, still sleeping. She lay there befuddled, disoriented and full of remorse. She knew what she had done was wrong. Well, not exactly wrong, but inappropriate. Of course, she could have lusty sex with a man she liked, but as a proprietress of a bed and breakfast chateau, it was certainly unacceptable to sleep with a guest. The one thing she was thankful for was having had her tubes tied early in her marriage to Andy, since neither had wanted children. At least her night of impulsive passion would not result in unintended consequences.

Cherise kissed François lightly on his forehead, glad he did not awaken. She searched for her panties and found them wadded against the wall where they had dropped. Grabbing her damp, wrinkled blouse and capris, she picked up her sandals quickly and tiptoed out of his room, closing the door as quietly as possible. As Cherise briskly walked back to her room, she prayed no one would be in the hallway. Thankfully, the chateau was quiet. She opened her bedroom door and quickly bolted the lock behind her, throwing her clothes over the back of a chair. She hated to wash off his touch, but she showered, dried her hair with a thick towel and sat on her bed thinking about what she would do. What would she say to him? Cherise felt she had behaved without reserve and her desire was entirely too obvious to François. She was also embarrassed by her physical hunger.

She was certain he must think less of her but it was too late to regret her behavior or his. It had happened because both wanted it, but that did not make it right. As Cherise went down the stairs, purposely conservatively dressed, she was filled with self-recriminations but, at the same time, she felt more sexually satisfied than she had been with Andy for a very long time. Her skin was glowing; her cheeks tinged a warm pink and she hoped Sandrina would not notice. She was thankful her maid went home each night, leaving no one in the castle, except a feral cat on the window ledge, to hear last night's unabashed cries of ecstasy.

Cherise met Sandrina in the kitchen, carrying a basket of bakery scones and fresh fruit. Sandrina could tell something was different. Cherise was very distracted, fiddling with the coffee pot, staring into space.

"Good morning, Sandrina," swallowed Cherise, clearing her throat.

"Cherise, you look upset. Did something happen?"

"Yes...and no, well I mean, I don't know Sandrina"

"What do you mean yes and no? Are you ill?"

"No, I'm fine. I'm just so embarrassed. I did something ridiculous and utterly unprofessional."

"Unprofessional, what do you mean?" Sandrina looked concerned.

"I...uh...I slept with one of our guests!"

With a gaping mouth, her wide eyes filled with extreme curiosity, Sandrina said, "*Mon Dieu!* Who?"

"François!" Cherise covered her mouth with her fingers and tilted her head back in disgust, groaning in remorse.

"Was he very good for you?" Sandrina inquired, in her charming French accent, breaking into a coquettish smile.

"Oh Sandrina, you are so French, young and uninhibited! I'm so embarrassed!"

"Well, was he?"

"Was he what?" Cherise pretended not to remember the question.

"Did you delight in each other?"

"Yes, of course. It was a night of lust-filled rapture and it's a long story," she said, her eyes rolling upwards, shaking her head in disbelief. "He wanted to sketch me. I knew it was not just about sketching and where this might lead, but I did it anyway."

"Hearts have a way of telling the head what to do. Did you pose nude?"

"God no! I had on my capris and a blouse." Cherise didn't dare tell her maid she'd left off her bra. "He had me drape my shirt over my shoulders so he could draw my back."

"Well, that hardly sounds malapropos…or slutty as you Americans would say. You just got caught up in the moment." Sandrina was rather enjoying the story told by her unexpectedly uninhibited proprietress.

"Yes, but a castle bed and breakfast owner should have her head tell her heart that sleeping with a guest is despicable. I'm beyond embarrassed and I feel so stupid," Cherise cringed.

"So, who is he going to tell? Other guests? There's no one here right now. Everyone who was here has left. I'm sure he is discreet. François is French and he is not going to parade his conquest in front of new guests arriving at Roufillay."

"Yes, I hope you are right. Nonetheless, I feel mortified. How will I face him?" Cherise stammered, pouring a pot of freshly brewed French roasted coffee into her cup. Sandrina smiled with a twinkle in her eye and, putting one hand on her little hip, whispered quietly to Cherise with delight, "Mademoiselle, you will face him with pride, with your clothes on and a cup of coffee. He's about to walk into the kitchen."

CHAPTER 8

Chippenham, England

"Brett, it's me, Kent. Pick up man!" he shouted, anxiously fretting as the voice message started rolling over to the answering maching.

"I'm here. I was in the shower—don't take the phone in there you know. Let me get a towel. What's up?" huffed Brett as he fluffed a towel, drying his hair, unaware of the water dripping off his feet on to the tile floor.

"What's up is that you're not gonna' believe this!" Kent said excitedly.

"Not believe what?" Brett said, as he struggled to put on his briefs with one hand, trying to avoid falling on the floor while holding on to the wall with his other hand.

"The spatters on the bottom of the obelisk were indeed very small spots of dried blood. I did the DNA sample myself and it is a match to Raleigh Aubrey. The hairs from the electric shaver were from Raleigh. You were right. This was no accident! I had goose bumps the entire time I ran the forensics. What are you thinking now?"

"Guess it looks like I am not retired after all. Now I have a killer to find. Odd isn't it, how the entire investigation at the time of his death showed nothing in the reports other than an accidental death?" Brett said, grabbing a flannel shirt and putting the phone on speaker mode so he could slip on some wool socks.

"Yeah, but when there was no apparent evidence to suspect foul play, the initial investigating inspector saw no reason to focus on murder.

The gruesome experience of finding him in that manner on the stairs probably shocked everyone, including the coroner who assumed an old man simply fell to his death," Kent shrugged his shoulders away from the graphic visual picture in his mind, a chill shuddered through him as if he had just opened the freezer of the refrigerator. "Do you think he had any enemies?"

"Everyone has enemies," Brett said, "but most people don't resort to murder. It's an enormous risk to kill someone so prominent. If someone else was in the house that night, that person may have killed Raleigh. What I wonder is how the murderer got into the castle. Were there any broken windows or jimmied doors?"

"Nope. No evidence whatsoever of a forced entry," Kent commented. "Doors were shut; alarm was on. That's what the police report here says."

Interesting. "Was Raleigh's wife, Diana home at the time of the accident?"

"Um…let me see, uh according to the report, yes. Notes indicate she was distraught, inconsolable and quite hysterical—unable to look at the body which was terribly contorted lying in a pile of broken bones, head bashed in."

"Kent, Spare me the drama. Remember I knew this guy. So, she was there. Did anyone question her?" Brett asked, now fully dressed. He sat down on the bed, shifting backwards to rest his head on the pillows flanking the headboard in his bedroom. Glancing out the diamond shaped, leaded window, he noticed it was starting to rain. He waited many moments for Kent's reply.

"Sorry this is taking so long. There is a lot to read here." Brett could hear Kent shuffling pages.

"Apparently there was no reason to interrogate her. With the wheelchair lying at the bottom on the stairs and blood everywhere, it seemed obvious Raleigh had taken a very bad fall. Um…says they talked to her, but there is nothing in the notes about any details of the discussion, other than she was very upset."

"Was anyone else there?" Brett asked, hoping there were other bystanders or witnesses.

"No," said Kent. "The servants had left at the end of the day."

"Oh, that's right. I remember now the servants did not live in the castle. It made Raleigh nervous to have other people wandering around at night. Those trusted individuals who took care of the place lived in the servant's quarters, outside the main gates, adjacent to the estate. Thinking about it, there were several outbuildings," Brett recalled, his memory shuttered flashback photos in his mind.

"Kent, was there an autopsy?"

"Not sure. Hold on a minute while I read thorough this stuff. Ah... yes there was. One of the EMT's was concerned Raleigh might have had a heart attack. Maybe that's why they did an autopsy."

"Did Diana agree to it?"

"Yes, apparently. It was performed the day after he died."

"What did the autopsy show?" Brett was scrawling notes so furiously his pen ran out of ink. He reached in the nightstand drawer and grabbed a pencil, pausing to learn more.

"Um...I'm flipping through reports...uh, let's see here—yes, a fractured skull, broken neck, broken back, punctured lung from a broken rib and several spiral fractures to his arms, and a broken femur, severe osteoporosis of the bones. That's about it."

Brett shuddered at the pain Raleigh had endured and prayed he had died instantly. "Any evidence of illegal drugs?"

"Nothing unusual, Brett, just prescription Vicodin for his severe pain and a small amount of alcohol—just wine. No serious narcotics or suspicious substances. What's going through your mind now?"

"Kent, I'm thinking, when you whack someone old with the force of the base a granite object, you could crack the skull enough to damage the brain stem so he would bleed out. The fall from several flights of stairs would have done the rest of the damage. Impossible to know where the fatal injury had come from. Very clever. Very well planned."

Brett continued, "Kent, you said the alarm had been on at the time the police arrived?"

"Yes, Diana had to let the police in at the gate from a control box in the vestibule and then disarm the alarm to let them into the castle."

"Interesting," said Brett, rubbing his forehead and squinting his eyes, tapped the pencil nervously on a pad of paper. "Here's what I think. Her husband is brutally bludgeoned by a murderer and pushed down the stairs in his wheelchair. Everything is tidy. I have a strong suspicion whoever committed this crime had a little help from the, fine acting skills of the so-called hysterical sobbing wife. Either she planned it herself or they planned it together. I'm not really sure who the killer is, but I suspect Diana wanted her husband dead and so had someone else."

Kent asked, "Couldn't she have done this by herself, hitting him with the obelisk?"

"Yeah, it's possible, I suppose, Kent, but it's not as likely she could have hit him hard enough to crack his skull and then run down the stairs. Also, the obelisk I took was on the left side of the console. There was another identical one on the right. If someone had been upstairs hiding, let's say in one of the bedrooms or the hall closet and he crept out to the console, if he was right handed, he would have taken the obelisk nearest to him. Yet the one with the blood on it was the farthest away from the closet. I'm guessing the murderer is possibly left-handed. Hard to tell though because the two objects were rather close together. We have no idea if the wife is left or right-handed, but unless she was a very tall, powerful woman, she could not have wielded such a forceful blow, and she would also have risked plunging down the stairs herself."

"Blimey, Brett, I'm impressed with your shrewd deduction. You've put together pieces of a puzzle everyone else had missed."

"I've had more time to think, and I am suspicious by nature. And you have to think *murder* in order to look for the possibilities and method of how someone might have killed him. A guy like Raleigh just doesn't simply tumble out of a wheelchair. When you are confined to one, you know how to control it so you don't fall. Sure, you could forget to set the wheel lock, but not likely. You could get to the edge of the stairs and black out from any number of maladies that might befall an older person…but again not likely."

"Where do you go from here, Brett?"

"Gotta' find a car."

"Something's wrong with your car?" Kent said, confused.

"No stupid. The car leaving the driveway that night."

"Right-o, sorry. Where do you look?"

"Needle in a haystack. I'm looking for a black classic vintage car, rare, expensive with lots of chrome, and a wheel mounted on the side. I'll spend some time on the Internet. I have a few ideas, but to find the car fitting this description, I need to go back and talk with the gardener at Brightingham. He's the only witness to that car and some guy with possible gray or dark hair. Not a lot to go on. Can you do me one more favor, Kent?"

"Bloody hell. Don't you think you've used up your favors?" Kent simulated a moan, dreading the next request.

"Well, please do it anyway. It's good for a couple of free beers," Brett joked.

"Okay, lay it on me. You're going to make me a drunken sot."

"Find out if Diana was seeing anyone. Check out the country club they belonged to, and find out who was in their social circle. Talk to anyone who might know if she was having an affair."

"Okay, I'm on it."

"Have a good Glenmorangie single malt scotch on me while at their club. It's one of the benefits of being a Yard boy, Brett cajoled. No 'Members Only' rules. You can get in anywhere."

"Yeah, lucky me, just the snobby-arse club type. Can't wait to pull out my silk ascot and my double-breasted navy blue blazer. I'll do my best to look the part." Kent laughed. "I should have gone into acting. Remind me to buy some cigars while I'm at it!"

Brett laughed too and reminded him, "Don't get cancer on my account. I'm not paying your hospital bills and don't get too bladdered in the bar."

CHAPTER 9

Somewhere Over the Atlantic

Andy Eden was not one to spend a lot of time analyzing his emotions, but flying 747's on transatlantic flights gave him more than enough time to think about life, whether he wanted to or not. He thought it odd that, when he was in California, he did not think of Cherise as much as when he was heading to Heathrow or Paris. Today it was Paris. The closer he got to Europe, the more he wondered about how she was doing. He could not think of any excuses to see her. They had stayed in touch only a few times by phone, and he knew better than to call her to chat. She had made it clear to him she wanted her distance, both physically and emotionally.

He had been the one to ask for a divorce, and it made little sense for him to call to check on up her or to give her the feeling he was prying into her life. Andy was aware Cherise had purchased property in the Dordogne, but did not know exactly where it was. Although he had dated Madeline, the stewardess who came on to him and made him feel valued and desirable, their relationship had faded even before the sex became boring. Andy missed Cherise. He hated to admit it. He missed her perfume and her clothes on the floor. He missed the peanut butter spoons she left on the counter, her laugh, and her habit of twirling her hair around her fingers. He even missed their arguments. Mostly, Andy missed having his wife on the other side of the bed.

For all the blame he'd put on Cherise for her career over-commitment, Andy now realized his constant travel, the difficult

71

time zone adjustments, and the long flights had all contributed to the breakdown of their relationship. He was not a giving person and yet he'd expected her to always be there for him. This was crappy stuff to think about, he realized, as he carried several hundred passengers all relying on him to arrive safely at their destination. The plane jarred and began to shake. Turbulence. "Let's move it up another three thousand feet," he said to his co-pilot. The plane settled into a smoother path, but the *Fasten Seat Belt* sign remained illuminated.

Oddly, Andy now found flying lonely. On his previous flights to France, he enjoyed experiencing different cities. Andy had fun flirting with the crew, lounging on the beaches in St. Tropez, and luxuriating in the occasional stay at the Hotel Inter-Continental in Cannes, feeling like a jet-setter in his crisp blue suit with silver wings. But now, a layover trip to the famed location had lost its thrill. The tanned, bikini-clad women all looked the same to him, the only variation, the color of their hair, or the size of their butts and breasts. None of it mattered now.

What Andy missed most was the woman he had fallen in love with years before. These were the images that surprisingly kept coming back to him at night in strange hotel rooms, mere glimpses of a photo album of his married life he had not paid attention to while he was living it. Now, in his memory, he recalled the many happier times he and Cherise had shared together. Simple pleasures like a walk in the park, a glass of wine at a local bistro, laughing and holding hands at a movie, or simply sitting and watching TV. These things he had taken for granted. Andy had assumed when he walked out on the marriage, the companionship and sex that had been missing would be replaced by someone who was interested in him and would make him feel better, younger and vital. Instead, he simply had found someone new, but the depth in a relationship was not there.

To his dismay, Andy realized the women he dated did not want to get serious, but they certainly loved to get him into the sack, later spreading gossip to girlfriends about how they had bedded the pilot. Or worse, they simply wanted to marry a pilot, period, as if he was a status trophy. The thought of being some young woman's trophy made his stomach lurch, and it had nothing to do with dropping altitude as he prepared for descent.

Andy felt emptier now than the times when he was home alone and Cherise was traveling on business. Hindsight was always enlightening, but no one had told him it would be so painful, realizing his mistakes. After this flight to Paris, Andy planned to only stay overnight, and the next day, fly back again to New York, and on to San Francisco where he was based. He was grateful for the layover, especially as lately he'd been experiencing blinding headaches he assumed were a result of frequent time-zone changes.

During this unsettled time, Andy was thankful he was a pilot, as he had nowhere to go or any reason to stay permanently. He may as well just be shuttling planes back and forth until he could figure out what to do with the rest of his life.

As the plane circled Charles de Gaulle, he dropped the landing gear when he saw the runway lights. Andy decided that, when he returned to San Francisco, he would find a permanent home. He hated his rental apartment and needed a real home base. It would be a good time to buy a condo, a place of his own, now that he lived alone. He had recently looked at a property on South of Market Street. *The Heritage* on Fillmore was one he liked because it was in close proximity to several blocks of highly-rated, trendy restaurants and jazz club entertainment bars. Prices for condos were reasonable, especially considering high-priced property in California. Andy had found one he liked at $600,000 for a one-bedroom, sufficient for his needs since he was seldom there.

The plane landed safely with a bouncing thump, the wheels hit the tarmac and taxied to its gate abruptly, bringing him back to reality. Andy was glad to be on the ground. He caught a taxicab to his hotel and wearily walked through the lobby to the reception desk. Two attractive stewardesses waved hello from the bar, calling out to him, asking if he wanted to join them for a drink. Feigning a polite smile, Andy offered a brief, "Thanks, but no thanks."

After checking in, the porter showed the pilot to his room, opened the door and set his carry-on bag on the luggage rack. One eye blurred as Andy removed several bills from his wallet and handed them to the porter, who pretended not to notice the slight shaking of Andy's right hand. The porter left quietly, closing the door behind him. Exhausted, Andy removed his clothes, wondering if was experiencing a migraine, without really knowing the symptoms. He recalled Cherise used to get a really bad headache when she was stressed and depleted. Assuming his symptoms were the same, Andy ignored the fuzzy vision in his right eye and compensated by turning his head so he could see through the other eye. He groped through the shelves in the room's mini-fridge, selecting a cold bottle of water. He gulped down three extra-strength aspirin to control his pounding head and went to sleep. He hoped he'd feel better in the morning.

CHAPTER 10

Chateau Roufillay, Dordogne, France

May quickly turned into June, and then July. Temperatures were warmer, bordering on hot, at mid-day. Jasmine flowers bloomed with fragrant scents that lingered in the evening air. Clouds billowed in fluffy compositions and mild rain showers raised the humidity but cleared the air. Guests arrived and departed successfully, obviously enjoying their stay, as confirmed by their glowing recommendations of their experience at Roufillay they shared with their friends. Appreciative visitors frequently commended Cherise for the great job she was doing, providing her a great source of satisfaction.

The symphony of the cicada-like insects in the Perigord region during the day became a constant white noise reminiscent of New Orleans and other places in the South, but also characteristic of the Dordogne. Evenings cooled the air, but were still very warm, with a high level of muggy humidity. Lavender bloomed in abundance on the hillsides, while bumblebees danced in and out of the flowers. White honeysuckle and purple clematis wound themselves together in a happy marriage, climbing the stone wall on the promontory, leaving a heady fragrance of blended perfume.

Cherise and François spent hours talking together during the evenings after the guests had gone to bed. Sitting at the weathered teakwood table at the farthest point of the stone patio, they sipped regional wine while admiring the view overlooking the winding, glistening Dordogne River. Sometimes they would walk through the woods, occasionally swatting at mosquitos as they walked along the paths. More often than not, they slipped into his room or hers, lustfully ravishing one another. But on this particular evening, they walked. Cherise no longer wished for anything else except François in her life. She braved the one question she feared most, with some hesitation she might get an unwelcome and upsetting answer. "François have you ever been married?"

Prepared for this question, he touched the small of her back while walking and said, "No. I never found the right woman."

"Oh, that's interesting," she acknowledged, happily kicking pebbles down the path.

Adept at changing the subject, he prodded, "Can we talk about you?"

Cherise dreaded discussing her past and kept the story simple—just that her marriage had not worked out and her husband had left her for another woman. However, something about François engendered her trust and she felt she could share her deepest emotions.

"Were you happy?" he asked her.

"I thought I was," she sighed wistfully. "My job took up so much of my time and Andy was often home alone when I was stuck at work. Sometimes I'd be home and he'd have flown to Europe. It wasn't an ideal marriage," she said with consideration, no longer feeling the sting of guilt. Together, they walked further along the path, watching feral cats chase field mice.

"What about your parents?" she asked.

"They are both dead," he said without emotion.

"Oh, really? I'm sorry."

"Don't be," he ground his teeth. "Let's change the subject."

Cherise thought it odd and a coincidence neither her nor François' parents were alive. He had no siblings, nor did she, making their bond even stronger.

"What about your parents?" he asked, hopeful the conversation would remain about her instead of him.

"It's odd, I suppose," she said. "I rarely think of them because I feel they are always with me in my heart. But now, talking like this encourages me to remember my parents with fond memories despite the medical difficulties they suffered before dying. I lost my dad to lung cancer when he was fifty, and my mom to leukemia, five years later."

"Do you want to talk about it?" he inquired, attempting a show of compassion.

"No, I'd rather not. I'm happy now. They are in heaven—I'm sure of it. That alone gives me considerable comfort."

"I understand," he said, unclear of his mother's soul's whereabouts and certainly hoping his father was burning in hell.

A red fox eyed them from a distance and warily disappeared into the thicket.

"Let's go back," she said. "I've become tasty food for the forest's late evening bugs."

François remained at Roufillay, helping Cherise almost every day except when required to travel to neighboring towns, including the picture postcard La Roque-Gageac or Rocamadour and he sometimes travelled to Paris by the TGV bullet train. He told Cherise that he had business to attend to and she understood.

One evening, expecting François' return, Cherise anxiously listened for his car in the driveway, and ran to greet him at the front door.

"I'm so glad you're back," she collapsed into his outstretched arms. "I missed you terribly while you were away."

"Me too," he said, hugging her tightly.

It was a pleasantly warm summer evening, a soft breeze gently rotating the air like a Bermuda ceiling fan. Guests had departed and Sandrina had gone home.

"Let's turn in for the night," François said, touching her breast with the tips of his fingers. Cherise felt romantic and could sense he wanted her, as they headed up the stairs, one flight at a time, ducking under angled beams. She lit the candles lining free-hanging shelves in her bedroom, the shadows dancing as the candles flickered. They shared pleasure until both were satisfied. After their lovemaking, François wrapped his arms snugly around Cherise's waist as they lay stretched across the soft cream-colored, feather-filled duvet. He stroked the small of her back and whispered into her ear, posing the question he felt was timed exactly right.

"Will you marry me? I want you to be my wife."

Without hesitation, Cherise turned over and looked at him in the glow of the candlelight.

"Oh yes," she asserted, embracing him tightly. Certain she had found her perfect life partner, Cherise repressed the thought that she had not known François very long. What did it matter? François made her deliriously happy and that was all she needed.

Cherise felt she and François had become a team. Together, they had managed the steady stream of guests, daunting paperwork, and perpetual phone calls to help lost travelers navigate the highway from Bordeaux or Paris, along with the general enormity of daily upkeep of Roufillay. François looked after the myriad of details of running the business and Cherise was glad to have a partner so invested in helping her succeed. François was so unlike Andy, who had ignored her success, or rather expected it, taking her accomplishment for granted and resenting it at the same time. Many times, François would sit and talk with guests, making them feel welcome upon their arrival and inquiring politely if they had enjoyed a good night's sleep. He charmed guests with his conversational skills, including his ability to listen intently while guests talked about their travels and shared their personal stories.

After a particularly hectic week, François looked at Cherise, haggard from a bone-weary day carrying sheets, fresh flowers and stacks of toilet paper, up and down the stairs to each room. "You look exhausted. I've been thinking we should hire a concierge to manage the paperwork and attend to the customers' needs while they stay at Roufillay."

Cherise resisted. "I don't think it's necessary," she disagreed. "I should be capable of doing it all with Sandrina's help. With your skills, I think we are doing just fine," she pleaded, feeling accountable she couldn't manage everything properly.

"We may be doing well," he said, "And we are both experienced business professionals. But at the end of the day, we are both physically and emotionally drained. There is little time for us."

François' comment, "There is little time for us" raised a red warning flag, alarming Cherise. She did not want a repeat of her marriage to Andy. François convinced her their guests required a higher level of personalized service, especially with travel reservations and sightseeing tours. Roufillay needed a professional concierge. Cherise finally agreed but told François she did not know where to find such a person. He informed Cherise he knew a capable woman in England with the requisite skills who might be interested. François advised Cherise that Colette Armond would be perfect for the job.

François suggested the new concierge live in the empty caretaker's cottage. Her duties at Roufillay would include assisting guests with their travel reservations, using her multi-lingual skills to book guests' hotels in other parts of France, Spain or wherever else they wished to go. There was much to explain and describe about local restaurants, the regional food specialties such as fois gras—often bringing horror to the minds of some guests, while others saw it as an epicurean delight—and countless other unique dishes including cassoulet, duck confit, noisettes d'agneau and coq au vin. Additionally, a concierge could suggest fascinating historic castles to visit if guests were traveling further up to the Loire Valley and sights to see in Paris.

Finally convinced, Cherise reluctantly agreed that Colette Armond would be perfect for the job. The new staff concierge could take charge of the reception desk during the day, and live in the guest cottage at night, giving the two of them privacy and freedom. François assured Cherise that Colette was professional, polished, skilled in languages and that having a concierge would be an asset to Roufillay. Cherise shrugged, sipping a sweet white aperitif from Monbazilac, finally settling on the idea. Colette would make her life easier, giving her more time to spend with François. She was not about to make the same mistake in a marriage twice.

All was perfect the day of their wedding. Several of Cherise's friends arrived from Sarlat, including the town's charcuterie proprietor. Living in a small town, Cherise and François were familiar with everyone who owned or worked in a shop because they purchased locally. The shop owners had become their extended family and friends.

Sandrina was the bridesmaid, dressed in pale lavender, carrying hyacinths and white roses from the garden tied with deep purple streaming ribbons. A local cleric performed the ceremony and together they spoke their handwritten vows. Her sheer, handmade lace veil was neatly placed by François' hands deftly behind the pearl and crystal headband, tucked securely with small combs into the two twisted strands of her upturned curls, while the rest of her sun-streaked blonde hair cascaded down her back. Under the courtyard wire canopy, entwined in white roses, François and Cherise were pronounced man and wife. When François kissed Cherise, following their "I do's," tears flowed happily down her face, dropping to the bodice of her ivory, satin beaded dress.

It was a glorious day, sunny but not too warm. Birds filled the air with their own music—starlings, robins and small yellow finches, fluttering to and fro under a cerulean sky dotted with billowing white clouds. Cherise was happier than she believed she deserved. Wedding guests tossed rose petals and scattered generous handfuls of rice, applauding their union.

She tossed her floral bouquet, tied with a pink silk ribbon, which landed in the arms of Amélie, owner of the local patisserie. Because Amélie was already married and the mother of seven children, the guests found this particularly hilarious. Everyone danced to lively music provided by a local band. The wedding reception went on into the night, guests quaffing champagne and gobbling up the white chocolate frosting atop the lemon custard filled cake. In the early hours of the morning, Cherise and François said merci and goodbye to their friends.

Even though they were exhausted, Cherise could not resist opening their wedding presents before going to bed. They stayed up in the early morning hours opening many wonderful gifts, each being personal and lovely, especially the hand-glazed pottery from the region. They savored the aroma of freshly baked fruit pies and homemade jam tucked into woven wicker baskets filled with crisp apples.

"Oh look at these!" she exclaimed with heartfelt gratitude. François and Cherise had received ornately designed, hammered silver platters, heirlooms passed down in generations from the families living in Perigord region. Several farmers gave them wonderful large glass canning jars filled with cassoulet of beans, duck, pork and sausage.

"This is good," François said. "You won't have to cook for weeks."

François presented Cherise a solitaire ruby pendant necklace, which she feared cost far more than she dared ask. She clasped around his wrist an engraved silver cuff with their initials entwined. Her heart was so full knowing if she had not moved to France, she never would have met François.

"Let's not take a honeymoon now," he murmured into her ear.

"You are right," she agreed.

"With our onslaught of impending guests, instead let's go somewhere special after the rental season has closed at the castle. Perhaps we could go to Monaco," he suggested.

"That would be wonderful," Cherise enthused, "I've never been there."

Unable to stand up or stay up any longer, the newlyweds walked up the staircase, single file, to avoid the slanted beams in the hallway. It had become routine to take the first flight by ducking their heads to the right, and on the second flight, tilting their heads to the left. This was the way to avoid a bang on the skull. Reaching her room, the nuptial bed beckoned. Sandrina had scattered rose petals on the embroidered pillows. Exhausted, Cherise slipped on a lace and satin nightgown she had selected intentionally for this special evening.

"You look absolutely beautiful," François said, taking her hand and lifting her onto the bed.

She nestled entwined in his arms, and whispered to him, "François, I cannot believe I am yours."

He thought it was the perfect utterance and he said quietly to her, while stroking her hair, "Yes, dear, you are completely mine."

François had accomplished the most important part of his plan. He had made Cherise fall in love with him. It had all been easy...very, very easy indeed.

Dawn broke early, streaming through the leaded glass bedroom windows that had blown open during the night. Cherise got up and dressed, selecting a linen skirt, flats, a cream colored top and simple jewelry. As she shut the armoire door, looking in its mirror she saw not only her reflection, but the face of a hopeful woman, whose previous marriage had disintegrated. She had not heard from Andy in a long time, nor did she expect to. She had not provided him her address and felt it was better if he could not call her. Her fear was her ex-husband would want her to return to San Francisco and would try to talk her out of living in France.

Nonetheless, she felt an unexpected pang for not telling him about the wedding. Perhaps she should have called Andy. Cherise rationalized that, since he was the one who had left her, it would appear as if she was getting even with him or trying to hurt him. So, she had not called him. She figured Andy was most likely flying to some exotic country and, even if she tried, she could not reach him anyway. Leaving a *"By the way, I am getting married—or I am married"* message on his recorder was unthinkable and unnecessarily cruel. Andy had wounded her deeply, but being hurtful and vengeful was not in her nature.

Watching François dress for the day, she admired his perfect physique revealed in his fitted tan slacks and black polo shirt. Curious, Cherise asked, "What time will Colette be arriving today?"

Dabbing his aftershave cologne, François said without hesitation, "She should arrive around noon. I have to go to Bordeaux to pick her up. It's a three-hour trip, one way, so I won't be home until later this evening."

"Why didn't she fly to Sarlat?" Cherise asked inquisitively, trying to fix her hair into a ponytail with a rubber band that wouldn't wind properly, causing her hair to sprout out like a haystack.

"Colette could not fly into the local airport, because the renovation on the runway is still not finished."

"Couldn't she have taken the train?" Cherise pondered, sitting cross-legged on the bed, with the palm of her hand supporting her chin, elbow resting on her knee.

"Normally, yes, but there was some problem with the rails—they are being repaired today," François said, with a pleasant smile.

"Oh, okay. I won't plan dinner, but we can all have a glass of wine when she arrives. I'm really looking forward to meeting her."

"Wine will be nice."

"Au revoir, my husband," she said, regarding him longingly

"Au revoir, Madame Delacroix."

He pulled her gently out of bed, kissing her fervently on the lips, holding her hips in his hands and pressing her into his body. She watched him turn and quickly depart their room, intent on getting to Bordeaux on time. She called loudly down the stairs after him, "Do you need something to eat on the trip?"

"No, I'll grab a bite on the way and I'm taking some croissants and cheese with me. I'll be fine."

Cherise heard the sound of the castle door close, the cold thud unpleasantly reminiscent of the finality of sealing a prisoner into a dungeon. But, she mused, if anything, she was a prisoner in a state of complete bliss. It amazed her that noises became far more apparent when alone—like the ticking of the clock on the nightstand and the sound of the red-headed, black and white woodpecker pounding its beak on the underside of the rafters rather than the nearest elm tree.

She liked the sound of *Cherise Delacroix—Mrs. François Delacroix*— she could not decide which she preferred but planned to order engraved stationery and thank you notes with her new name. Hearing the engine roar to life on his sports car, Cherise leapt out of bed and dashed to the small window in the hallway so she could watch François confidently maneuver down the winding driveway. She reminded herself that maybe she did deserve such happiness. François was passionate and so very considerate of her feelings and well-being, even to the point of ensuring that she did not have to work so hard as proprietress of Roufillay.

Andy had never been as sensitive and caring, except during the early years of their marriage. Somehow, later in their marriage, he had become oblivious to the long hours she worked. What a blessing it was to have a man in her life who put her needs first. How did she ever find someone so perfect, so caring? Cherise believed she was the most blessed person in the world. She no longer felt like a failure in either her marriage or her job. Roufillay was a success. She was married to the man of her dreams and the scars of her past had healed. Cherise was not particularly religious, but at that moment, she raised her blue eyes up to the sky to where God might reside, and thanked Him with all her heart for her perfect life.

CHAPTER 11

Chippenham, England

Brett distractedly drank several cups of strong black coffee, not bothering to shave, while poring over vintage car magazines. He discovered auto varieties new to him, including a Broomstick Jaguar XK120 which, although built in 1993, was not a rare vintage car. Brett entered various word combinations on the Internet...*vintage car, old classic cars, rare English cars.* He came up with a few possibilities, but had no way of knowing if any of these cars were the one that the groundskeeper Henry had seen the night Raleigh died.

Brett found several Lagondas, from 1933 to 1936, all rare and expensive, up to 300,000 euros, depending in which country the owner sold them. He found several rare Aston Martins, titled *Pre-War,* and there was a 1924 model worth over 1,000,000 pounds. After hours of research, Brett discovered a likely possibility—a 1931 S-type *Invicta.* The car was very rare and there were only a few in the world, often collected by the highest bidder. All were convertibles.

Brett's instincts were alerted by this particular *Invicta* model's name. *The Black Prince* was manufactured in the 1940-1950 timeframe. Somehow, he thought it might appeal to a sinister person—but decided that was probably wishful thinking. Also, a car manufactured in the 40's or 50's would not be as rare as a 1931 S-type. He rubbed his head in frustration and then folded the downloaded computer printed pictures and stuffed them into his trench coat pocket.

He grabbed his lunch, locked up the house, and dashed to his car. Brett drove through the unrelenting downpour, heading to Brightingham to see the groundskeeper, Henry Tabbits. He thought to himself, if Henry could remember the car or at least rule out some of the models from the pictures he had brought with him, it might help him narrow down the make and model. Finding out who owned such a vintage car was going to be difficult, but not impossible. After all, he told himself, the impossible just took longer. It's why he did what he did. It just made the challenge greater, and in the end, the result was worthwhile.

Brett shivered in the car and turned on the heater. "Damn, damp drippy weather," he muttered to himself in disgust. Reaching for a pastrami sandwich he'd prepared before the trip, he chewed each bite slowly, enjoying the zesty mustard and sauerkraut that dripped down his chin onto his clean shirt. Brett was glad he was meeting with Henry and not a woman who would think him a slob—a smelly slob with disgusting bad breath. Brett reminded himself the point of the trip was to talk to Henry the groundskeeper to see if he had ever spoken with Diana and ask if he knew what the servants thought of her. Brett did not know how he would ask the questions and wished he had thought to ask the groundskeeper more about Raleigh's young wife when he was there a week ago.

As he drove up to the entrance gate, he discovered it was closed even though it was mid-day.

"Drats!" Brett growled aloud in frustration. He rang the buzzer, once, twice and on the third try, he heard a faint voice, "Yes, who is it?"

"It's Brett Maxfield. Is this Mrs. Weatherly?"

"No, it's Cicely. I'm one of Carl and Anna's maids."

"Oh, uh…I met with Miriam Weatherly just last week and she introduced me to Henry Tabbits. I wanted to ask him a question about some bugs that are eating my laurel leaves."

Brett thought he should have come up with a better reason for being there. Did bugs eat laurel leaves? He chided himself for being inept. Maybe he should have said mites or worms, he thought to himself.

"Mr. Maxfield, I'm terribly sorry," the maid said, her voice cracking and weak. "Uh, oh dear, sir, Henry passed away yesterday morning.

Apparently he had a stroke while working at the pond, and fell in. He drowned. No one found him for hours. Mrs. Weatherly is not here right now, and we are all quite grief-stricken. It was dreadful! Did you want to leave a message for her?"

Gasping, Brett mumbled, "I'm so terribly sorry. Please tell Mrs. Weatherly I stopped by and give her my condolences."

Brett numbly stared through the gate at Brightingham's imposing facade and looked down at the gilded gate buzzer, jolted by the news. He turned, opened the car door, and sat in his dark green MG, listening to torrents of rain pouring on the tan convertible canvas top, pounding erratically like a woman beating an old dusty rug. He took the vintage car pictures out of his pocket and stared at them on his lap with a sense of despair. With no one to identify the car, maybe his detective days, post-retirement, were over.

CHAPTER 12

London, England

Diana Dupree, for all her beauty, had an unusually conflicted personality as well as a reputation for being an opportunistic woman. Much of her selfishness and desire for wealth were a result of losing both of her parents in a car crash when she was five years old. An only child without any living aunts, uncles or grandparents, Diana was a product of the foster care system, shuttled back and forth to more homes than she cared to count or remember. A few families had been kind to her, but she never felt genuinely loved. Some foster parents abused her, verbally and physically. Some ignored her needs, instead using the foster care system for the money. Diana could remember hearing their arguments at night, yelling obscenities to each other, during their fights about her.

"Why did you bring one more mouth here to feed?" "If you would just get off your damn butt and get a job, I wouldn't have to keep bringin' extra kids here for the money. I only do it for the money." "You think I can stand these little bastards running around here all day?"

Often a foster parent's home included several children and Diana simply blended into the group, having no identity of her own. Early on she lost the ability to become attached to anyone and developed her own survival techniques.

When she was seventeen, Diana experienced her sexual awakening in an encounter with a lonely neighborhood widower. She quickly learned her body could give others pleasure as she discovered her body responded in ways no one had ever told her about. When she was old enough to escape the foster system, poverty was something Diana intended never to tolerate again. Her memories of eating out of garbage cans at the back of restaurants disgusted her and she was determined to improve her distasteful lot in life. The tools Diana had were her looks and her figure. She would learn how to use them to her advantage vowing to find wealth whatever the cost.

Diana never considered herself a prostitute. She considered herself a survivor who was clever enough to save money from her trysts to buy expensive dresses, fine shoes and sheer lacy undergarments. As Diana grew to a young woman, she quickly learned how to entice men in bars in fine restaurants and hotels. Waiting for the right man in the bar to sit next to her and offer to buy her a drink was quite easy. And Diana could choose. If she did not think the man was wealthy, which she assessed by how he was dressed, she could always decline his offer. Certain restaurants seemed to attract better prospects, as did certain hotel bars.

"Let's go to my room," he would say, grasping her arm in anticipation. Diana never left the bar accompanying a man, so the bartender couldn't accuse her of prostitution. If the bartenders suspected, they never said anything to her or to the management, for which she was grateful. Diana's whispered words were always, "No, just give me your room number and key and once we are away from the bar I will meet you up there in fifteen minutes." She would smile and seal the deal with a purposeful enticing wink, tracing the top of her breasts with her finger.

This courtesan life Diana had crafted for herself gave her an opportunity to consider going out with select, carefully chosen, older wealthy men who treated her to fine restaurants and outstanding cuisine. If a man attracted to her was married, Diana was unconcerned. In fact, a married man traveling on business was easier because she knew some unsuspecting wife was at home, far away. Condoms were cheap and sex was a small price to pay for sleeping on expensive, high thread count sheets and sipping fine wine. Dining at exclusive restaurants made Diana forget her emotionally troubled background. She made up so many stories about where she was born and where she lived, she had trouble remembering her own lies. In her head, Diana wished any of her fabrications were true.

"I want you to model for my agency," one professionally dressed man said to her, after meeting her in a fine hotel bar.

"Oh, do you think I'd be any good at it? I've never done any modeling," she inquired.

"With your looks and figure, you'll be a standout," he said.

"I'd be grateful to give it a try," she said. "What do I have to do?" Diana lilted with brief hesitation.

"Just come to my office in the morning. Here's my card. We'll do a photo shoot and try various lines of clothing to see what suits you best."

This encounter changed her life. Diana Dupree's face served her well and allowed her access to designer labels which she got to wear after trunk shows. Some clothes she stole, generally one outfit at a time, and they were never missed at the larger fashion shows. Diana was not an A-list top model, because she was not tall, certainly not the requisite bone-thin emaciated type and, in fact, she was quite well-endowed. However, her exquisite facial beauty ensured success and she earned enough money to pay her rent on her small apartment.

If she was very lucky, Diana would meet someone who belonged to a country club or owned a yacht or private jet and simply wanted her to be an attractive trophy on his arm to accompany him to prestigious events. Occasionally a liaison lasted for years, but ultimately one or the other tired of the relationship. Diana was unable to compel anyone to marry her. Either the man did not ask, or if she asked him, the answer was no. It appeared Diana's lot in life was to play the courtesan...the harlot...descriptive words she hated. She envisioned being a chatelaine living as the mistress of a vast castle. Diana Dupree dreamed of being adored, of being appreciated, but most of all, being loved.

Diana had never felt truly loved. Men adored her, but appreciation never led to marriage. She knew marriage was a remote possibility, and most of the time she did not care, as long as someone kept her living in luxury. She remembered the charming, exceptionally wealthy sheik's proposal of marriage. She had considered marrying him, but it would have meant living in Saudi Arabia, and the sheik already had several other wives. Being part of a harem where she was not unique or distinctive did not interest her. Although Diana realized she probably was not capable of loving anyone, she desperately wanted someone to care for her and give her the life she'd never had.

In 2004, when she met Sir Raleigh Aubrey, Diana Dupree had been dining at an upscale restaurant in London. She accidentally bumped Sir Aubrey's arm on the way to a reserved table with her date, Jacques Poundstone, a respected member of the Queenswood Golf Club. Just as Raleigh was lifting a glass of Chateau Margaux, the red 1985 Grand Cru Classe vintage wine spilled over the lord's expensive suit, tie and the linen tablecloth.

"Oh, I'm so terribly sorry!" Diana blushed, embarrassed. Sir Aubrey was gracious, claiming it was nothing.

"Please. I insist on paying for the cleaning bill. Here's my name and phone number." Diana quickly jotted her contact information on a piece of paper thinking she'd never hear from him. With everyone in the restaurant looking at her, the least she could do was to offer to clean his suit.

When Sir Raleigh Aubrey called several days later, Diana was surprised. He was charming on the phone and offered to take her for a walk in the park and then to dinner so he could get to know her. Surprised by his interest, Diana realized Sir Aubrey was different than other men. No one had ever said they wanted to get to know her as a person, which meant for the first time, Diana had something to offer a man besides her body.

Diana accepted his dinner offer. He asked her what music she enjoyed and they talked about books and current events. Raleigh did not make her feel cheap. They spent more and more time together, and Diana realized Sir Raleigh was delighted to be in her company. He made her laugh, and she was an expert at making him feel desirable and interesting, even though he was in his late seventies. It was the first relationship Diana had with someone who seemed to be interested in what she had to say. To her surprise, when Raleigh asked, Diana discovered she had opinions of her own to share about almost every topic.

After many pleasant dates in London where he kept a flat in posh Hyde Park, Raleigh invited her to his castle in Windermere-on-the-Lake, in Cumbria. Diana had no idea of the Camelot-sized property or that Sir Raleigh Aubrey was a very prominent person of considerable wealth. She learned his wife had died many years before of ovarian cancer and she could sense the older man's need for companionship. Diana realized this was one man she actually liked and felt she could manipulate into marriage if she tried hard enough. Raleigh was kind, lonely and willing to indulge her with anything she wanted. Diana loved the idea of living as a wealthy woman in England. She was so close to the life she wanted. She could almost touch it and nothing was going to get in her way.

Windermere, England, 2004

One evening, after dinner in his vast dining hall some thirty meters long, having dined on fine Herend china, solid gold chargers, heavily engraved Towle silver, and more crystal glasses for wine than she had seen at a wedding, Sir Raleigh discretely insinuated he wanted to be intimate with Diana that evening. Waiting for the staff to leave the dining hall, Raleigh leaned toward Diana and whispered,

"I would be honored if you would spend the night."

"Of course," she replied. "It would be my pleasure." She straightened the folds in her emerald green shantung silk dress that showed off her porcelain skin, chestnut red hair, and abundant breasts, knowing she was irresistibly enticing and prepared to give him whatever he needed or wanted.

"Can you help me navigate the stairs?" Raleigh asked, without a hint of frailty. "Certainly," she said. "Let me take your arm."

As he walked with her slowly up the enormous stone staircase, lined with carved balustrades, he balanced with his cane, carefully taking one step at a time, bending slightly from the waist. Holding his arm, Diana glanced upwards at the 17th and 18th century tapestries and enormous oil paintings. She could imagine a life like this.

"Where are we going?" she mused.

"I want to show you the upstairs and my room. I like to do all my writing there," he breathed with a new intimacy.

Sir Raleigh Aubrey's bedroom suite was off the main hallway. It was furnished with an intricately carved four-poster bed, a large gilded gold writing table with a leather inlaid top, an antique armoire, several silk sitting chairs and a soft 18th century pale aqua and cream Tabriz carpet. Heavy red velvet drapes and silk red and beige corded tiebacks hung attached to the frames of the leaded windows. A gold beveled, ornately scrolled mirror tilted slightly from the wall, and two matching tall blue willow spice jars flanked the mantle atop the fireplace. Glancing upwards, Diana stifled a gasp, never having seen such beautiful, carved wood coffered ceilings.

He sat on the edge of the bed and removed his dinner jacket. Not entirely sure what he expected, Diana sat next to him, folding her hands in her lap. Raleigh turned toward her, placing a wrinkled, liver-spotted hand on her cheek. He kissed her on the mouth, lightly and then with more intensity. Diana moved one of her hands toward his belt. He stopped her and buried his head in the cleavage of her breasts kissing them softly. She again tried to remove his belt buckle and he gently restrained her hands, clasping them together.

"No. Please don't," Raleigh said firmly. She looked into his eyes, rejected and confused. "It's not you, Diana. It's my age. I have spinal stenosis and severe osteoporosis. War injuries have taken their toll and I cannot satisfy you in the way I feel you deserve. I don't want you to see this aging body. It will frighten you away."

"Oh no, no, I promise, it won't." she said. "It does not matter to me what your body looks like. I just want to please you."

He asked her to undress, slowly and sit in one of the red silk bergere chairs with the ottoman situated across from the bed. Eyes greedy, he requested she pleasure herself while he watched. He wanted to see her hands stroking her body, reaching a climax, naked and writhing in sexual heat. Diana obliged him, finally understanding that Raleigh did not want to be touched, did not want the embarrassment of being unable to have an erection, and to avoid having her look at the frail, bent frame of the man he used to be.

As she touched herself, stroking her hands over her breasts and her nipples, Diana moved one hand between her thighs, pulsating back and forth. She watched him watch her, occasionally closing his eyes, as if remembering how desire felt, while lifting his beard and neck upward as if he were participating in her pleasure. Raleigh continued watching her with lurid intensity, breathing heavily and observing her climax as if it was his own. A true voyeur—he was experiencing her pleasure through his eyes and in his mind as if it was happening to him. She delighted in this and, when finished, Diana walked naked towards him and sat down on his bed.

He lightly touched her breasts, while she kept her arms at her side, whispering to her that she was exquisitely beautiful. He carefully positioned her on his bed, covering her gently with the silk sheet and told her to sleep, while stroking her hair. As Diana drifted off, Raleigh got up slowly, using the bedpost for support, gained his balance and limped to one of the bergere chairs. He sat down, with a grimace, searching for a comfortable position. Watching her sleep from a distance, he decided he had to keep her. This exquisite creature belonged in his life. Comforted by her presence, he slowly slid into slumber.

Over the next few months, Diana spent more and more time with Sir Raleigh, convincing him she truly loved him. He was smitten and wanted to own her like the many other fine possessions he had obtained. When he asked her to marry him, Diana felt she had finally accomplished what had been impossible in the past—a marriage proposal, a life of wealth and prestige—all she had dreamed of and with an elderly man she did not have to sleep with. Who could have asked for more? She had her own room and was merely obliged to provide visual excitement for him in his bedchamber when he requested her presence. After her exhibition, Raleigh would kiss her, and Diana would retire to her own room. Raleigh preferred to sleep alone, in silk pajamas soft on the skin, covering his bent bones protruding out of his back like broken twigs.

Diana and Sir Raleigh Aubrey, preferring a civil ceremony, were married in London at the courthouse close to the famed Covent Garden theatre district near Piccadilly. After the ceremony, Raleigh had wanted to attend a newly opened musical, *Wicked*, but she pleaded with him to instead take her to Harrods to go shopping. Despite attempts to keep the wedding a secret, several photos made the tabloids and the *London Dispatch*. The paparazzi had gotten wind of the marriage and, with their cameras clicking incessantly, caught them together leaving the courthouse steps, despite Sir Raleigh Aubrey's best attempts for privacy.

Friends and business colleagues in London could not help but gossip and word of the May-December marriage got out. Raleigh told Diana he did not like other people being involved with his private matters, and knew some friends and former business colleagues would not approve of his marrying someone so young and beautiful. Sir Raleigh wanted to spare himself their disdainful glances and knew his friends would taunt him that his new young wife was after his money. Raleigh sensed their concern was possible, even probable, but he did not want to hear it from others or be forced to believe it. He was happier than he had been for a long time and he wanted to be left alone to live out his days in Brightingham in peace. When Sir Raleigh attended occasional board meetings in London, he often dropped Diana off to shop at the best places, suggesting she buy whatever she desired, and as much as she could carry.

Wandering through the quaint shops, she smiled to herself. Diana Dupree became Lady Diana Aubrey the moment they signed the wedding certificate. What had seemed impossible to her had finally happened. She was married to a wealthy man. For once in her life, she had status, even though it would probably become a sordid topic of discrete discussion in some circles. Diana was no longer a model, nor was she a child of the streets, unwanted and unloved. She was somebody—she was Lady Diana Aubrey and finally she was loved.

After returning to Brightingham, Diana showered her husband with attention daily, serving him breakfast in bed, laying out his outfits, and fetching lunch on a tray, including his favorite newspapers, magazines and books. Up and down the stairs she climbed, several times a day, never complaining, knowing this kept her in shape. Diana could have taken the lift, but it was a hassle to pull the gate across, close the door and attempt to balance the food or clothing on her arm, while trying to push the elevator button. The walk from the lift to his room was too long, so she made peace with the stairs.

When Raleigh was in the mood to talk, Diana listened to his stories about the war and the invasion of Normandy. Being a companion and wife, interested in her husband's past life, she felt she was doing a kindness. It was an odd experience to trust since she was not used to having kindness reciprocated. Diana could be blunt and less than tactful when ordering the servants around or when she felt her needs were not immediately being attended to. The servants did not live in the castle, but in the caretakers' cottages, which were outside of the back entrance gate to the property. Every morning they dutifully arrived through the coded back entrance gate to cook and clean the castle and then, much later, after preparing dinner and finishing cleaning up in the kitchen, they returned to their little homes.

It was a pleasure for Diana not to make her own cup of tea if she preferred having the staff attend to her wishes. She spent her days waiting on her husband, walking the grounds, disdainfully refusing conversation with the groundskeeper because, in her mind, those in servitude were beneath her. By distancing herself from the staff, except to make requests or give orders, Diana perceived that she was elevated to a more lofty position. She did not like the disapproving glances some of the servants gave her, but their smirks and snickers were a small price to pay for living a life of luxury.

The majority of her free time, Diana spent reading books. There was so much she needed to learn about the world, about art and music. Raleigh readily discussed any topic with her, answering any question she posed to him and she quickly absorbed knowledge like a dry sponge dropping into the ocean for the first time.

Effortlessly, she embraced certain household duties for herself, such as planning Raleigh's meals with the staff, which they did not object to since Raleigh continued to order the same favored menu choices he had dictated to the staff for years. If there was a business event Raleigh needed to manage, now as his wife, Diana enjoyed orchestrating all that had to be done. She helped him manage the many business calls he had to return, comfortably speaking in French, English, Italian and Spanish. Her proclivity for learning other languages she had picked up from her previous liaisons had paid off. Diana was conversationally adept, and could converse readily and with ease, switching from one language to another. Much to her amazement, she never thought learning various languages would serve her so well.

Although Raleigh no longer built and developed country clubs, he remained on several advisory boards and numerous art and charitable foundations. Because it was common knowledge he was exceptionally wealthy, everyone wanted and requested philanthropic funds for their favorite charity, for new commercial building projects or prospective start-up business ventures. Brightingham had been paid for years ago and had no mortgage—only yearly taxes, which he could afford easily with revenue from the business he had sold years before he had met Diana. His advisory board stipends covered the food and utilities, the servants and groundskeepers. Nonetheless, a great deal of bookkeeping and business journal entries were required. Rather than have his accountant bother him constantly with every detail, Sir Raleigh was glad to turn it all over Diana to manage.

"I'm so pleased with everything you've done to help me with my business dealings," he smiled with relief.

"I'm happy to help you, Raleigh. I've learned so much from you. It's the least I can do," she'd responded.

He was gratified his young wife was genuinely interested in his business affairs. Raleigh could not know that Diana did nothing without a deliberate purpose. She was intensely interested in all of his business dealings because she knew eventually his wealth was going to be her wealth when he died. Childless, Raleigh would have bequeathed his money to charity had he died before he met her, but she would make sure the only charity in his life was the protected future of Lady Diana Aubrey.

Sir Raleigh continued to delight in Diana's skills and was glad to have someone who was as much a personal secretary as a wife. It gave him time to relax and listen to Puccini—his favorite was *Madame Butterfly*. With additional assistance, now provided by Diana, Sir Raleigh finally had the time to start working on his memoirs, a promise he had made to himself long ago, to write about his service for his beloved country during the war.

Raleigh summoned his attorney to Brightingham late in the winter, and he changed his will, making Diana the beneficiary to inherit the castle and all his assets if he died. He had no children from his previous marriage or living relatives and Raleigh was delighted to leave his entire estate to his wife rather than to charity. He had already donated much to hundreds of charitable organizations over the years and he felt that, should he die first, Diana deserved to continue her life of extraordinary ease and comfort.

As winter turned to spring, the seasons blended into disconcerting boredom for Diana. She began to feel unsettled and agitated. Hating to admit to herself what was all glitz and glamour when new, was now starting to feel like servitude. Thoughts she could not repress were forming in the back of her mind.

Sitting in her room late one night, Diana realized she didn't feel the rage and insecurity she'd had for years because she was no longer afraid of going hungry or felt the need to resort to trading sexual services for money. The trauma of eating out of garbage cans had faded from her memory. She had blocked out much of her past because she did not want to remember it. Her life with Raleigh provided all the wealth she had dreamed of. However, it wasn't enough.

"I can't believe I feel so trapped," she said aloud to herself. Thoughts were swirling in her head conjuring up feelings she did not want to acknowledge. "He's boring. I'm tired of listening to the same damn stories of his life, over and over. If I have to hear about the invasion of Normandy one more time, I will just shit," she said to herself in disgust. "I'm young. I want to go into town to shop, to be seen, and to sleep with someone who can satisfy me."

Diana was aware she could not continue to contemplate this train of thought. Infidelity would not be tolerated by her husband. She missed the company of people her own age and being among vibrant and exciting people. Remaining with Sir Raleigh was starting to make her feel old.

Sir Raleigh Aubrey began going to bed very early and sleeping late in the mornings. He was experiencing more trouble getting out of bed and was unable to go up and down the stairs without assistance. The lift was too far away and Raleigh did not want to be in the elevator with his servants. So, with Diana at his side, they navigated the stairs with his arm holding on to her shoulder, one step at a time, taking an eternity. She had to help him to the bathroom, which she dreaded. Getting him on and off the commode was daunting and disgusting, waiting for him to defecate, often taking half an hour or more.

"Raleigh, are you done yet?" she would ask in frustration, sitting on the bed or in a chair, listening to gross body noises that should be private. Diana would open a window to prevent herself from gagging. His severe osteoporosis and spinal stenosis was painful requiring Vicodin, administered twice a day, making him groggy and constipated which was even worse. Diana abhorred having to call a servant to come up to his room to clean up the splatter on the loo. It was a blessing, perhaps, he slept most of the time, but that meant relentless daily boredom. At the end of each day, the servants would return to their cottages and Diana felt deserted in the vast mansion, engulfing her in the terror of being alone with someone who was nearing death.

Raleigh began to drink excessively and demanded she bring him brandy or whisky. He was unable to move easily and hated being in bed. The more he was confined to his room, the more he bellowed and yelled for her to come running to him to preform meaningless tasks. Raleigh would ring for the servants for no reason and they became tired of his ranting and raving.

Gradual dementia eroded his once sharp mind and Raleigh settled into a fog, not remembering what day or even which year it was. His sporadic lucid moments were filled with manic energy, writing his memoirs of World War II, so transfixed, he refused to eat. Inevitably, Raleigh became permanently relegated to a wheelchair, which he profusely protested. He was reconciled and less angry when he realized he could get in and out of it by himself by clutching onto furniture in the room. With some limited independence, Raleigh could wheel himself to the window and look out over the spectacular, manicured gardens. He appreciated small pleasures that graced the grounds often spotting a blue heron or red fox or even watching and listening to a woodpecker hammering against an oak tree.

As days blended into weeks, the old man could no longer walk independently and became completely confined to his room. He was helped into his wheelchair and out of it to go to the bathroom (a task his wife relegated to a male servant during the day). Sir Raleigh Aubrey had become a permanent invalid, stuck in his room. If he wasn't writing, often in dementia-infected gibberish, Raleigh would roll himself to the window, gazing out in despair. Mostly, he slept in the wheelchair, now a prisoner of his condition. He looked like a ghost, confined to inescapable hours of resigned self-pity.

Diana felt trapped, miserable and utterly panic-stricken. If she tried to leave, even for a brief trip into town, the old man screamed at her and called her ungrateful. She knew it was dementia and the pain talking, but her temper began to flare. She lost patience with Raleigh and called him names. She said awful things about his decrepit body, knowing her words hurt him deeply.

"I feel like a caged animal in a museum of luxury," she barked at him.

When he asked her to disrobe and undulate in front of him, she was now repulsed and screamed at him "No, I won't and you can't make me!"

He yelled back at her and said "If you don't do what you're so damn good at, I will write you out of my will, you no-good bitch!"

She fled out of his room, screaming back at him, "Do what you damn well please!" and threw herself on her bed in her own room, sobbing.

While the rain pounded the windows and shutters slapped wildly against the stone ledges, Diana stretched out on her bed and thought about Raleigh's threat. She looked at the floral draped canopy attached to the four bedposts overhead and sat up, fearful and distraught about the possibility of being poor, alone and back on the street and once again needing to find someone to take care of her. The cold, calculating girl she'd needed to become growing up returned, tapping on her shoulder, reminding her of the pain she had suffered. Diana was determined to survive. She needed to think. She might lose everything. If Raleigh wrote her out of the will, all of this would have been for nothing.

Had he not started drinking and been so demanding maybe, she told herself, she could have tolerated remaining his wife until he died of natural causes. She did not plan on dealing with the dementia. Providing nursing care for him was an awful burden. She hated every minute, watching him drool and cleaning up after him when he was incontinent. Continuing this misery was unthinkable and revolting to her. Diana wanted out of this marriage, but not without the wealth she had earned and deserved.

Shivering, she grumbled quietly to herself. "How am I going to do this? How will I manage?" She weighed the prospect of selling some of her jewelry, but it would not be nearly enough to live the lifestyle she wanted. "I want to travel, to stay in the best places, to meet important people," she thought to herself, checking off her priorities.

"What I really want is to meet someone who will make me feel alive again." Diana said, out loud.

She resolved to come up with a plan—a way to keep Brightingham for herself. Chewing on her thumbnail, she knew what she needed to do. Barefoot, she crept out of her room, down the staircase to the library where she flicked on a desk lamp. She opened the real estate section of the *London Dispatch* and luxury property magazines and researched other castles with similar property for sale for several million pounds. That would do. With the eventual sale of Brightingham, Diana was going to be a very, very wealthy woman and now she needed to devise a scheme for her survival.

The morning after their terrible fight, Diana entered Raleigh's room, smiling pleasantly. He was gazing out of the window, sitting in his wheelchair, looking forlorn and humiliated.

"Look, I'm sorry for the things I said last night. I'm sorry for my behavior," she pleaded, hoping for a reprieve.

Raleigh had awakened sober, and the fog of his dementia had faded for the moment. He recognized Diana and felt remorseful, begging her to forgive him as well. Diana touched him gently on the forehead, leaning over his shoulder. She moved to the front of his chair, knelt down putting her head gently on his lap. Forced tears spilling from her eyes onto his robe she wheedled, "Let's take a round-trip Mediterranean cruise—a chance for both of us to get away from the confines of the castle. A change of scenery and fresh sea air would do you good," she smiled convincingly.

Startled, Raleigh balked, saying he would be too much trouble. Knowing how to get what she wanted, she dropped her nightgown to the floor. "Raleigh, I promise that on the cruise, I will do whatever you want, as often as you care to look." He stared at her, considering.

"They have excellent accommodations for people in wheelchairs, highly competent doctors and your physician has agreed to increase your medication so you'll be in much less pain. Please, Raleigh? We both need this." To her delight, he finally agreed to the trip.

Diana immediately contacted the travel agency and booked a stateroom on a luxury cruise ship. Boarding her elderly husband onto the ship, wheelchair and all, would be a challenge, but possible. She could keep him on painkillers and booze so he would sleep most of the time, especially in the early evening. Finding someone to kill Raleigh was going to be harder. Confident in her charms and Diana determinedly packed her tightest fitting dresses, uplift bras, thong panties, exotic perfume and most expensive jewelry. She was sure someone could be bought for a price to carry out her plan.

The Mediterranean, South of France

Diana was pleased with the cruise she'd selected, visiting some lovely ports-of-call, including Nice, Cannes and St. Tropez. The weather would be warm and a pleasant change from England's damp climate. Once onboard the ship, with the help of a porter, she got Raleigh settled comfortably in their large stateroom on the fifth deck. There was enough room for his wheelchair and Raleigh would be able to look out the balcony windows. Against one wall was a desk where he could continue writing his memoirs on good days and read his beloved history novels. The ship's daily itinerary provided plenty of activities to enjoy. The evening dinner no longer required formal attire, but Sir Raleigh preferred to wear a jacket, so she obliged by helping dress him.

On this evening, Diana attired herself in an alluring white satin and chiffon cocktail dress and jewel-studded, high heeled sling-back shoes. Other passengers stared admiringly at them, sitting at their private table in the dining room. Raleigh preferred not to meet people he would never see again, and he did not have patience for senseless conversational chatter. Diana ordered from the menu for both of them, selecting his favorite scotch and a vintage wine for dinner. Raleigh observed the waiters fawning over his wife, serving her every need with obsequious attention. He enjoyed watching others dote on her, knowing his young attractive wife was his own private possession.

A daily routine emerged. After dinner, Diana would wheel Raleigh back to his room and give him his medication. By that hour, he usually had consumed two scotch and sodas, wine with dinner and he was tired. Raleigh welcomed going to bed. Diana stayed with him, dutifully performing for him, if he wished. If he was overly tired, he told her to enjoy the musical performances on the ship or to browse the many shops, stocked with beautiful jewelry, handbags and clothing. This evening, as her wheelchair-bound husband fell sound asleep, she refreshed her make-up and went up to the cocktail lounge on the lido deck.

Attired in her stunning white satin and chiffon knee-length strapless dress and emerald jeweled necklace, Diana was glad she had remembered to dab her signature intoxicating perfume on her wrists, behind her delicate ears, and in her décolletage before starting the hunt. She looked around the dimly lit lounge, admiring the sophisticated silver and black art deco bar and large mirrors reflecting the glass shelving supporting expensive liquor bottles. Exotic neon rope-lighting lined the matte black, faux-finished crown molding. Floor-to-ceiling glass windows jutted out on a precarious slant, leaning over lower decks, providing an unobstructed ocean view. The vaulted ceiling was romantically studded with simulated twinkling stars. Sitting cross-legged on a bar stool, her curve-hugging dress showing off her gorgeous legs and ankles, Diana ordered a dry martini…and then another. In the mirror she watched a decidedly handsome stranger approach her from behind.

"Hello," he said. "Are you waiting for someone?" He sat down on the bar stool next to her, wondering if she was alone. If she was, he said to himself, then he would be damn lucky. Her perfume awakened his senses as he leaned toward her slightly.

"Well, yes I am," Diana said with a teasing tone in her voice, "but it is not what you might think." She looked at his deep blue eyes, noticing his jet-black hair, slightly gray at the temples and his striking countenance. He was dressed in a black suede dinner jacket, black shirt open at the neck and light tan slacks. This man was stunningly handsome.

"And what should I think?" he said, gazing into her lovely green eyes laced with impossibly long black eyelashes. He admired her ample breasts cradling her emerald necklace, making her even more desirable. "I see, unfortunately, you are taken, by the impressive size of your diamond ring," he smiled charmingly, looking at her left hand.

Diana laughed. "*Taken* is a funny word if you knew my circumstances."

Intrigued, he leaned in toward her. "Can I buy you another drink?"

"Yes. I'd like that," she flirted, picking the olive out of her martini and popping it seductively into her mouth, staring into his eyes.

"Let me introduce myself. I am François Delacroix."

She thought the name fit him. "You sound terribly French."

"And you, pretty lady, sound terribly English."

"Good guess. I am. My name is Diana Aubrey."

The disco music started to blare and although she liked dancing, it was not on her mind. She cupped her hands to her ears, pretending to be unable to hear him. He took the cue. François asked if she would like to go outside on the lido deck. She agreed. He guided her, his hand caressing her waist, leading her through the automatic sliding doors to the promenade which circled the ship's upper deck. The air was slightly chilly, but surprisingly comfortable for the time of year. As they walked past unoccupied wooden deck chairs, they were drawn to the metal railing. Moonlight illuminated the gulls as they swooped over the glistening silver waves.

Diana turned toward him, eyes gazing into his. As François looked at her, leaning against the railing, he had never seen any woman more exquisite with chestnut hair cascading down her backless dress, her porcelain skin slightly creamier than the white dress clinging to her voluptuous curves. He looked hungrily at her crimson, full lips and felt an irresistible magnetism.

"So, Diana, what brings you to this cruise? Are you going to stay in France?"

"No. I am taking a round trip cruise with my elderly invalid husband. Just a change of scenery."

"That must be nice for him and for you as well," François said.

Taking a chance on what she was about to say—but then Diana was very good at taking these risks—she decided to offer him the bait.

"It would be nicer for him," she sighed, "if I wasn't trying to get out of this awful marriage."

Stunned, but inwardly delighted, he removed his jacket, gallantly wrapping it around her shoulders.

"Do you want to talk about it?" François said.

Opening her evening bag and taking out a handkerchief, she blotted fake tears easily conjured after years of artful deception.

François listened intently, pretending to be sincerely interested in her plight. It was a long, but incredibly interesting story. And she was obviously very wealthy. He certainly hoped she would be his next income producer. Usually he had to spend weeks on a cruise to identify the right woman. Here it was, only the third day of the cruise, and Diana was exactly what he was looking for…and maybe more.

"Will your husband be wondering where you are?"

"Oh, no. He's flat out on Vicodin and booze and other medications for his osteoporosis and spinal stenosis. I will be lucky if I can wake him in the morning for breakfast. He's in his late seventies and his spine has given out, so it's easier for him to be in a wheelchair. He has early dementia and, at times, does not know what's going on."

François put his hand on her shoulder, and then moved it slowly to her waist. She did not flinch. It was a signal he was hoping for. He planned his words carefully.

"I'm sorry your marriage is not working out. I agree it would be a terrible thing if he wrote you out of his will, after all you have done to take care of him."

"Well, I have not been a total saint either. I do have needs."

She purposely turned toward him, hoping the bait was taken. She moved in close, tossed her hair and lifted her head, her lips slightly parted. François kissed Diana lightly at first to see if she would respond. She fully opened her mouth, allowing his tongue find hers. His kiss left her breathless. She wanted him desperately. It has been too long since she had experienced a virile man pulsating inside her. Every bone in her body ached for him. She felt his breath caress her neck as he pressed her body to his.

"Do you want to do this?" he asked.

"Yes, François. More than anything." She pleaded into his piercing blue eyes.

Other passengers were ambling toward the ship's railing where they were standing and the sea air was getting cooler, misting slightly.

"Come to my cabin," François uttered softly, tracing the top of her breast with his finger just under her necklace.

"We shouldn't go together. Tell me your floor and cabin number and I will meet you there in fifteen minutes."

106

François whispered into her ear the location of his cabin, then turned and walked away, without a glance.

Diana was pleased with herself. She knew Raleigh would not awaken and she would enjoy an affair she desperately needed. She planned to be the most desirable woman François had ever slept with and would do everything to him and let him do anything to her. Under the influence of her considerable charms, she was sure she could convince him to kill Raleigh.

She knocked on François' cabin, several decks above her own stateroom and he opened the door wearing the luxurious terry robe provided by the ship. He was unconcerned that it opened slightly when he walked. It was obvious that underneath the robe he was naked.

He bolted the door and Diana walked over to him. Without losing contact with her eyes, François shrugged off the robe and it dropped to the floor. She marveled at his aroused Adonis-like body. Standing close, she reached her hand down, caressing him with her fingers. François asked her if she was on the pill or if he should put on a condom. Diana assured him her tubes had been tied years ago. Relieved, François permitted himself to respond to her touch.

Diana knelt, taking him in her mouth until he could no longer endure the wait. François pulled her up slowly against him. The zipper on her dress slid down easily. She wore no bra and the tiniest thong panties. François caressed and fondled every inch of her body, kissing her mouth and her voluptuous breasts, her nipples hardening in response. Grappling with abandon, they knocked over a small table, spilling a bottle of white wine, as they fell onto the bedspread. Diana mounted him, fully moist, and let him enter her. He grabbed her buttocks. She moved, circling her hips slowly and intensely, up and down with titillating precision. She felt wildly alive.

François fondled her, pulling her breast into his mouth and finally exploded into her. Their heated passion continued for hours. Diana was insatiable and even though he was exhausted, François found himself entering her, intensely coming again and again. Drained and sated, they lay together, drenched with sweat. François had never expected someone so classically beautiful to be so wildly uninhibited in bed. She was intoxicating.

Afterwards, he watched Diana open the cabin's window, allowing the fresh salty sea air to cool them off. He knew he would feel the marks of her fingernails on his back for days.

Diana's head was spinning but she forced herself to concentrate on her agenda. Hoping he was vulnerable and would not ask her to leave, she said in her softest, most beguiling voice,

"François, I want you to help me kill my husband. His days are filled with excruciating pain and I want to end his life. I don't want to be trapped as his caregiver any longer. I'm too young for this depressing life. If he dies, his will states specifically that I will inherit everything."

Waiting for the shock on his face, shadowed in the moonlight, she was thrilled with his calm response.

"Diana, if I agree to kill your husband, you will have to do everything I ask and the murder must be planned so no one will know we've ever met. And, it will cost you a great deal financially since you will inherit everything when he dies."

"François, I will be glad to give you any sum of money you want to get out of this marriage. However, I don't want to be penniless and I won't live on the streets ever again," she said, pretending to cry.

"Diana, I promise to take very good care of you. I will devise a plan to keep you safe and out of the country so no one will know where you went after his death. You will simply disappear."

"Fine. I can do that. Let's work out the details," Diana wiped her eyes. They plotted and planned every nuance, down to the minutest detail until both were agreed on the exact plan for ending Raleigh's life.

"Don't you need to be getting back to your room? It's nearly 4:30 in the morning?"

"No. I'm not worried. He's dead asleep," she said with a trace of dark humor, climbing on top François again.

Afterwards, they rested in each other's arms, agreeing they should not be seen together on the ship again, and that they could not risk another tryst. Diana congratulated herself that she had accomplished the improbable in finding François. How lucky she was to so easily find someone willing to help kill Raleigh. François lay on the comfortable bed, stroking her back and smiling to himself, thinking that cruise ships remained a fantastic source for finding desperate women—lonely attractive wealthy women willing to do anything. He had killed before and was a master at committing flawless crimes. Diana was just the means to an end…but what a delightful derriere she had.

At five in the morning, Diana returned to her cabin and slipped in her key card, knowing the door was locked. Raleigh lay on his side, drooling into his pillow, snoring like a horse. He looked pathetic and repugnant. She sat on the sofa in the sitting area, pulling off her dress and damp undergarments. Her lilac silk nightgown would be perfect for Raleigh to see the first thing in the morning. She lay in bed, legs still quivering and her mouth remembering the taste of François' lips on hers. Never had she suspected she would find someone so easily or so soon to help her eliminate Raleigh. Looking at his bony frame through the sheets and listening to the snoring, she knew this intolerable situation would not go on forever. In a few days, she would be back in England and her nursemaid days would soon be over. She could play the part of the dutiful wife a bit longer.

CHAPTER 13

Bordeaux France, 2007

One year had passed at Roufillay. François waited for Diana at the airport in Bordeaux, as planned. He thought about how he had met her on the cruise, what she looked like, how she felt to his touch. He smiled smugly, thinking about how their plan had succeeded perfectly.

Now seeing her after such a long absence, waiting patiently by the curbside, he noticed Diana was drawn and pale but still extremely attractive. He knew that while Diana had lived in Switzerland during the past year, she had enjoyed the experience. She repeatedly raved about the beauty of the Jura mountain range and charming towns. Diana had mentioned to François on more than one occasion that she was pleased people had left her alone, did not pry into her personal life and respected her privacy. This was one of the great things about the Swiss. Diana tried to remain a recluse, as he had wished, but whenever he'd called to check in, Diana told François she was terribly lonesome, missing him desperately.

He stopped the car at the curb, got out and rushed to her, kissing her fervently and holding her tightly. François breathed in the scent of her hair, inhaling her heady French perfume, *Bal à Versailles*. Diana clung to him and he knew the long year had been worth the wait.

"François! It's so good to see you. I can hardly believe I'm here."

"I know, Diana. It's been a very long time, but I promise you it will be worth the wait."

He quickly hoisted her single bag of luggage, strapping it to the back of his car. The convertible top was down and she disdainfully frowned with pursed lips indicating to him he'd better promptly put it back up. She got into the sports car, having to crouch down somewhat to fit comfortably. Exhausted from the trip, she drifted in and out of sleep, reflecting upon her life during the past year.

For Diana, now "Colette," it had been a year of a life as a wealthy single woman. She had lived in François' villa on Lake Geneva, expense-free but it had been an emotionally very long year indeed. She had followed every instruction and was sure she had not made any mistakes. Lake Geneva was a perfect place to hide where no one knew her identity. She'd paid cash for her basic necessities, even including groceries, as he had demanded, and she'd left no credit card trail. François had indicated he did not expect her to be a nun while she stayed in his villa. He accepted the fact that she was young, vibrant and had sexual needs to be fulfilled. When she did sleep with an attractive man, she made sure to book a room at the Hotel Eden Palace au Lac on Lake Geneva.

Adept at using skills from her former encounters, Diana was sometimes tempted when she met a man at the bar who was traveling on business who desired a tryst with no strings attached. Sleeping in a handsome man's room, she indulged in the occasional one-night stand, discretely leaving the hotel during the night or before dawn. Diana expected to be paid in cash for her services, which she found ironic and humorous, having experienced both poverty and wealth in her past. Without conscience, she would hop a taxi back to François's villa. She was careful to never use her former name, *Diana Aubrey* or her new name, *Colette Armond.*

The long year had finally come to an end, exactly as planned. In time, Diana would have all the wealth she felt she deserved and be with François. With that comforting thought, she finally drifted off to sleep as he continued to drive.

When she woke, Diana gazed at her surroundings, admiring the pastoral scenery. She was delighted to finally be in France with her lover. François briefed her on her new alias, describing details of her new representation as "Colette Armond." Displeased, Diana argued about her role having to act as a concierge at Roufillay. She was not happy to learn she would be required to live and sleep in the caretaker's cottage.

"Why can't I stay in the main castle?" she asked, pouting her lower lip like a petulant child in disbelief that she would be relegated to servant's quarters.

"You cannot stay in the castle," François explained. "There are booked guests in all the rooms."

"Oh," Diana said, "Well, of course I understand about the guests. That was stupid of me. It's not a problem, really." François patted her thigh, offering a bit of comfort. "We will have plenty of time together once this charade is over."

The concierge duties were acceptable to her, but the idea of not staying in the chateau in an adjacent room near François was distressing. He reminded her that, however frustrating, these were necessary details and she had promised to do whatever he'd asked.

"I just want to get on with the plan. I'm tired of waiting so long to have a satisfying life. The very idea of having to live in the guest cottage, separate from you and imagining you with your wife in the castle is frustrating," Diana whined.

"I understand," he nodded. "It's not easy, but you'll get on with Cherise, I'm sure."

"We'll see," she speculated. In her mind, she was determined to dislike Cherise even before she met her.

"What's your wife like?" Diana asked.

"Well…" François faltered, carefully choosing his words, "She's a very good business woman, capable and has an outgoing personality."

"Humm, uh…" Diana wrinkled her forehead, staring at his countenance while he was driving. "What I wanted to know, is she pretty?"

Not wishing to elaborate, François assured, "She is attractive in her own way, but not a raving beauty like you are, my dear."

Diana remained agitated knowing that, even as part of his plan, any wife of François presented an emotional burden. She hated visualizing François kissing and enjoying another woman's body. However, Diana acknowledged that, at François suggestion, she too had slept with a few men during the past year and she had kept her end of the bargain, always sleeping at the hotel, never at his villa, as he had requested. Now, after a long year apart, she was finally in France and Diana remembered that she had to accept every part of his plan without question. Without any accessible money of her own, she had no choice.

In preparation to meet Cherise, Françoise advised Diana, in her newly contrived role as concierge, to dress plainly, to avoid all jewelry except simple earrings or a bracelet, and to eliminate heavy perfume. François wanted Diana to appear attractive but professional and business-like.

If asked, she was to have been born in Suffolk, with parents who had died in a car crash, and she would have no siblings. Diana, as Colette Armond, had fashioned her life first as a chambermaid, eventually acquiring expertise as an event planner. François suggested that Diana never discuss her modeling background, instead, emphasize her language skills had been attained during her studies in school and through employers she had worked for. There would be no reason for anyone to suspect her life had been any different. François counseled Diana to keep the lipstick light, subdue the overt sex appeal and concentrate on a demeanor that would be business-like, reserved and highly capable.

"I want you to assist Cherise in any way she needs help with the business and remember you cannot look at me in any way that would cause her to wonder about us." And, from this day forward, I will only think of you and speak to you as Collette. It is critical for me to never accidentally refer to you as Diana. You must understand and accept the necessity of this."

Diana laughed out loud and called him ridiculous. François touched the back of her neck and reminded her she owed him this and more if he asked…a small price to pay for her husband's death. He had housed her in his villa for a year, paid the rent and she did not suffer for food or shelter. François enjoyed the control he had over her. For him, it was all a game, and manipulation was a big part of the satisfaction. He had promised Diana he would share the 5,000,000 pounds from the sale of Brightingham. That was their agreement. Convinced, Diana quietly slept the rest of the journey, her head against the closed convertible top, wind blowing across her face from the small open window, all the way to Roufillay.

When they arrived at the castle, Diana was unprepared for the size of the imposing structure and the resplendent grounds. A family of ducks, including fuzzy brown ducklings tottering obediently, crossed the path as they drove up the long driveway. Diana repeated out loud to herself, *"My name is Colette—Colette Armond."*

Red and yellow rose bushes were in full bloom, humming with hovering bees. Well-manicured green shrubs were interspersed with crimson and pink rhododendrons, lilac azaleas, and deep purple tulips.

"Oh my," Colette exclaimed appreciatively. "This is really very pretty." Winding through the tall grove of trees, an amber-colored spotted fawn stopped in their path, stared at the *Invicta*, then darted off into the woods.

"You see how charming this countryside is? It's almost as lovely as England," François commented, as he shifted the car's gears to ease the steep climb. Colette nodded, mentally morphing into her new character's persona. "Yes, she said in a contrived English accent, "It's quite lovely."

Colette's small suitcase was strapped to the back of the car, barely containing enough clothing for her new life. François assured her she could purchase whatever she needed in Sarlat. She was startled by her first view of the castle entrance with a gothic wood and iron door so massive, a smaller entry door had been fashioned within it. Centuries ago, riders on horseback rode directly into the castle, hooves clopping deftly across the stone floor, returning from a day's journey. Iron pillars were set into the floor and near the top of each pillar hung a large forged circular ring, fastened securely to each pillar, used to tie the reins after a ride. Although this castle was not Brightingham, Roufillay was much more than she'd expected.

Now in character as Colette, she stood in the entry hall looking up at the enormous iron chandelier, was startled by Cherise's voice.

"Hello, you must be Colette. I'm Cherise. I am so pleased to meet you," she said enthusiastically, extending her hand.

"Yes, I am too," Colette said, dropping her head while attempting to fix her wind-swept chestnut hair. Looking up, she experienced a chill along her spine. Cherise was much prettier than she'd expected. Colette reluctantly offered her hand, knowing whatever short amount of time Cherise grasped and held it, would feel like an eternity.

Cherise thought Colette a bit shy and, although she wanted to give her a hug, she sensed that would make Colette uncomfortable. Instead, she smiled at the new concierge. "Welcome to Roufillay. I know you will be a great help to me."

Colette stood, her arms at her sides, and quickly replied, "It is my pleasure" in English, French, Italian and then Spanish, tilting her head elegantly, hoping to garner status by impressing her employer with her linguistic skill.

Cherise raised both eyebrows in delight and gave Colette a warm smile of approval. François stood impassively, watching the two women interact.

"Oh," Cherise said to François, "these language skills are going to be incredibly helpful to our guests. I'm so glad you brought Colette here. She *is* everything you told me and more." Colette managed a weak smile, feeling her facial muscles pull upward as if by a marionette's strings.

"Let me show you to the caretaker's cottage here on the grounds," Cherise said. "I'm sure you must want to get settled after the long drive."

"Yes, I am rather tired. It's been a long day," Collette nodded.

François unfastened the leather straps, releasing Colette's luggage on the back of the *Invicta* and lifted the small heavy luggage case off the car's trunk. He mused that it was a magnificent automobile but with such limited storage it was virtually impossible to carry anything more than the clothes on one's back.

As they walked to the caretaker's cottage, Colette could see that it had the charm of a bed and breakfast inn. Its honey-colored Dordogne stone block walls had aged gorgeously, enhanced by chartreuse moss and ivy clinging to the walls. Red clusters of pyracanthus berries decorated bushes tucked under a small-paned window facing the castle. The rooms were small but very charming. A two-story living room was warmed with aged hewn wood beams enhancing the ceiling. Light blue and white checked wallpaper, peeling at the ceiling, coordinated with the yellow, blue and white floral window coverings with braided tie-backs that gracefully framed the windows. A small blue sofa, dark wood carved armoire and a yellow club chair with a floral needlepoint pillow furnished the living area.

Beyond the living room, Colette could see the small kitchen, with its stone floor, knotty alder wood cabinets, cast-iron farm sink, four-burner gas stove and small refrigerator. A large rectangular wood table in the center of the kitchen was surrounded by chairs covered with cheerful Provençal yellow and blue paisley cushions, fastened to the backside of each chair with tiny rope ties and tassels.

A small hallway, barely large enough for two people to walk through at the same time, led to a modest but adequate bedroom and adjoining tiny bath containing a modern toilet, pedestal sink and claw foot tub with a hand-held shower. French doors along one wall opened to a small balcony with a view of the Dordogne River.

Colette looked for the closet but there was none. She glanced at François, rolling her eyes, her pursed lips and a furrowed brow hinting displeasure at the lack of storage. He pointed to the armoire in the living area. She let out a sigh, wondering how long she would have to reside in the small cottage.

Acting her role, with a show of enthusiasm, Colette uttered, "Cherise, everything is charming. It's perfect," thinking to herself the entire caretaker's cottage would fit into her entry vestibule at Brightingham. Humility did not come easily and every reminder of destitution made her feel like the child she had been in the hated foster homes. She bit her lip, holding back tears, as Cherise turned and asked thoughtfully, "Is there anything else I can get you?"

Colette thought she should say something and added politely, "Some bottled water and some fresh fruit would be wonderful." She would have preferred a bottle of brandy, but wisely didn't ask, for it might have ended her new career and François would be livid. She'd do her drinking in private, on her own time.

Cherise responded, that she would have Sandrina, the maid, bring the water and fruit to her right away. François wished Colette good day, and he and Cherise left the cottage. Walking, with François by her side, Cherise asked him if he planned to invite Colette to the chateau for a glass of wine.

"I think she will be too tired from the trip and long drive from Bordeaux. Let's do it another time," François suggested. Colette's stiff demeanor had indicated she was not in the best of moods, but he was certain she would eventually settle down.

As Colette watched the two walking along the short gravel path to the castle, their hands entwined, she seethed. Looking at the remarkable view of the castle from her little caretaker's window, Colette was quite certain they could not hear the crash of the ceramic pitcher of flowers thrown against the stone wall in the kitchen. Wiping her tears with her arm, she picked up the shards of pottery and mess of flowers, knowing Sandrina would be there soon with the water and fruit. If Sandrina caught her on her knees on the floor, she would say she had accidentally knocked over the pitcher and was terribly sorry. Lying was exceptionally easy for her. Playing the role as the concierge of Roufillay was going to be a bitter pill to swallow, but she would do it....for the money.

CHAPTER 14

Chippenham, England

Buzz…buzz…buzz, the mobile phone vibrated in Brent's pocket. He left the ring tone turned off because it always startled him by ringing at the wrong time in places like the theatre or the opera where the sound of a cell phone ringing wasn't acceptable. He looked at his cell phone caller ID and saw it was Kent Olson.

"Hey Kent, buddy, what's up?"

"Did you enjoy my call?"

"Yeah. Tingles in my slacks, making me laugh every time it goes off."

"I wanted to get back to you about Diana Aubrey."

"Anything interesting?"

"As you suspected, this woman sort of disappeared. But I was able to find out she sold Brightingham through a real estate agent at Sotheby's. After several requisite drinks at their former club I encountered two squiffy chatty patrons who were willing to gossip. With the buzz I acquired in the name of duty I was lucky to leave still standing, but I got a lot of information. It wasn't hard to reach the selling agent."

"What was the selling price?"

"5,100,000 pounds."

"Well that's a nice inheritance to soothe the grieving widow," Brett smirked.

"Actually mate, that's the thing. Seems to be a problem."

"What problem. Didn't she get the money?"

"Well she did. The agent provided a certified check for the five million pounds and received a separate check for her own commission on the sale. Diana was the sole inheritor of Raleigh's estate."

"Then what's the problem?" Brett asked, confused.

"It's odd. The money was never deposited to her account at the Bank of London, nor any other bank in England that I could trace or find," Kent said.

"Well, if she deposited the check, it has to show up somewhere."

"True. It's traceable. Should I look into it?

"Yes, I need your help with that, Kent. I have to find the money in order to find her. Do you know what happened to Diana?" Brett asked, intrigued.

"She's disappeared. There is absolutely no trace of her. I checked airlines, ships and railroads—nil. Can't find anything proving she traveled. Do you think she's dead?"

"Maybe she wanted to disappear. It's all starting to make sense to me, pal. Somehow, I doubt she is dead. She's probably very much alive," Brett pondered. "The question is, where? Does she have any family?"

"No. I checked to see if she had any brothers, sisters, family etc. and nada, zip zilch. Her parents were killed when she was five. Grew up mostly in foster homes—no grandparents either. There was a photo in the tabloids and the London Dispatch mentions their courthouse wedding, but it did not say much. Apparently was a private civil ceremony."

"Kent, what was her maiden name?

"Uh…let's see here. Her name was Diana Dupree. She was a model. Not a high fashion runway type, but for lesser-known couture designer labels. Quite a looker too. Reddish hair, not too tall, nice legs and rather busty for a model."

"Interesting. She's no dummy. Managed to marry well above herself."

"What now, Brett?"

"I don't really know. Gotta think about this."

"Wanna get a couple of pints at the pub?"

"Why not, Kent? Let's drink up. Our clues are going nowhere. This case is starting to irritate me. Maybe I should just give up. I don't have any idea where she went, what she did with the money, and where she is now. I have no idea where the alleged killer is either, or where to find the damn vintage car. This sucks."

"You're just a retired old fart trying to be an ace detective again."

"Thanks, Kent. That really helps a lot."

"Skip the pint. I'll buy you a scotch, Brett. In fact, I'll buy you several."

Brett decided it was a good time to drink away the frustration. Maybe tomorrow would be a better day.

CHAPTER 15

Roufillay, Dordogne, France

François emailed Colette regularly from the laptop in his room to the guest cottage, connected to a server in his locked third floor art studio. After their marriage, he'd told Cherise he required a private place to write and paint. His new wife gladly allotted him the extra room in the chateau since they did not need it for revenue. François slept in her bedroom, which they now called their master suite. Cherise had become accustomed to her husband working late in his studio, writing poetry on his laptop, he'd said. Occasionally he read his free verse to her, but most often he chose to paint. She respected his creative privacy. Cherise had no idea what he was doing on his computer, nor did she care.

If François wasn't writing or painting, she assumed he was managing his investments. From time to time, François was immersed in reading, often perusing financial magazines or the prospectus of a new emerging company looking for financial backing. Cherise no longer had any interest in business corporations, preferring to read a compelling novel instead. She admired his business acumen and was certain his investments provided all the money they needed. François routinely deposited funds into their joint account they kept separate from the Roufillay business account.

Planning her trip to France, Colette had packed the laptop that François had provided her the year before, tucked between her sweater, suit jacket, skirt and slacks. She had it shipped through baggage from

Switzerland. She did not want to carry a laptop on the plane, and he had emphasized caution that no one should see the emails they had written to each other. François indicated she would be required to create spreadsheets for Roufillay, including a new software program to assist with account management of the castle, so that Cherise would be relieved of keeping track of details by painstaking handwritten entry.

François had provided an accounting software disc and made her upload it on her computer. Colette balked at first, but she recognized having a specific task would give her something to do in the evenings and it provided a legitimate reason for them to talk privately to each other, undetected, without creating suspicion.

During the past year, while she lived in Switzerland, François reluctantly allowed Colette to send emails to him from his home. He'd insisted on placing calls from non-traceable purchased phones with blocked numbers. After the call had been made, the phone was trashed. François never called Colette from his cell phone. No one knew she was in Montreux. The money he wired went directly to his accounts so it would simply appear that he was paying his property tax and monthly utilities, as usual. The cash stipend he had provided her a year ago was sufficient for her food and personal necessities. Now, the opportunity to manage the revenue and expense of running Roufillay, placated Colette, reminding her of her own future financial standing.

Colette made herself invaluable right from the beginning. A well-attired older couple, traveling from Spain and staying at Roufillay, had difficulty understanding the various routes to the Loire Valley in France and how to find a specific hotel listed in their travel guide. Fluent in many languages, Colette explained everything to them in Spanish, and then placed a call, making reservations in flawless French. They marveled at her expertise and told Cherise how much they appreciated having someone competent to help them with their travel plans. The elderly couple wanted to see several well-known chateaux outside of Paris. Colette assisted with their request and recommended various excellent restaurants en route—well-memorized preparatory homework required by François during the past year.

Suggesting places of interest for them to visit on the way to Paris, including Chenonceau, stretched across the Cher River, Colette encouraged the couple not to miss the extraordinary architecture of Chambord. She told them the double helix staircase design was attributed to Leonardo Di Vinci. They nodded excitedly while she emphasized, that of course, they would want to consider booking a full day of Versailles. If they had time, she suggested they could visit picturesque Chantilly outside of Paris, to see their magnificent horse stables or Chateaux Cheverny and Chaumont. There were more sights to discover including historic cathedrals like Chartres and famous wineries with wonderful reds, whites, Pouilly Fumé and Muscadet. A person could spend months in France and not be able to see everything or fully experience the culture. It was easy to set up itineraries for guests.

The days and nights went by quickly. There was a lot to do and Colette did not have time to feel sorry for herself during the day. She rather enjoyed the game of impressing guests, and Cherise, whenever she could. When François was listening, Colette outdid herself linguistically, making certain he would never regret having brought her to Roufillay.

After weeks of pretending to be the perfect concierge, Colette began to hate rising in the morning. She had to force herself into the dowdy business clothes, pale lipstick, hair pinned in the requisite grandmotherly bun. She felt spinsterish and twice her age. Blouse buttoned up close to her neck, covered with a navy jacket, purposely closed to hide her ample feminine assets, her outfit had become an unbearable annoyance. Her breasts were flattened and constrained in utilitarian bras she would never willingly have purchased for herself. No lace, just plain cotton knit fabric with wide athletic straps—an ugly garment making her feel completely prudish—totally abhorrent, in her mind. The little local village shops lacked elegant designer clothing and, other than some lovely leather jackets and purses, were stocked primarily for tourists. Colette would have had to drive to Sarlat for attractive clothing, but she dared not buy anything other than the conservative outfits François insisted upon.

Every evening after working in the castle, Colette would walk to the cottage, throw her clothes in a pile, and sit naked in a hot bath. Frustrated, missing François' sensual touch, she would sink into the warm water with a sigh and grasp the hand-held shower, opening her legs wide, straddling the porcelain tub on her back, until the pulse of the water and her hand brought her to a climax. She longed to be feminine and desirable to François once again. Colette slept naked without a nightgown between her body and the coarse cotton sheets that rubbed like sandpaper against her delicate skin. She was becoming unhappier by the day, impatient for François' plan to succeed. Reminding herself to be patient for the wealth she needed and the man she desired in her bed, she opened a bottle of wine and drank herself into a fitful sleep.

A month went by quickly and Colette was becoming increasingly irritated but she knew she could not let it show. Besides being impatient, she was extremely physically frustrated. She had asked François to stop for a quick interlude on the drive from Bordeaux the day he picked her up, but he would not. He'd said it was too risky and someone might recognize him. Of course, he had been right. Colette had to tolerate and accept that François was always right. Alarmed, Colette was aware she was once again without any money of her own. She received a modest salary as a concierge, but it was laughable in her mind, especially compared with the lifestyle she was used to at Brightingham.

Some days, Colette reflected on her life as Lady Diana, the person she used to be in what seemed another lifetime ago. She uneasily recalled her past behavior, conspiring to kill Raleigh. It seemed despicable yet, she rationalized, she had put him out of his wheelchair-bound misery. And anyway, what other choice did she have? If she had deserted her aging husband, he would have written her out of his will. Diana had enjoyed the luxurious lifestyle at Brightingham, but she just could no longer tolerate the old man she was married to. Remembering how he drooled when he slept, she sighed, justifying to herself that his death had been a kindness. Colette lulled herself to sleep with comforting thoughts of her future. Soon she would be wealthy again. Yes, soon she would have everything—money and a vibrant, daring and exciting man to share her life.

During the early morning hours when she had time to herself, Colette considered whether she was actually "in love" with François. Perhaps she loved him or perhaps she loved the idea of him, mostly because she had never truly allowed herself to love anyone. She wanted him because François was a wealthy, virile and handsome man. Colette's ambition was to regain wealth and have someone who could satisfy her physical needs.

Acting as Colette even when they were alone, she asked François if he loved Cherise. It was a question that haunted her. He assured her that, although he liked Cherise, he had never been in love with anyone. François told her candidly he would not allow himself to become so enthralled with a woman that he would lose his edge. His ability to remain emotionally detached was essential and he had become an expert. Colette understood and accepted his answer because she was very much the same.

CHAPTER 16

The phone rang in the castle with a loud ring-a-ding, sending Cherise scurrying to the front reception desk, littered with papers, ledgers and tourist brochures.

"Hello, Cherise?"

"Oh my gosh! Is that you, Cindy?"

"Yes it is. I'm so sorry I couldn't be there for your wedding."

"I know," Cherise nodded. "You had to be at work launching the new product line."

"Boy, was that a bummer. I really wanted to fly to France to be there with you. How is everything going?" Cindy asked.

"Much better now. François hired a concierge to handle the travel arrangements and keep track of the revenue and expenses. It's so much easier than when François and I were trying to do everything ourselves."

"I'm glad. The reason I called is that I have to be in Paris next week for a product presentation and wondered if I could visit you."

"Oh, absolutely! Tell me when you are coming and we will book a room for you. Do you want me to pick you up at the airport?"

"Thanks, but I'd rather drive, if it's okay with you. I'm dying to see the countryside, as it's my first time in France."

"This is a wonderful surprise. I feel I've not seen you in ages and I can't wait for you to meet François."

"Me too. I'm so excited. I hope the room won't cost me an arm and a leg. I've seen the place on the Internet—took my breath away!"

"Of course not. The room is on us," Cherise added. "We've had a very profitable summer. We just want you to enjoy yourself."

The week went by quickly and Cherise asked François to assist Colette as best as he could so she could prepare for Cindy's visit. Cherise asked Sandrina to clean a lovely room for her friend and include a vase of fresh pink roses with some sprays of jasmine. Cherise knew the approximate time Cindy would arrive, so when she heard a car drive up the road, followed by a knock on the door, she was certain it was her friend. Scampering across the kitchen floor like a rabbit, she ran to the entryway, shifted bolts and opened the massive door. Cindy set two small suitcases on the cobblestone floor and extended her arms for a hug, shaking her head at the same time in disbelief. As Cherise embraced her, Cindy looked up at the enormous chandelier with her mouth agape, finally managing to blurt, "This is just unbelievable. I can't comprehend you actually live like this. You've outdone yourself."

"Well, we love it." Cherise grinned. "I'm so glad to see you. It's been way too long. Let me get François to help you with your bags and we will get you settled in your room."

Cherise cupped both of her hands to her mouth shouting, "*François? François, darling, Cindy is here!*"

He gracefully sauntered into the entry foyer, his face not betraying his ambivalent thoughts about this stranger. Knowing she was a business friend of Cherise, François decided that a somewhat restrained hug would be correct. Cindy was speechless. Her friend's new husband was stunning, his perfect physique accentuated in neatly pressed cream linen slacks that clung to his body and a light blue turtleneck matching his eyes. As he walked toward her, Cindy extended her arms, delighted to get a hug instead of a handshake,

"Gosh, it is so wonderful to finally meet you," she gushed.

"It's good to meet you too. Let me help you with your bags," he offered.

"That would be great," Cindy agreed. "I wish I could stay longer than two days."

"Well, we will make the most of it," Cherise smiled. "We have other guests here, so we can't go out to dinner. We'll eat in, if okay with you?"

"Oh absolutely fine. I've already had so much food. Everything tastes so good here," Cindy patted her stomach. I don't want you to go to any trouble."

"No trouble at all," Cherise said, while François went upstairs with Cindy's bags to the room reserved especially for her.

Cindy leaned forward as close as she could to Cherise's ear and whispered, "That husband of yours is a dream. Gosh, you have a castle, a gorgeous husband and a great business. And you were the one who said you didn't plan on meeting anyone for a long time."

"Yeah, I know. I could not have predicted this happening in my life. Can I get you a drink—perhaps a glass of wine?" Cherise smiled, heading toward the wine cellar.

"That'd be great. I'm exhausted from the drive. I had no idea it was such a long way from Paris," Cindy sighed, awkwardly straddling a bench cushion in the kitchen.

Cherise took three wine glasses out of the cupboard and set them on the yellow checked tablecloth. "How about some cheese and crackers to go with the wine?"

"Wonderful," Cindy said, flipping her blonde bangs off her forehead, glancing around the room in a stupor. "You know, despite the lovely warm summer day, it's actually a bit chilly in here."

"Castles," Cherise nodded. "The walls are three feet thick and it never gets hot in here, which is a good thing because we don't need air conditioning. Can you imagine what that expense would be?"

"Probably my entire year's salary," Cindy declared, pulling her navy cardigan around her shoulders. "When can I have a tour?"

François returned to the kitchen, cradling a bottle of French wine and poured equally into the three glasses. Cherise picked up her glass, "Let's toast to friendship and you being here, dear Cindy. I'll give you a tour in the morning after the guests leave."

"Let me toast to both of you and your wonderful life here. I'm very impressed!" Cindy enthused, raising her glass in the air.

Cherise set out a silver platter of select local cheeses, assorted crackers and fresh strawberries. They sat companionably together in the kitchen drinking the local wine and enjoying the pungent Cabécou goat cheese. "You know, it's such a nice evening, why don't we sit outside on the patio," Cherise suggested. She arranged the tasty hors d'oeuvres and wine glasses on a copper serving tray while Cindy slipped on her flats so she could navigate the bumpy cobblestones.

They walked past the courtyard's two-story massive stone block walls, verdant with moss, ivy and climbing white roses. Cindy nearly tripped on the uneven cobblestones and found the gravel path easier to navigate. Her past awkward tumbles and gawky near misses were an embarrassment she hoped to avoid at Roufillay. Steadying herself, she walked along looking at the ground rather than the distant scenery, to assure that her feet knew the direction where her body was going. François, Cherise and Cindy sat on elegant outdoor furniture arranged on the patio promontory cliff, facing the Dordogne River. The sun was starting to set, blazing red on the horizon.

"So how was your presentation?" Cherise asked.

"It went well. Our new product line is very much in demand in Europe. I think the Paris office won't have any difficulty working through their distributors," Cindy said enthusiastically.

Cherise nodded, "I'm so pleased work is going well for you."

Cindy observed François sitting absentmindedly, and she was anxious to engage him in a conversation.

"Uh, excuse me, François. I understand you are quite interested in technology?" Cindy asked, admiring his piercing eyes and the small cleft in his chin.

François felt a stab of worry in his temple, as he feigned a composed response, realizing Cherise had informed her friend of his business interests. "I try to keep abreast of the latest software technology developments," he commented, subtly changing the subject. "How was your trip?" he asked Cindy.

"Oh…it was great, although it was a long plane flight from San Francisco. I took a night flight so I was not totally exhausted when I got to Paris. I slept on the plane with a little help from Ambien."

Trying to get the conversation back on track, Cindy took a few more sips of wine and inquired,

"What technology companies are you most interested in?"

François took a long, calculated swallow of wine not liking where the conversation was going.

"I am interested in any cutting-edge company doing well," he said. "Will you excuse me for a moment, I've forgotten there is something I need to attend to."

"Of course," Cindy commented. "I can't wait to catch up with Cherise."

The two friends chatted while fireflies floated above tall grass, twinkling off and on like little iridescent orange bulbs. A half hour or more passed, and François did not return. Cherise continued chatting as if nothing was unusual, assuming François was responding to nature's call. But Cindy was uneasy when he did not return. "What happened to François?" she asked, peering over her shoulder at the castle courtyard door.

"Oh, I don't know. He probably had to deal with a guest's request or perhaps help Colette manage something. Or maybe he had to use the loo," Cherise quipped.

"Humm," Cindy said. "I would have enjoyed talking with him more."

"I'm sure you will have time tomorrow," Cherise assured her friend.

"Oh, and I want to meet this Colleen-person…the concierge who is so amazing."

"No, not Colleen," Cherise corrected her. "It's Colette."

"Oh right, sorry," Cindy smiled. "Where is Colette from?"

"Uh, I believe England," Cherise answered, unconcernedly.

"Don't you actually know?" Cindy asked, her face contorting into an unflattering expression.

"I didn't ask a lot of questions. François said he knew she was from England and had done concierge work before."

Scratching her head while swatting at a mosquito, Cindy asked, "Did you see her résumé?"

"Gosh, no," Cherise frowned, feeling pressured. "I let François take care of it. He highly recommended her, said he knew her and that was enough for me."

Cindy munched on a cracker piled high with cheese. "I see," she said, wrinkling her brow. "Then you don't know very much about her."

"No I don't," Cherise said, feeling uneasy. "But she's been a godsend and she's very good at her job."

"You're lucky. You've told me François is a wonderful business partner and you have this great concierge to help. And then there is Sandy who is the maid?" Cindy asked.

"No, not Sandy, but close. Sandrina. She was the maid with the previous owner. You'll like her. She's absolutely darling and very efficient."

A familiar sound buzzed around Cherise' ears as she slapped her forearm. "I think the mosquitos are having dinner as well out here. Let's go inside," Cherise remarked.

They returned to the chateau and found François in the kitchen spreading pâté on fresh baguettes. Cindy decided her concern about François' momentary disappearance had been ill-founded. Even so, Cindy did not know why she felt uneasy. She had so wanted to like him, but instead, she sensed he preferred his distance and that he did not want to get to know her…but maybe he was just tired or preoccupied.

Cindy shook the disquieting thought out of her head and sat down for dinner. François sat next to Cherise on one bench and Cindy sat opposite both of them, thinking they made a very handsome couple.

They ate quietly with Cherise doing most of the talking about their life in the Dordogne and the experiences they had shared running the chateau. François cleaned up the dinner dishes and then excused himself, saying he had to take care of some emails.

Cherise offered to take Cindy on a tour of the castle the following afternoon when the last had guest checked out. Cindy said she would enjoy a quiet breakfast by herself and had brought along a good murder mystery she had picked up at the airport in San Francisco.

"Let me show you to your room," Cherise said. "I'm sure you're exhausted."

Nodding affirmatively, Cindy followed Cherise through the lobby to the staircase.

"No elevator?" Cindy asked. Laughing, Cherise explained that when the castle had been built, elevators didn't exist. Up the stairs they went, to one of Cherise's favorite rooms decorated in several shades of blue, furnished with an off-white four-poster bed, two club chairs and an ottoman in bright red fabric. The room was enhanced by a coordinating red, navy and blue oriental rug.

"Oh this is gorgeous," Cindy said. "I think I am about to have the best sleep of my life."

"Sleep late," Cherise smiled. "Lots going on in the morning for us. You can come down for breakfast any time before noon. Sandrina will have the croissants, jam and juice set out for you whenever you are ready."

Kicking off her shoes, toes sinking into the plush rug under feet, Cindy slumped on the edge of the bed in disbelief—this was a fairytale. She grumbled to herself about all the reasons why she didn't have her own prince charming. Exhausted, she plopped herself onto the fluffy duvet, nestling her head on the down pillows and, in no time, she was fast asleep with her clothes on.

The sound of crows, in noisy conversation in a nearby oak tree, slowly woke Cindy up.

Discovering no blanket under her arms, she was disoriented, realizing she had slept in her clothes. Her eye makeup felt like glue and one eye was stuck shut. Her skirt resembled wrinkled laundry stuffed into a duffle bag, looking like it had never been ironed. She got up and walked to the window, opening the closure, deeply inhaling the garden's fragrance. Her nose welcomed the fresh warm summer air into her lungs, along with the local pollen, which made her sneeze. She had hoped her allergies would not bother her in France, but to her disappointment, they came along with her on the plane. Cindy reached into her carry-on bag and found her make-up and some nasal spray she knew would give her a headache, but at least she would be able to breathe.

It was already eleven-thirty in the morning, not allowing much time to shower and dress for breakfast, but she recalled Cherise had encouraged her to sleep late. The shower was divine and the thick cream bath towel was heavenly. She made a mental note to ask Cherise where she had purchased such a luxurious plush towel, especially impressive because she had heard large towels in parts of Europe were scarce commodities.

Dressing, Cindy chose apricot-colored slacks and a matching top, applied fresh makeup and blow-dried her hair. She could hardly wait to see François again and meet the wonder woman Colette. As she navigated the stairs with caution, she bumped her head into a slanted beam, and nearly missed a carpeted tread. She mused that falling down the stairs would not make a very sophisticated entrance. Hearing voices, she noticed François and a woman at the reception desk. She watched François talking animatedly and wondered if the woman was a guest.

"Oh, good morning! Or should I say good afternoon?" François inquired suavely.

"I'm sorry I slept so late." Cindy said, rubbing the sore bump on her head.

"Not a problem at all. Let me introduce you to our concierge, Colette Armond."

Studying Colette's features, she was surprised at how attractive she was with her auburn hair styled in an impeccable French twist, setting off her flawless skin against her white blouse and sensible navy suit.

"I'm so very happy to meet you," Cindy said. "I've heard so much about you."

"Thank you," Colette said, not extending her hand. "I understand you are a friend of Cherise?"

The concierge's soft voice provided relief from the awkwardness of not shaking hands. Cindy explained that she and Cherise had worked together for the same corporation in San Francisco. Colette wrinkled her forehead, assuming that somehow Cindy and Cherise were an alliance, giving her one more reason to dislike both of them.

"That must have been nice." Colette managed, not interested in delving into either Cindy or Cherise's background.

"We did enjoy working together while it lasted." Cindy sat on a kitchen bench, studying Colette and François—something about the way François looked at Colette was unnerving, unnatural—perhaps too familiar? Of course not. This had to be her imagination. François once again excused himself and disappeared.

Like two lionesses facing one another to protect their pride, Colette took an immediate dislike to Cindy and vice versa. Each could sense the other's antipathy.

"So what brought you to France?" Cindy asked pointedly.

Wishing this guest would evaporate, Colette evasively indicated François had contacted her to fill the position.

Cindy knew she should not pry, but could not contain herself. "Oh…how did you come to know François?"

Colette felt her throat constrict and fumbled for an answer. "I, um, we um…"

Silence broken by the phone ringing was a relief for Colette and she quickly switched to French. The conversation went on for some time.

Cindy watched Colette handle whatever the conversation was about with obvious aplomb. It appeared she was booking a reservation, jotting information into a registration book. She mentioned something in French about confirmation, directions and other things Cindy could not understand. She desperately wanted to continue their conversation, quite determined to find out more about Colette, despite the palpable tension. When Colette hung up the phone, she glared at Cindy asking rudely, "Is there something I can get you?"

"Uh…no. I was just wondering…"

"Oh there you are, Cindy," Cherise chirped cheerfully, entering the kitchen. "I can take you on a tour now if you would like. The last guest left a bit early."

Cindy thought it was propitious timing and agreed. Colette watched Cindy depart and if daggers could have flashed out of her eyes, Colette would have shot them straight into the back of Cindy's skull.

Cherise was enthusiastic about showing Cindy the castle. Imagining herself as Eleanor of Aquitaine, Cherise grandly announced Cindy's name as they entered the formal dining room, enjoying her friend's audible gasps. With animated gestures, Cherise pointed out the details of the immense living room with its enormous fireplace, stenciled beamed ceiling and lovely oil paintings. Cherise laughed at the number of times Cindy blurted out, *"Unbelievable!"*

"Would you like to take a walk on the grounds?"

"Oh, I would love to." Cindy said fervently.

As they left through the side entrance to the castle, they were greeted with a friendly tail-wagging black and white King Charles Cavalier spaniel.

"Is that your dog?" Cindy bent down to greet the fluffy creature.

"I wish, but no, he's not ours. François is allergic to dogs and cats, so we cannot have any pets. This is Tulare. He belongs to the groundskeeper."

"I thought it might be nice for you to have a dog when François is gone. You said he travels on business?"

"Yes, he does, but not that often. And, with the guests coming and going, honestly, I don't have time for a pet."

As they walked down a narrow gravel path, butterflies flitted over the wild flowers and bees buzzed in the purple clover. It was warm, without excessive humidity. The sky was hazy, sun filtering through pleasantly without uncomfortably penetrating their skin. Struggling to decide whether or not to bring up her concerns, Cindy finally felt compelled to say something.

"I met Colette this morning." Cindy commented, stepping cautiously on stones in the small creek flowing across their path.

"Isn't she amazing?" Cherise effused.

"Well. Yes. I suppose." Cindy sighed, a frown wrinkling her forehead.

"Didn't you like her?" Cherise sensed something was bothering Cindy.

"She's very efficient. Her French is quite admirable and she seemed to handle her responsibilities very well. But, there is just something unsettling. I cannot put my finger on it," Cindy asserted, wishing she had not been so forthcoming.

Cherise, taken aback and clearly stunned, hid her thumbnail digging into her clenched hand. She did not know what to say or how to respond but felt herself becoming defensive.

"We could not run this place without her," her voice sounding curt, even to her.

"I know," Cindy soothed. "I'm not criticizing her abilities. It's just something in her manner. Like a shoe that does not fit correctly."

"Oh? What do you mean?" Cherise asked, looking at her friend in dismay.

"Well, I tried to talk to her about how she had known François and she really did not want to tell me anything. How well do you know her?"

"Cindy, I saw no reason to question François about how he knew her. We were so busy at the time and I was overwhelmed. When François suggested we hire her, I hesitated, but then realized I couldn't manage all the bookkeeping and the guests at the same time."

Sensing the conversation was not going anywhere productive, Cindy wisely dropped the subject. "I understand. I'm sorry. It's my nature to be so inquisitive."

Cherise seemed to relax and she pointed out a white heron landing at the side of the pond, letting the conversation settle. "Don't you think François is every woman's dream?"

"Yes, of course. He is drop-dead gorgeous and he seems to make you very happy."

"You sound hesitant. Gosh, don't you like him either?"

Fumbling for words, Cindy took a deep breath. "I am sure he's a wonderful person—it's just that he makes me uneasy. I can't explain it."

"He made me very uneasy when I met him, that's for sure," Cherise interjected, anxious driblets of perspiration forming on her upper lip. "He's so handsome. I think it's unsettling to anyone at first," she added convincingly.

"Probably," Cindy agreed. "You are going to think I'm being obnoxious, but I wonder if you did a background check on François?"

Cherise stopped walking and looked aghast at Cindy, a perplexing sense of anger rising as she groped for an explanation. "I did not do a background check on him, my gosh. It's not like he was an employee I was hiring. He was a guest here and we fell in love. It's as simple as that!" Cherise was adamant.

"Is it?" Cindy stared at her, knowing this was not going to help their friendship. "I saw him looking at Colette. It was like he knew her, of course, but not the way one looks at an employee."

"You are imagining things. She's just an employee. François' never done anything except be the perfect husband and business partner. I think you've been in the corporate world too long, where everyone is suspicious of everyone else's ulterior motives."

Knowing she was treading on fragile ground, Cindy said she was sorry to have shared her misgivings and agreed that Cherise was probably right—she'd spent too much time with office politics, mergers and acquisitions, where executives had to be duplicitous for survival.

"I think we should get back," Cherise stated, still miffed.

"I agree. I want to take a nap before dinner," Cindy demurred, attempting to dispel the tension permeating the air between them.

"Of course. Can I fix you something to eat?"

"Uh, no please don't go through any trouble. I'd love to go out for dinner if you can recommend a good restaurant in town. Might give me a chance to do a bit of shopping."

"All right. I'll have Colette make a...no, I mean I will make a reservation for you."

Neither Cherise nor Cindy slept well that night. Cindy wished she had not brought up her concerns, feeling that her outspokenness had been unwise. At the same time, she knew that if she had not spoken to Cherise about her concerns, she'd feel responsible if Cherise got hurt. Cindy did not trust François nor did she trust Colette. It made her sick to think this way. Cherise was a woman who deserved a good life and she needed to be with a man who would always be there for her. Cindy determined that, when she got home, she would research their names on the Internet to see what she could discover. Of course, if it was something troubling, she doubted she would tell Cherise, anyway. She had already said enough to risk fracturing their friendship.

Cherise stared at the ceiling after François fell asleep. Other than an occasional bat screeching and the symphony of crickets chirping loudly below her open window, it was a pleasant evening. She wondered how her friend could have misgivings, not only about her husband, but about

Colette as well. She tried not to be angry with Cindy, but as much as she wanted to pretend it did not bother her, the concerns her friend raised were deeply troubling. Sleep finally came when she decided that Cindy had not spent enough time with François or Colette to appreciate either one. Comforted, she curled up against François' arm and welcomed pleasant dreams.

The next morning, Cindy packed up, stuffing clothing back into the suitcase haphazardly, aware of the need to hurry. Just as she zipped the suitcase closed, there was a knock at her door. Barefoot she walked to the door, wondering if it was Cherise.

"Good morning, Cindy."

"Oh, Sandrina—yes, hello. Good morning."

"Are you ready to leave?" Sandrina offered a courteous smile, brushing her bangs away from her forehead.

"Yes. I'm all set. Thank you," Cindy glanced once more over her shoulder at the room. As lovely and restful as it was, her thoughts had kept her up most of the night, worried about the previous day's uncomfortable conversation. Sandrina brought her bags down and handed Cindy a prepared a box lunch for her to take along on the train. They arranged for Cindy to take the train back to Paris rather than drive unfamiliar roads. François would helpfully return her rental car to Paris and he would return to Roufillay on the train the next day. As they walked through the hallways, past the vestibule, Cindy looked for François and Colette, but neither was in sight. She sighed inwardly, thinking it was just as well because she had no idea what to say to either of them.

Cherise drove Cindy to the train station in Sarlat. They intentionally chatted about subjects that would cause no distress for either of them— the weather, recipes, make-up and of course, office gossip. Arriving at the train station, Cherise opened the trunk, removed the suitcases, and set them on the curb.

Cindy paused, settling her purse on her arm in a comfortable position, and determinedly turned to Cherise. "I want you to know how much I enjoyed my stay. Your home—your castle—is extraordinary. Honestly—I'm so very happy for you."

138

Cherise gave her a hug, but not an overly warm and affectionate embrace—more of a 'glad you are leaving' hug. Cindy felt the limp arms around her and she was regretful.

"I'm so sorry, Cherise, if I upset you in any way. I had no right to imply your husband and concierge are anything but absolutely wonderful. You are my dear friend. Please forgive me," her voice croaked out the best apology she could muster.

"Not to worry," Cherise said. "It's already forgotten."

As Cherise drove back to Roufillay, she pondered female relationships. Maybe it was Cindy herself who was responsible for her two failed marriages. If her friend was so distrusting about people's motives, how could anything good ever happen in her life? She reflected that, with an attitude like hers, Cindy would probably remain single for a long, long time. Cherise prided herself when it came to accepting people as they were. It was so much easier living life and trusting people, rather than suspiciously wondering about people's motives.

The rest of the day was a hectic round of catch-up chores in the castle. Both Cherise and François were anxious to fall into bed early, worn out with the challenges of running a bed and breakfast chateau. As he was brushing his teeth, François casually inquired if Cindy had gotten to the train on time.

Cherise raised her eyebrow and replied, "Yes, traffic was minimal."

Rinsing his mouth with a final gurgle of water, he swallowed, wiping his lips with a washcloth.

"Don't you think your friend is a bit…how shall I say…odd?" François asked, testing the waters with his wife, rinsing his toothbrush under the faucet.

"Well, she's a good person and she cares about me," Cherise defended, curling under the duvet covers.

"She asks a lot of questions," François muttered, wetting his hair with a dab of gel, admiring his reflection in the mirror. With a nod of self-satisfaction, he turned off the bathroom light, crossing the room to the bed.

"I think it's her business nature. She's very good at what she does, Cherise reflected.

"Whatever you say my dear," François yawned and crawled under the covers. He held his wife, planted a kiss on the forehead and flipped over on his side, pretending to have fallen into a deep sleep. However, sleep was the last thing on his mind.

The storm, black thunderclouds raging, blew fiercely up the river without warning, customary for the Dordogne. Torrents of rain fell sideways in sheets; gale-force gusts bent trees to the breaking point. An observer could see lightning approaching, following the path up the Dordogne River. From the castle turret window, it was both electrifying to watch—and terrifying to hear—making a person's bones shake. First the lightning then, holding one's breath, counting seconds until the loud thunder clap shattered the air. Petrified, a watcher would anticipate the next loud bolt and flash.

A lightning rod had been installed above the writing room in the castle turret, next to Cherise and François' bedroom. This safety measure ensured the castle remained grounded and would not catch fire and burn to ashes—a common problem of historic homes and castles.

Cherise tossed and turned in her bed, trying to sleep with her pillow over her head muffling the storm. With a crashing bang slamming against the bedroom wall, the windows and shutters blew open, cascades of rain poured into the room. Draperies blew horizontally across the room as if animated by some unearthly force. She sat up, panic-stricken, and reached out her arm toward François to ask him to shut the windows.

She was startled. He was not in the bed. "Shit!" These storms scared the wits out of her. Deciding he must be in his art room, she yelled to him, but there was no answer. She got up and tried to close the windows, barely controlling the force of the wind as she leaned her full weight into the window latch to shut it. She tiptoed to the west window and peered out cautiously. At that exact moment, a lightning bolt, resembling an upside down tree branch, illuminated the sky. In the intermittent flash of light, Cherise was shocked to see François furtively walking to the caretaker's cottage. Her heart thudded in her chest. Stunned, Cherise stared bleakly, rain dripping down her shoulders, soaking the rug. It was nearly three in the morning. What was he doing running to the cottage? Was Colette okay? Maybe something was wrong.

Not thinking or considering what she was doing, Cherise dashed barefoot down the narrow stairs, one flight at a time, banging her knee on the wood banister, and bumping her head on the low slanted beam. In her nightgown, she ran to the side castle door, and stood in the rain, deliberating. *Shall I go…or not go down to the caretaker's cottage?* Finally, deciding if there was an emergency or something might be wrong with Colette, she should go and offer help.

Gingerly navigating the gravel driveway, doing her best to avoid sharp stones on her bare feet, Cherise approached the cottage, dodging muddy water trapped in puddles. She knelt down in the brambles, straining to see through the gauze curtain in the window.

She spotted François in the kitchen standing with his arms on his hips while Colette's back was toward the window. In the glow of the candlelight, it appeared they were having a fight. Colette's arms were flailing. François was yelling at Colette. *What was going on?* She thought about knocking at the door, but was hesitant to interrupt them. She realized she was flimsily dressed in nothing more than a wet cotton nightgown and looked ridiculous.

She crept, knees bent like a cat stalking a mouse, to a smaller window. Shaking her head and swatting the rain out of her hair, Cherise strained to hear their argument above the sounds of the storm. Shivering in the cold rain, she crossed her hands over her arms. She could hear François shouting and Colette was yelling back at him. Another bolt of lightning and rumbling clap of thunder muffled their conversation. Cherise could only catch snippets of François' words snapping at Colette, "Dammit, everything is going according to plan…be patient."

Now frightened that François might see her, Cherise knew she had to get back to the castle. Blindly, she ran alongside the cottage and caught her nightgown on a thorny bramble bush. She tripped and fell, sliding in the mud, skinning her knee on the rough pebbles until it bled through her nightgown. She knew she had only moments to get back up into her room, to come up with a story about why she was so wet…*Oh God, she could not think clearly*…the rain, the wind blowing wildly.

Sprinting up the stairs, dripping glops of mud as she bolted across the carpet like a hare sprayed with buckshot, Cherise ripped off her bloody, torn nightgown, clutching it in a ball. Footsteps. She heard him coming up the stairs and threw the wet nightgown it into the hamper, hiding it with a towel on top. She jumped into the shower, turned on the water to wash off her bloody knee. The shower nozzle streamed warm water, masking her already soaking wet hair. She was shaking and her mind was racing.

François entered the bedroom and was alarmed to see the light on in the bathroom and hear the sound of water running.

"Cherise? What are you doing up? Are you okay?"

"The storm was so violent, it just shook me and I could not calm down. I decided to take a hot shower. Where were you?" She regretted saying it the minute her words came out of her mouth.

"Oh I went to see if Colette was frightened. She is not used to the storms we have here in the Dordogne," he answered, his vocal cords constricting in his throat.

"Well, dammit, I'm not either! You know I hate them. I could have used you to comfort me." It was the best lie she could come up with. It was also true.

Cherise considered telling him what she'd heard in the cottage, but knew it did not make any sense to her...*what plan, what was going according to plan?* She needed time to think. He started to step into the shower with her, and she felt faint.

"François, please not now. I'm too rattled, and I banged my knee on the bed. It's still bleeding. I need to put a bandage on it. Maybe I will get some hot tea. I'm not sleepy."

He studied her bleeding knee. "All right, dear, finish up and come back to bed when you are ready."

He did not think her behavior unusual and decided she was just upset about the storm. François tossed his wet clothes on a chair and climbed into bed. Pulling the covers up over his shoulders, he turned on his side, his eyes fixed on the window. Shaken by the fight with Colette, he wondered if he could successfully implement his plan.

Quietly closing the bathroom door, she bandaged her knee and decided she would throw out her torn, bloody nightgown the next day. Right now, Cherise knew she had to return to bed. She quietly removed a fresh nightgown from her dresser drawer and crept in beside her husband, still shaking and listening to the lessening storm, which had faded to a slow, steady rain. She finally heard him snoring, and was grateful not have any further conversation. Sleep eluded her, thoughts raced through her mind as she lay in bed, staring at the ceiling beams in the dark, listening to the rain. Cherise wondered in her gut if something was seriously wrong, but had no idea what it could be. Why would Colette and François be fighting? What did François mean when he'd said *'everything was going according to plan'*? Was he talking about her job or something else?

Exhausted, but before allowing herself much-needed sleep, Cherise decided she would not confront him. Until she figured out what was going on, she decided it was better to keep the information secret. It was the first night during their marriage she had no desire to cuddle up with her husband.

The next morning when François awoke, Cherise was still asleep. While he was dressing, he looked down at the rain-soaked bedroom carpeting and stairwell steps, noticing the mud tracks. François did not realize the muddy footprints were not all his.

CHAPTER 17

Chippenham, England

Brett sat pensively, one arm resting on the other, knuckles tucked under his chin. He shifted in his favorite old brown cracked leather chair in his living room in Chippenham, opposite the fieldstone floor-to-ceiling fireplace, staring absently into the crackling fire. He had been uneasy for weeks, feeling he had failed Raleigh and wishing he had never gotten involved in the mystery of his death. Removing his reading glasses, he began chewing on the earpiece, occasionally swirling it in his mouth, pondering what he should do next. He nervously rubbed his forehead as though, by doing it long enough, the solution would come to him.

He had not forgotten that when solving a crime, when all else failed and clues were obscure, two things were usually certain. The first point was to follow the money. The second crucial element was to look for small mistakes and inconsistencies, not just the large ones. Any killer, no matter how polished and accomplished, always made mistakes sooner or later. The difference between an average crime-of-passion killer and exceptionally good pre-meditated killers was that they never made big mistakes...but inevitably and over time, small ones were unavoidable.

He slid into his ratty leather slippers and made a call to Kent, not caring too much what time it was.

"Hello?" a hoarse, sleepy voice answered the phone, sounding like a dead person coming to life.

"Kent, it's me, Brett."

"Mate, do you know what time it is?" he groaned in disbelief.

"No. Sorry, Kent. Didn't look at the time."

"Blimy, it's two in the morning!"

"You're right, I'm sorry. Shake out your cobwebs. I need help."

"It'll cost you," Kent purposely yawned as loudly as possible.

"Yeah, yeah, I know, but it's important," Brett said urgently.

"It had better be," Kent muttered, sitting up on the edge of his bed, bleary-eyed in his boxer trunks. He turned on the bedside table lamp.

"Remember when you said the money was never deposited to Diana's bank account?"

"Ah huh."

"Well, I got to thinking."

"Can't you do this thinking during the daytime?" Kent stifled another yawn, rubbing his eyes and looking around for a pencil and paper.

"It's the coffee. I still drink too much damn coffee and it keeps me awake. Can't help it."

"Lucky me," Kent mumbled. "I'd prefer you were an alcoholic. At least you'd be out cold some of the time."

"Very funny. Let's get serious here, okay? You said she had sold Brightingham for 5.1 million pounds and that Sotheby's had managed the sale. The agent got a commission right?"

"Yes, 100,000 pounds."

"The new owners were the Weatherlys. Check the Weatherly's bank and find out if they wrote a check for the full amount directly to Diana Dupree Aubrey."

"Don't have to. I remember it was two checks. One to Sotheby's for the 100,000 pound commission and the other check was written out to Diana for five million pounds. I have the file here at home. Let me go get it."

"Thanks. I'll have another cup of coffee."

"Is this going to go on all night?"

"Might."

"Bollocks. Ok, I have the file. What do you want to know?" feigning a serious yawn.

"Check the Weatherly's bank and find out where the five million was deposited. If it went to another bank, the wire transfer will show up."

"Follow the money?"

"Yes, follow the money. I have a hunch. Call me tomorrow."

"Can I go back to bed now that I am not the least bit tired, you ass?"

"Sorry."

"You say that entirely too much."

"Do I? Ring me tomorrow or as soon as you have got this. Call my cell phone please."

"Yeah, yeah, vibrate, vibrate."

"Thanks, Kent. I owe you."

"I'm keeping count. You're going to make me a rich man someday."

Brett ended the call and paced around his living room. He kicked off his slippers and flopped down on the sofa with his arms behind his head, thinking. Five million pounds had to be traceable. Where did it go? Pondering the possibilities, he drifted off in a fitful sleep. It was nearly dawn and having forgotten to set the phone on vibrate, it rang loudly in his pocket. He sat up, looked at the silent alarm clock in a stupor. Pushing his hair out of his eyes, he fumbled for his cell phone while struggling to sit up on the sofa, squinting out the window at a surprisingly clear day. Brett focused on Kent's words.

"Brett, apparently the check Diana received through the conveyance company from the Weatherlys was sent to a bank in Switzerland that wire-transferred the money from the Weatherly's bank to a Swiss bank account, in accordance with Diana's solicitor's instructions."

Brett started ranging about the room like a hunting dog chasing the scent of a hare.

"Give me the name of the bank in Switzerland. Nothing worse than a Swiss bank account—can be nearly impossible to get any information out of them."

"Brett, do you think Diana is in Switzerland?"

"Maybe. It's a possibility. Kent, check the major credit card companies. See if any transactions were made by Diana Aubrey in the last year. Might be a slim chance, but it's all I have to go on."

"You never give me anything easy to do. This is all giving me a piss-ass headache."

"Drink some coffee. Caffeine is good for that too."

"You are a real pain, Brett."

"I know, but I can feel it in my blood. Somewhere, somehow, she made a small mistake."

CHAPTER 18

Chateau Roufillay, Dordogne, France

Cherise repressed her anxiety about François' argument with Colette. She avoided him, busying herself with guest requests, check-ins, and departures. She provided instructions to Sandrina so that she herself could go to the market in Salart to buy the food and supplies they needed. Finding excuses to calm her nerves, Cherise did laundry when there was none to do. She washed blankets and towels that were not dirty and vacuumed clean carpets, giving herself time to think. Surreptitiously she watched Colette during the day, noticing that during her working hours assisting guests, everything seemed normal. Colette's demeanor with her was pleasant but distant.

François, unaware of Cherise's knowledge of the bewildering conversation she'd overhead the night of the storm, behaved as he had always done. During the day, when guests had left the castle to sightsee, he spent hours in his room. Occasionally, François went to Bergerac, or Moissac for the day. Evenings, he continued to be attentive to Cherise, which left her feeling befuddled. Sometimes he would bring her a glass of wine, lean over her shoulder and kiss her neck, adding to her confusion.

François made love to her at night with intensity and passion. She tried to respond with the same passion, but could not. Instead she found herself obsessively wondering about *the plan* in the context of the argument she had overheard. When François wanted to make love, Cherise could not concentrate on being enticing and sexy. She went through the motions, acting passionate, but her mind was elsewhere. Cherise finally admitted to herself the bonds of trust with her husband had broken.

Aware his wife was distancing herself emotionally, one night François directly asked her what was wrong. Convincingly, Cherise tremulously smiled and said she was just tired, that running the chateau was so much more demanding than she had expected. She hedged, telling him she simply did not have the energy to feel sexy whenever he wanted her. It worked. François gave Cherise the space she requested.

François was actually relieved that Cherise was less interested in him, as he discovered he was feeling a miniscule bit of compunction about his plan. He really did like her. Maybe he even loved her in a twisted way, but he knew he was not capable of truly bonding with anyone.

Grateful François did not insist on more intimacy, Cherise was relieved because she did not feel like having sex and hated acting out a climax. She just wanted to be left alone with her thoughts. During the day when she was not busy, she pondered the relationship between François and Colette. Cherise knew she had been blindly trusting—of his words, his love, his story. Perhaps that had been stupid on her part. Maybe Cindy had been right. What if he was not who he said he was? What if Colette was not who she said she was? What if *they* planned to harm her? What was their fight about?

She brooded about how they might hurt her, and perhaps, God forbid, kill her. She was a woman of significant financial means and Cherise reluctantly acknowledged this was a motive for murder. But how? Guests were scheduled to check in and out at the fully-booked chateau. No one had opportunity to harm her with castle guests coming and going. Cherise scolded herself, shaking her head. This sort of thinking was ridiculous. She had to stop imagining these absurd concerns. François loved her. He would never harm her. The *plan* must have something to do with Colette's job at Roufillay. Perhaps she missed her home and was homesick. That would make sense. François had determinedly relocated her to Roufillay to help with running the business and maybe Colette was upset and lonely. But why fight about it?

Cherise believed people acted with the best motives and she felt unsettled by these nagging thoughts. If she were at risk of being harmed, what could she actually do to prevent that? She told herself to calm down. The chateau was booked and she would not be alone.

Guests were scheduled to arrive and depart for another week. Increasingly paranoid, Cherise wondered if Colette might try to poison her. She inspected her food carefully, ingesting only what Sandrina brought fresh from the market each morning.

Although Colette rarely joined them for dinner Cherise finally convinced herself they were not trying to poison her. If they were teaming up for murder, how would they do it? Would François suffocate her in bed? No. There would be a dead body to contend with and she was sure that would not be logistically feasible. Cherise desperately wanted to stop such frightening thoughts but she could not. What if she could not trust François? She ruminated, going back to the unlikely story that he had run out in the storm to comfort Colette. If he had been concerned, he could have called her on the phone. There was no reason to run to her cottage. This was the basis of her distrust.

Something in her gut made her wary and Cherise realized the queasy feeling would not disappear without investigation.

She considered taking a trip, but had nowhere convincing to go. She wished she could talk to the police, but then decided against the idea. It would be impossible to keep a secret in a small town like Sarlat. Everyone knew her and François, and if one person saw her enter the police station, gossip would flourish, undoubtedly getting back to him. She could not risk it.

The evening after the last guest had checked out, Cherise had difficulty sleeping. She uneasily mused that soon Roufillay would be closed for the season, leaving the chateau relatively empty. Restless, she got up, went to the bathroom, returning to the bed. The windows were open, the air balmy and still. Surprised to discover François was not sleeping under the covers, Cherise listened for any sound coming from his art studio. Perhaps he'd ventured downstairs to read in the library. Now wide awake, Cherise decided a little snack might be calming, maybe some chocolate or fruit. She slipped on her cotton robe, quietly navigating down the stairs, one flight after the other.

She walked soundlessly across the sitting room, lobby reception and past the grand entryway to the stone vaulted kitchen. She brewed a pot of Earl Grey tea and selected a crunchy Deltana apple from a bowl of fresh fruit, deciding to nestle on the cozy sofa in the corner of the grand living room. The immense fireplace mantle loomed above her head. In the moonlight, Cherise marveled at the beauty of the oil paintings, the tapestries on the walls and the architecture of the hand-stenciled beamed ceiling. She loved each and every detail of Roufillay—her chateau, her castle, her home.

Tiptoeing to the open window, she looked up at the full moon in the sky. Admiring the silver moonlight illuminating the grounds, she nonchalantly glanced in the direction of the caretaker's cottage. As she lifted the cup to her lips to take a sip of hot tea, she startled. Hands shaking, the cup and saucer smashed to the floor, tea spilling in every direction. She gasped and clenched her fist against her heart. By the light of the full moon she was horrified to see her husband in the cottage with Colette, lying on her back, pumping her with wild abandon on the kitchen table. Cherise stood frozen, unable to move, watching them. Because there was no wind, she could hear ecstatic cries faintly emanating from Colette as she writhed under François.

Devastated, Cherise bent down, picked up the shards of broken cup and saucer and numbly staggered back to the kitchen. Shaking and frightened, she put her head against the hutch and began to cry. Her ragged breathing matched her rapid, fractured thoughts. Cherise was furious, so angry she wanted to storm in on both of them, screaming, *"How could you both do this to me?"* She realized in that moment, François could not have ever really loved her. So much arrogance, using their property to indulge in an adulterous liaison with the concierge. What gall he had!

With this knowledge, Cherise realized she was uncertain of everything she had assumed. Knowing her husband would eventually return to their bed, she hastily devised a plan realizing she had two choices. The first was to yield to her raging emotions and confront François. The other choice was to take control of her own life and stop trusting the man she had so blindly loved. She had become weak and dependent. The strong business woman she had once been in California would have never let something like this happen twice. Angry with herself, Cherise determined she was not going to permit any man to tear her heart out again. She had not seen her divorce from Andy coming and she certainly did not see this catastrophe either. Cherise told herself, "Enough is enough." She scolded herself for her gullibility, her wishful romantic illusions that her husband was perfect, rather than the reality he was bored and unfaithfully screwing the slut concierge in the guest cottage.

Gritting her teeth and squaring her shoulders, Cherise vowed not to let François take advantage of her. She would not be a victim again.

Cherise climbed back into bed, waiting for him to return. She heard his footsteps on the stairs and the bedroom door creak open. In the shadowed bedroom, she saw him enter the adjacent bathroom, heard the toilet flush, and felt the jostle as he slipped into their bed. He wrapped the covers over his shoulders on the far side of the bed as though nothing unusual had just happened. Cherise felt a momentary reckless desire to kill him. Head throbbing, she forced herself to face him in bed, "Having trouble sleeping?" she asked, veiling the scorn in her voice.

"No, I just had to go to the bathroom," François assured, his arm on her shoulder. "I was hungry, so I went down to the kitchen to get a croissant."

"Oh," she murmured, revulsion turning her stomach. He lied so easily. She slid away from his shoulder. "I think I am coming down with the flu," she stammered, bolting into the bathroom. Staring in the mirror at her pale face, she gripped the sink and watched the blood drain from her face, feeling faint. The walls weaved back and forth as she slid along the wall to the floor, clammy and sweating. She leaned over the rim of the toilet seat and vomited.

"Are you all right?" François called to her. He abhorred illness and had no intention of getting up unless necessary.

"I'm fine—better now," she uttered in a raspy voice. "Just go to bed," she yelled back at him. "I think I'm going to be sick again and prefer to stay here."

"Do you want your robe?" he offered.

"No!" she screeched, aware she sounded shrill.

"If you need anything, let me know," he expressed, hoping to sound helpful, as he pulled his pillow around his ears to muffle the disagreeable sounds in the bathroom.

Cherise collapsed on the cold bathroom floor, sick, but not with the flu. Her husband had deceived her. Her heart ached, wondering how long he had been lying to her. Sharing a bed with him was now impossible. The very idea of being next to him filled her with loathing. No longer able to share intimate space with François, Cherise unearthed an extra blanket from a cedar chest, removed her pillow from the bed and curled up on the sofa at the far end of their bedroom. She wondered if she ever hated anyone more than she hated François now. How could he do this to her? Was he bored with her and their life? Was indulging in an adulterous affair on their property normal for someone like him? What kind of man would do something so unthinkable and so risky? Tears streamed from her eyes but she managed to stifle her sobs. Dabbing her runny nose with a tissue, she breathed shallow rapid intakes of air like a wounded frightened animal until exhausted, she finally dozed off to a disturbed sleep.

CHAPTER 19

Cherise woke the next morning and noticed François had already left the bed. Apparently, he had decided not to wake her, she surmised, which was just as well. She curled up on the sofa, clutching the light blanket under her chin, wishing she did not have to get up. Her eyes were painfully swollen. She licked her parched lips, wishing for a drink of cool water. A hot shower would help—or at least she hoped it would. Despite the bile still gurgling in her stomach, she knew she would eventually have to go downstairs and face him. Besides, she desperately needed coffee and some food. There were no guests at the castle and because it was Saturday, Sandrina would not be working. Cherise was glad not to have to face anyone, even her loyal friend and housekeeper who had frequently asked if everything was okay, sensing in recent days that Cherise was not herself. However with no one in the chateau, alone with François, she found herself feeling concerned—frightened, really. Yesterday had been the most awful night of her life. If her former divorce had been painful, her current sham of a marriage was becoming hell.

She wandered into the kitchen, looking like she'd barely recovered from a terrible illness—hair dripping wet from the shower, pink robe tied around her sore stomach, her face devoid of makeup, displaying a swollen nose, ruddy blotchy face, and a mosquito bite bump on her forehead. For the first time in her marriage with François, Cherise was unconcerned about looking wretched.

"My dear, you look so pale," François uttered with concern. "Do you have the flu or something worse?"

"If I had the flu, I'm over it now. I'll be fine, really." What she really wanted to tell him was that he was a lying bastard and she would find a way to derail his plan. But since she did not know what the damn *plan* was, she could not say anything.

François casually mentioned he was going to Sarlat to obtain a specialized part for his car and that Colette had asked to accompany him to go clothing shopping. Cherise convincingly agreed, effectively concealing her distain and emerging anger at both. In truth, she was glad he would be out of her sight. Cherise wanted Colette off the property. Their excursion would serve her purpose.

Cherise deemed it necessary to search François' room and Colette's cottage. As she watched the *Invicta* thunder out of the driveway, swerving on the first sharp hairpin turn, she knew she should wait at least ten minutes to be certain François and Colette were far from Roufillay.

Dashing down from the third story, taking two steps at a time, Cherise sprinted to Colette's cottage. Taking out her own set of keys, she opened the cottage door. In the bedroom, she wrenched open dresser drawers seeing nothing but clothing, underwear, nylons. Then she looked under the bed. Nothing. She searched under chair cushions and the rug finding nothing. She was not even sure what she was looking for. Her heart was racing and a pounding rush in her ears.

Cherise stared at the kitchen table where she had seen François and Colette the night before, controlling her tears. Her anger propelled her and she continued her search. Nothing suspicious in the small bathroom, in the tub, sink, tiny medicine cabinet and toilet. No pills. Nothing unusual. Walking toward the living room, Cherise noticed the armoire door was ajar. She recognized Colette's small leather suitcase and she yanked it out onto the floor. Ripping the zipper open, she flipped the lid and unzipped smaller side pouches, discovering a small black purse. Her fingers shaking, she pulled out the purse, opened it, and out dropped several passports. The first passport identified her as *Colette Armond*—correct height, weight and nationality. Cherise examined the second passport and nearly fell over backwards. *Diana Aubrey.* Same photo—same height. Who the hell was Diana Aubrey? Clearly it was the same person as Colette Armond.

Cherise returned the passports to the purse, stuffed it back into the zipped pouch, and shoved the suitcase to the back of the armoire where it had been. Which way had it been facing? Toward the front? Oh god, think…no it was facing the back. She had opened the zipper right to left, so it had to have faced the back. Cherise did not want anything to look disturbed. She left the armoire door slightly ajar as she had found it.

Heart racing, she dashed back to the castle, running up three flights of stairs. She tried to open François' art room but it was locked. Because this was his domain, she had no idea of the whereabouts of the key. Hurrying downstairs again, to the back hall laundry closet where Sandrina kept the maids' keys, Cherise snatched the large, wrought-iron key ring, ran back upstairs and, breathless, she fumbled to find the studio key. Her hands were shaking. She tried several keys. None were right. Fearful François and Colette might return soon, she feverishly fumbled with the keys, dropping them jangling on the stone floor. Selecting a key at random, she inserted it into the door lock and miraculously felt the bolt open with a click. She left the key in the lock.

The room looked much as she remembered but she noticed the screensaver movement on his computer on the corner table. Cherise needed to access the Internet. Shaking her head in amazement that his laptop was plugged in and running she muttered aloud, "Sloppy arrogance." Cherise clicked the Internet icon and waited for the search engine to appear. She typed *"Who is Diana Aubrey?"* Heart pounding, she perched on his chair, waiting in anticipation. The search engine pulled up three lines of data. The first, *Sir Walter Raleigh Aubrey marries model Diana Dupree.* She clicked, revealing a photo of an elderly white-haired man leaving the steps of a building with a woman, unmistakably, the person she now recognized as Colette. Feeling sick to her stomach and sweating profusely, Cherise typed, *Who is Diana Dupree?* Information was sparse. She had been a model and there were several runway photos.

Clearly, this Diana Dupree woman was voluptuous, not the least bit timid and very unlike her persona as Colette Armond.

Cherise typed, *Who is Raleigh Aubrey?* Wikipedia provided extensive biographical information, concluding with a news story, *Sir Raleigh Aubrey, longtime resident of Brightingham castle dies in a tragic accident, falling out of his wheelchair...crushed bones...* Cherise she put her hand to her throat and swallowed, unable to read the rest of the article.

Horrified, she ran into François' en suite bathroom, involuntary waves of nausea emptying her breakfast into the toilet bowl. Concerned François would discover his bathroom had been occupied, she grabbed a cleaning agent from the closet hallway, scrubbed it clean and flushed the toilet again. Thankfully, the window was open and plenty of fresh air wafted in with the breeze. She had to get out of there. Double-checking that she had returned the Internet back to icon mode, she was certain nothing looked disturbed on his desk. She put the chair back where she found it. She hastily turned the key that had opened the room, locked the door behind her and left quickly.

Extremely relieved François and Colette had not yet returned, Cherise's mind was racing. She wished when Colette returned with François, she could walk up to her and say, *"Did you have a good day, Diana?"* and watch the shock on her face and François', knowing it would cause a calamity, so she thought up a better plan of her own. However, Cherise now realized there was every reason to suspect her life might be in danger.

CHAPTER 20

Bordeaux, France

Cherise' plan was to go to Bordeaux. She would make a plausible excuse to François, telling him she wanted to buy some new cushion fabric for the kitchen benches to replace the tattered ones and also purchase new clothes only found in a bigger city. Sarlat, the closest city to Roufillay, had limited high-end clothing and no large retail fabric and upholstery store. She decided to take the train, permitting much-needed time to relax along the way. She knew it would not be hard to convince François she needed a little vacation from the exhaustion of the bed and breakfast routine.

It was difficult to acknowledge to herself that buying a chateau on a whim, and then falling for a captivating guest at a time when she was vulnerable from a recently failed marriage, had been a result of her own impetuousness. Wanting an escape from the anguish of her past life in San Francisco, she had cast off her business sense as well as her common sense, retreating into a fantasy world to live in a castle in a foreign country.

Both angry and disgusted with her own gullibility, Cherise assumed that during her time in Bordeaux, François would undoubtedly find his way into bed with Colette, and both would be delighted Cherise was off the chateau premises. Guest season over, Sandrina would not return to the castle until Roufillay reopened in the spring.

The weather was turning cooler so Cherise packed a warm wool sweater and jacket that coordinated with her skirt. She was glad she would have uninterrupted time on the train ride to consider how she would explain her story to the police.

Surprisingly, François did not question or argue about her trip to Bordeaux. In fact, she thought he looked relieved. Cherise departed Roufillay, her brief wifely embrace designed to convince François of normalcy. After a pleasant drive to Sarlat, she boarding the earliest train leaving for Bordeaux. Cherise welcomed her escape to a larger city.

Built on a curve of the Garonne River, Bordeaux was a fascinating city. The Grand Theatre was one of the best classical constructions of its design in France. She looked forward to seeing the Esplanades de Quinconces, and the Place de la Bourse, now converted into a splendid hotel. Departing the train station, Cherise hailed a taxi, directing the driver to an address on Rue St. Remi. Entering the stone building with its tired furnishings, nondescript windows and old metal desks, she was greeted by a disinterested, frumpy desk clerk. She was middle-aged, obese, overly rouged. Her reading glasses hung on a chain around her neck, and a chewed pencil was stuck in a bun in her overly-dyed blonde hair. This was not an auspicious beginning.

"Bonjour, Madam." The clerk glanced at the size of the diamond on Cherise's ring and then grudgingly raised her eyes to her to her face. This well-dressed stranger had interrupted her good moment, as she swallowed another chocolate, enjoying the daily newspaper. "Eh, bien, what can I do to help you?"

"I'm Cherise Eden, I mean Cherise Eden Delacroix….uh, I'm Mrs. François Delacroix. I must see the chief inspector. I have a very good reason to fear someone is going to try to kill me." Her dramatic words sent a shiver up her own spine.

Intrigued, the clerk finished her chocolate and put down the newspaper. "Oui, Madame, I will get the inspector for you. His office is down the hall. I will be back in a moment and convey to him what you have told me." She slowly waddled to an office in the back, reappearing with a very short, slightly balding portly gentleman, who was coughing and wheezing. Cherise took a deep breath as the inspector walked toward her.

"Bonjour. I'm Pierre Molyneaux, Chief Inspector for this district.

What can I do for you?" He wiped his red nose, extending his hand to her, commenting about the misery of allergies. "Had them all my life, but they are the worst in early fall."

Cherise had rehearsed what she wanted to say on the long train ride, deciding the truth was better than any contrived story. She asked for privacy, knowing the desk clerk had already heard enough to start gossiping with her friends. Pierre motioned for Cherise to follow him to his office in the back of the building. The room was not oppressive, just confining because it was rather small and without any windows. He flopped down in a black leather chair behind a large metal desk and motioned for her to sit in one of his two club chairs with worn brown fabric on the seats and arms. Cherise composed herself. She explained she was American, originally from California and now the owner of Chateau Roufillay, in the Dordogne. She told him she had recently married François Delacroix and the rest of the implausible story.

As the details of her experience unfolded, Pierre leaned in toward her more than once, rubbing his head, observing her closely to ascertain whether this tale was true or something imagined by someone who might not be mentally well. But as Cherise continued, providing details and explanations of what she had discovered in both the armoire and on François' computer, it became evident that she had either read a good mystery story, was in need of psychiatric attention, or this attractive woman actually was telling the truth.

Inspector Molyneaux inquired if François was wealthy. Cherise stated that her husband had income from various investments of his own and that he had never asked to borrow any of her money. The earnings from running Roufillay went toward business expenses, utilities, employee wages for Sandrina, Collette and the groundskeeper, food, and general maintenance. The bed and breakfast was a profitable venture and any surplus money was deposited into a joint bank account. The inspector asked Cherise if she had actually seen the bank statements. She nodded and indicated all earnings had been accounted for. No money had been withdrawn. Pierre rubbed his chin, trying to ascertain what François' motive or intent might be.

Cherise's tale sounded bizarre, yet intriguing to the inspector. Who would make up a story like this? She'd described running in the rain to a cottage in the middle of the night in a storm, mud and blood on her nightgown, and then running up the stairs to her bedroom to take a shower to hide the blood and camouflage her wet hair from her husband. Madame Delacroix was either a very creative storyteller...or perhaps this series of events actually had happened.

He leaned forward intently, nodding and taking notes when necessary. He asked her to repeat certain details and asked intentionally redundant questions to be certain she said the same thing twice. Although it was brazen act for her husband to have an affair on the grounds of their property, the inspector had heard far worse. Infidelity, in itself, was nothing new. Because Cherise remained professionally composed and was obviously intelligent, he let her talk at great length. The inspector was impressed with her poise and professionalism, especially when she presenting him both her business card and the brochure from Chateau Roufillay. At the end of the interview, Inspector Molyneaux was convinced she required police assistance.

"Please, she pleaded, I need your help. I have nowhere to turn." Repressed tears welled up in her eyes, impossible for her conceal her anguish. "I have no family in California except for my ex-husband and his mother. I wouldn't dare call them. And the friends I have in Sarlat all know each other. I could not confide any of this with my maid, ,Sandrina. Until I was certain of my facts about François' infidelity I had no reason, early on, to suspect either my husband or Colette. Please help me. I'm afraid for my life."

"But, Madame, I don't see what we can do to help you. It's out of our jurisdiction," Pierre sighed, easing back into the leather chair.

Cherise stammered, "I understand, but I wanted to tell you this in case something does happens to me, you will understand this was *not* an accident."

Alarmed, the inspector watched her despondent tears sliding down her cheeks. She swiped them away with her fingertips, sitting quietly, waiting for his response.

"What do you think he plans to do to you—with this woman, what's her name, Colette?"

"Yes, it is Colette Armond, now, but that's not her real name. It's Diana Aubrey. I don't know when or how she changed her name, but she had been married to Sir Raleigh Aubrey in England who died in a tragic accident. I'm really uneasy about his death. Apparently he had been confined to a wheelchair and he fell down the stairs and was crushed, but I don't think that's what happened."

"Are you saying it was not an accident?" Pierre leaned forward with renewed interest, and sneezed. He reached for a tissue box on his credenza and blew his nose, considering it might be possible Sir Raleigh Aubrey had been murdered by this Diana-Colette person, but there wasn't any proof, and anyway he could not get involved with that situation. Inspector Molyneaux made a mental note to check this news story on the Internet and he had an additional idea, as well. "Please go on, Madam Delacroix," he nodded.

"Inspector, Molyneaux, I have no proof, other than my husband's infidelity and the passports I discovered. François may be who he is, or not. But clearly, Colette is not who she claims to be."

"Yes, yes, very interesting," blowing his nose into his newly discovered pocket handkerchief loudly and apologizing profusely.

"Please help me inspector," Cherise pleaded. "I cannot go to the local police in Sarlat, as it would get all over town within a couple of days and someone undoubtedly will tell François. Can you imagine what might happen if he found out?"

"Ah yes, that is true in a small town like Sarlat, or any small town, anywhere. "Madame Delacroix...um," he hesitated, flicking his fingers in the air as if it became obvious he suddenly had thought of something.

"Please call me Cherise."

"Cherise, I have an idea, if you would be open to this suggestion."

"I'm open to hearing anything that might save my life."

"I have a friend. He is a retired Scotland Yard detective who called me just the other day. He is planning to visit. A murder case in England has not been going very well for him. I need to talk with him, and am thinking perhaps I can convince him to stay at your castle, as a guest, no?"

"I don't see how that would be possible...we are closed for the season."

"My dear, can you not reopen for a special guest, someone who just missed the season due to say, 'personal problems', for a week or so?"

"Well I suppose I could convince my husband. A single guest I could manage myself. I've already released my maid, Sandrina, until next spring."

"Good, good. Then I will contact you when I have more information. I should hear from my friend today or tomorrow. Where are you staying?"

She provided the inspector her hotel contact information, the Chateau Grattequina, near the center of Bordeaux. She rose from her chair to leave, overcome with gratitude.

"Merci beaucoup," she smiled and bestowed an impulsive hug just as he sneezed once again. Cherise asked the desk clerk if she would please call for a cab.

Cherise tentatively relaxed during the cab ride to her hotel. Determined, with new-found resolve, she would tell François she required an extra day in Bordeaux. It was important to purchase just the right fabric for the kitchen benches and some new clothing…or he would be suspicious.

CHAPTER 21

Chippenham, England

Kent called Brett very early out of spite, hoping to wake him up and annoy him. However, Brett was already awake, mapping out travel plans for Bordeaux to visit his friend and fellow detective, Pierre Molyneaux. The trip was supposed to be a vacation, but maybe it could be both pleasure and pursuit.

Without gloating, Kent explained to Brett that he had traced a single transaction on a Visa card at a small exclusive clothing shop to a Diana Aubrey in Montreux, Switzerland. Kent was able to obtain this information by faxing the shop owner his credentials from Scotland Yard, stating he was investigating a death.

Brett called a travel agent, requesting flight reservations to Montreux, connecting in Geneva with a final leg to Bordeaux. He packed light, taking his tweed jacket with suede patches on the elbows, decent shoes, and some oxford shirts. He owned only one tweed jacket but it was in good condition and comfortably worn. He shrugged into his trench coat before closing the front door since it was chilly and misting heavily outside. Some days he wondered why anyone chose to live in England with its predictably inclement weather and persistently damp climate.

Montreux, Switzerland

After an uneventful flight, Brett arrived in Geneva, rented a car and drove to Montreux. He had always liked Switzerland. Montreux was especially beautiful in the spring, when all the shrubs and flowers were in full bloom along the Lakeside Promenade Fleuri on Lac Leman, but even in the fall, Montreux was lovely. Lac Leman stretched from Vevey to Villeneuve, dotted with cafes and the splendid Hotel Eden Palace au Lac. Castle Chillon, on the edge of the lake, dated back to the 11th century. Poet Lord Byron was attributed to have scratched his name into a pillar. The original dungeon remains inspired the gristly tale, "The Prisoner of Chillon." where François de Bonivard had been chained for five years during the 16th century. Brett had vastly enjoyed his tour of the castle years ago.

He drove through the Montreux city streets, stopping in the shopping districts. He went from store to store, showing photos of Diana to proprietors and clerks, inquiring if anyone had seen her or knew who she was. Brett thought the likelihood of finding someone who recognized her was slim, but he would not rest until he had exhausted the search. He parked his rental car and decided to walk through one of the upscale shopping districts. Brett entered a very expensive and exquisite shop, *La Soie Belle*—Beautiful Silk.

Brett showed the shopkeeper his photo of Diana Aubrey, and was gratified when she nodded her head that she recognized this woman. Brett asked if she knew where Diana lived and although she did not, she thought probably in the nearby exclusive residential neighborhood since Diana often visited the shop. She would purchase small items and always paid in cash, except for one time—the Gianfranco Ferre designer blouse she said she simply must have, mused the shopkeeper. That blouse was the only item she had ever charged on her credit card. Brett, alert, realized this was a valuable piece of information.

"Did you process the transaction?" he asked the shopkeeper, hopefully.

"No, I did not. I was busy with another customer, but I recall my sales associate helped her. She later told me about it and we were both quite surprised since that was the only credit card purchase she'd ever made."

"Thank you," Brett smiled wryly. Diana had finally made a mistake. In his profession, Brett knew that people who were in hiding or those who have committed crimes eventually slip, becoming careless. The fugitive assumes his identity is protected because he lives in a foreign country. After time passes, he (or she) relaxes his guard. In this instance, Diana used a traceable credit card for her purchase. Big mistake.

With his success at *La Soie Belle,* Brett was encouraged that Diana might live near this neighborhood. He probed the local markets and boutiques, querying the merchants about Diana's photo, "Do you recognize this woman?" Wearily, Brett entered an awning-covered produce market featuring exquisite chocolates and pastries. Brett exhibited Diana's photo and the proprietor recognized the woman, a frequent customer. He recollected her name was not Diana. He knew her as Colette. Brett asked the proprietor if he knew where she lived.

"Yes, I delivered groceries to her home one evening when she was not feeling well." Brett presented his credentials and the owner provided Colette's address.

Brett drove up the winding, hilly streets, and parked at the front of an attractive villa, overlooking the lake. He rang the buzzer. If the woman Diana/Colette answered the door, Brett's cover would be as a prospective real estate buyer, engaging her in a conversation about the property. He rang the buzzer again and waited. No one answered. The property was surrounded by shrubbery, hidden from the neighbors. He looked furtively over his shoulder to determine a stealthy way to enter the villa. Brett discovered a locked side gate. He scrambled over the gate, wishing he had not worn his good clothes, and sauntered to the back terrace, admiring the spectacular lake view. He cautiously peered into the floor-to-ceiling arched wood shuttered windows.

The house was nicely furnished, but it appeared to be unoccupied. No papers or magazines on the tables. Nothing on the kitchen counters. Everything had been wiped spotless, as if a maid had cleaned up after the occupants departed. Breaking in crossed his mind, but decided against it. There was sure to be a security alarm. He appreciated that the villa was protected on both sides by thick bougainvillea and tall leafy trees, preventing neighbors from seeing him skulking around like a prowler. Wishing he was more agile, he clumsily climbed back over the gate, momentarily catching his coat on the gate's hinge, but managed to free himself without tearing his sleeve.

Brett wondered why the property seemed unoccupied. If Diana was not there, then where was she? Was she no longer residing in the villa? Had she moved elsewhere in Switzerland or maybe to another country? With so many unanswered questions, Brett groaned in frustration. He checked the mailbox before leaving correctly assuming he would find nothing. Any piece of mail with a return address label would have provided useful contact information. If she had moved, there would be a forwarding address. He made a mental note to check the post office. Brett wanted to know whether she owned this property…or did it belong to someone else?

To answer this question, Brett drove to the Montreux town hall to unearth the records of the villa ownership. A helpful clerk went to a back room, returning with a dusty green ledger with tattered edges, the binder spine falling apart with age. Peering up and down the columns with his index finger, he located the address. The records showed the villa had been owned by Madame Marie Bercier in 1997, and then it had been purchased by François Delacroix ten years ago. It appeared the taxes and utilities had been recently paid and there was no reason to suspect anything unusual. It was possible that Diana Aubrey (or as Colette) might still reside at the villa. Brett did not understand why this woman had assumed two names. Where she was now was anybody's guess. And where was the villa's owner, François Delacroix?

Frustrated and tired, Brett returned the rental car to the airport and sat in the terminal lobby until his flight gate for Bordeaux was posted. He was exhausted and depressed. It had been another long day of possibilities and failures. Brett considered the reality that, on one hand, he might be getting close, only to find this entire case had gone cold. There was no information regarding François Delacroix's whereabouts and no one in town had responded affirmatively to Brett's inquiries. Without a photo, it was impossible to identify François Delacroix. Brett tried an Internet search on François Delacroix, but there was no current or specific information. On some level Brett was not surprised, but he doggedly continued to think, culling his brain.

Bordeaux, France

Brett arrived in Bordeaux, refueled by the tuna sandwich he had purchased before boarding. He slept during the flight and felt restored and hopeful when he awoke. Picking up a Renault airport rental, he drove directly to his hotel.

The bar was open and Brett slumped on the barstool, downing one scotch and then another, pondering his next move. With one hand clasped loosely around his glass, he flipped a coin, "*heads you quit, tales you go on,*" he mumbled to himself. His bleary eyes watched the cascading coin land with a 'plink' on the counter. It was not in his nature to give up. If he remained on the case, he felt productive and purposeful with the opportunity to avenge Raleigh's death. If he abandoned the inquiry, the downside would be a sense of failure; the upshot would be returning to his quiet life in Chippenham. Brett recognized that, although his life in Chippenham was comfortable and without worry, he admitted to himself he was bored. The idea of returning to his cluttered cottage full of old furniture, dusty books and scattered newspapers was depressing. He took one more sip of the fourth single malt scotch on ice and lurched up to his room, dropped onto the bed, and fell into a deep stupor, shoes still on his feet.

Awaking the next morning with a brain-splitting hangover, he drove the rental Renault to Inspector Pierre Molyneaux's office on Rue St. Remi. College friends, Brett had not seen Pierre in years. Brett strode into Pierre's office, looking for his buddy. Spotting one another, each grinned, the years dropping away. More portly than Brett remembered, Pierre waddled toward him, two outstretched arms reached out to engulf Brett in a bear hug, followed by happy back slaps. Pierre was considerably shorter than Brett, and he grinned up at his friend, his chubby cheeks reddened and his bald head nodding, comical yet endearing.

"Alors, it is good to see you, Brett," as he reached into his trouser pocket, grabbing a handkerchief for the rousing bout of sneezing that ensued.

"Got a cold, Pierre?"

"No, Brett. It's these damn allergies. Dust and pollen bother me. If I go to the sea that bothers me, which makes no sense and it is the one thing that makes other people feel better. I am allergic to everything from sea air to peanuts and, of course, wool. I get dreadful hives. And then animals—Mon Dieu, things like furry dogs, and cats—oh, don't even talk about cats," he shuddered, waving his wrists in the air as if to brush off invisible animal hairs.

Brett smiled, nodding sympathetically, trying desperately not to laugh at his friend's animated cartoon-like gestures. "So tell me, what's so important, Pierre, that you wanted me to come all the way down here? I mentioned I wanted a vacation, but I sense there is something else on your mind."

"You first, Brett. I want to know what you've been up to as a retiree who is not so retired, I hear? Tell me about the case you are working on in England," the short inspector grasped Brett by the elbow, leading him back to his office.

Brett described the tragedy that had happened to his friend Sir Raleigh Aubrey and the rest of the frustrating starts and dead ends of this case. Pierre listened intently. When Brett mentioned that the empty villa in Montreux belonged to a man called François Delacroix, Pierre jumped out of his chair and began pacing the room animatedly. Brett was concerned for his friend, who kept uttering, "*Holy shit, Merde, holy shit!*" His friend calmed enough to explain to Brett that a distraught woman, Cherise Eden—well Cherise Delacroix—had been in his office just yesterday, claiming that her husband, François Delacroix and a woman at the chateau by the name of Colette Armond, might be planning to kill her.

Brett stood up, exclaiming, "*Holy shit! You've got to be kidding me! What are the chances that my case is tied to this? What an unbelievable coincidence. Colette Armond may be the name she is using, but she is really Diana Aubrey, who has gone missing over a year after Raleigh's death. Diana was Raleigh's widow.*"

Brett joined Pierre, each pacing the small office. At one point, they bumped into one another and laughed, breaking the tension. Pierre showed Brett the brochure describing Chateau Roufillay. Looking at colorful photos of castle and grounds in the brochure, Brett was impressed. Missing in the brochure were photos of Cherise or François Delacroix. Brett frowned and squinted his eyes, in an attempt to visualize her. Reading his mind, Pierre stuck out his chin, rolled his eyes and, with a tilt of his shiny balding head, he teased Brett in affectionate camaraderie, "Don't worry, she's very, very pretty."

Using his time wisely, Brett's immediate goal was to meet Cherise Delacroix while she was still in Bordeaux. Pierre considered Brett's request and described his emerging plan. If Brett agreed, the strategy would be to arrive as a guest at Chateau Roufillay, checking in for one week. Undercover, Brett would have time and opportunity to observe François Delacroix and Colette. Enticing and possibly dangerous but Brett was keen to try. Risk was minimal that he would seem anything other than a tourist traveling through the south of France.

Pierre enjoyed talking with Brett over several bottles of red Bordeaux Medoc and a sumptuous duck confit dinner, reminiscing about college and their lives after. It was a pleasant evening and they shared many memories and much laughter. Before leaving the café, Pierre called Cherise to schedule a meeting with Brett the following day at her hotel. Nodding his head, Pierre gave a "thumbs up" to Brett in confirmation. Brett said goodnight to Pierre, feeling energized and optimistic. Tomorrow would be very interesting. Brett had no intention of dealing with a hangover the next morning so he avoided the lure of the hotel bar. Not wanting to admit to himself, Brett was intrigued with Pierre's words about how pretty Cherise was and he wanted to look his best when he met her.

When Brett returned to his hotel room, he sank into a comfy club chair in the corner, facing a window with a view of the rooftops in the city. The sun had dropped below the horizon, casting a blaze of amber ribbons, stretched across the dusky sky. Brett opened the window, feeling the warm breezes fade into evening chill. Lying down on the bed, he sighed contentedly, imagining what Cherise might look like. He closed his eyes welcoming a good night's sleep.

CHAPTER 22

Cherise woke early and decided to stroll to Cathédrale Saint-André. The air was sunny but chilly. She crossed her arms around her cashmere cardigan and pulled it closer to her neck. Rather than looking at the people passing by, she kept her head down, affecting anonymity, while wondering what their lives might be like. Although she did not know anyone in Bordeaux, she was concerned someone might recognize her.

Pigeons flapped from one side of the street to the other, ignoring her footsteps. When she reached the cathedral she gazed up at the tower, admiring the architecture. She did not pray often yet found herself yearning to sit in a holy place, surrounded by people of faith. Selecting an empty walnut wooden pew, Cherise sat, observing the visitors, some sitting in silence, others lighting votive candles. She sat, overwhelmed by the Romanesque architecture and enormous stained glass window above the altar. It made her feel small and insignificant. Not knowing how to pray she mumbled to herself, "God please help me…if you can hear me, I'm so frightened."

She remained longer than she'd expected, feeling the inexplicable comfort of being in the safe haven. Cherise looked at the worshipers in the church, wondering what they were praying for. Cherise wished she had someone to light a candle for her. She wanted to light one, but felt embarrassed, not knowing the procedure or how much money to put into the canister. Eventually, she got up and quietly left through the enormous carved stone portals. As she turned her head back toward the cathedral as she walked away, Cherise noticed the statue of the Blessed Virgin and Child on top of the spire and the flying buttresses flanking the sides of the church. She wondered if the Virgin Mother answered prayers or was it the Child she was holding. Cherise offered a silent prayer to both of them.

Knowing she was to meet a stranger the next morning, she wondered what Brett Maxfield would be like. Could she trust him? Would he be empathetic or judgmental? What if he did not believe her? Inspector Pierre had assured her Brett was not only very bright but also exceptionally competent. Reluctantly, she told herself she had to trust someone.

Cherise pondered what she would say to Brett and how she would describe her predicament. When she thought about the things that had happened to her, she felt bereft and completely alone. In a moment of self-flagellation, Cherise wondered if her husband's infidelity was, in some way, her own fault. She chided herself for her lack of judgment when she had first met François and wondered now how she could have been so blind to his character. She winced as she remembered the evening when he had persuaded her to sit for the drawing. How clever and audacious he had been, taking advantage of her vulnerability.

Introspectively, she flipped through the pages of her mind, re-reading her life with Andy. Remembering him, their good years and the unexpected divorce made her sad. But François' intentionally manipulative actions made her more than sad and terribly upset. Cherise felt very, very angry. And that anger gave her strength.

As Cherise took off her clothes and slipped into the comfortable hotel bed, she hoped tomorrow's meeting with Brett would provide an anchor to hold her steady, in what had felt like an ocean of sequential rushing tides, crashing into the shore and continually pulling her back out to sea.

The next morning, Cherise felt more composed. She pushed the window of her hotel open to admire the lake, the breeze urging the small whitecaps. The garden below her window was overflowing with lavender and pink peonies, their last blooms bowing to the ground, too heavy to hold their heads up to the sun. A butterfly fluttered hesitantly, passed and then returned to sit on her window ledge. She marveled at the beauty of its wings, hovering before flying away. Cherise remembered a legend recounting that butterflies flitting around a person were the deceased souls of loved ones, bringing luck. Smiling, Cherise hoped this was a good omen. She showered, feeling the hot water cleansing her distraught soul. The stream drizzled over her head, down her back, her legs, flowing through her toes. If only she could wash her problems down the drain as easily, with the citrus scented shampoo, life would be so much easier, better, and satisfying.

While blow-drying her hair, she mentally rehearsed what she would say to the former Scotland Yard detective, Brett Maxwell. She dressed sensibly, wanting to convey intelligence and professionalism. Checking her watch, Cherise realized she had only a half hour to snatch a quick breakfast in the hotel café. As she crossed the elegant lobby surrounded by tall marble pillars, illuminated by large chandeliers suspended above the black and white marble tiled floor, she noticed guests in animated chatter. No one spoke or took notice of her, which was a comfort.

Cherise enjoyed a hot chocolate latte and a fresh buttery blueberry scone. Attempting to read the local paper was futile as her nerves prevented her from concentrating. She had agreed to meet Brett on the terrace. Inspector Pierre Molyneaux had described Brett and her eyes searched the area for someone who fit his description. As she scanned the terrace she noticed there were two couples sitting at tables and an elderly woman sitting by herself, a tiny white Maltese nestled at her feet, gnawing on a biscuit. In the corner of the terrace, under a cascading leafy shade tree, she spotted a man she was certain must be Brett Maxfield. He fit Pierre's description and appeared to be watching her as she moved toward him. Cherise cautiously approached his table and he stood up immediately, as if he knew her.

"Hello, I'm Cherise Delacroix. Are you Brett Maxfield?"

Extending his hand, Brett acknowledged her question, pulling out a chair for her to sit down. An attentive waiter arrived at the table and Brett ordered black coffee. Cherise selected an ice tea, anticipating her mouth would start to run dry when she spoke.

"Would you like to order anything else?" he asked.

"No, I'm sure I can't eat anything. I'm terribly nervous and don't know where to begin."

"Just start at the beginning. I hope there is something I can do to help you," Brett offered reassuringly.

Sitting on the sunny cafe terrace, overlooking Bordeaux Lac, Cherise relaxed her tight shoulders. Her initial impression of Brett was positive. He had an easy, unassuming demeanor that made her comfortable immediately. She thought him attractive in his blue oxford shirt and khaki trousers. While he talked, she studied his eyes, noticing they were the same shade of blue as his shirt. The lines on his face, especially around his eyes, made him appear scholarly and she liked the sandy color of his hair, which was short, but not too much so. Intuitively, she trusted him, quickly getting Brett up to speed by telling him Inspector Pierre had called her early that same morning to explain his plan calling for Brett to go undercover at Roufillay. Now, sitting across from Brett, he appeared to be the answer to her prayers. Cherise explained the entire disturbing story, trying not to sound desperate or unhinged.

Brett listened to her intently, watching her anxious face and hand gestures. He observed a great deal of sadness in her eyes. He found himself more involved than he'd anticipated. Pierre was right. Cherise Delacroix was very pretty and Brett liked her smile and the way she twisted her hair while talking. It was obvious to him she was a bright woman who had made some bad choices. Brett needed to learn more about her—to encourage her confidence and listen nonjudgmentally. Treading with caution, he asked her many questions. The more he learned, the more Brett was convinced something ominous was going on. He shared the details of his investigation, describing to Cherise his case in England, including Raleigh's death and his suspicions that Raleigh had been murdered. Brett postulated that his case was linked with her situation.

Hearing his theory, Cherise became even more alarmed, realizing François had quite possibly been involved in Raleigh's death. However, there was no proven connection between François and Raleigh. It was just a gut feeling and it gnawed at her.

They discussed and reviewed the details of the plan for Brett's guest stay at Roufillay. It was decided he should retain his real name, Brett Maxfield, a very common name in England. Retired from Scotland Yard years ago and no longer an active agent, Brett need only provide his current identification, his driver's license and a credit card. Cherise was relieved Brett would stay on the premises of Roufillay in an undercover role. Brett had been following the trail of Diana Aubrey for some time and this arrangement would permit him to observe both Diana and François unobtrusively.

Pondering the fortuitous odds that Brett Maxfield's path would cross with hers at this precise moment, Cherise stood up to say goodbye. Finally she felt the grip of panic unclench, replaced by a glimmer of hope. Maybe the Blessed Virgin or the Child in the statue's arms had actually heard her prayers.

With a determined sense of purpose, Cherise finished her shopping, buying fifteen yards of yellow and white checked cotton fabric for the kitchen benches flanking the large wooden breakfast table where guests enjoyed their morning meal. Next, she went to a fine boutique and indulged herself, purchasing two wool skirts and three luxurious cashmere sweaters for the colder months knowing these elegant garments were not available in Sarlat. An attractive pair of shoes caught her eye. Cherise's favorite perfume and an expensive pearl necklace were wrapped in designer-embossed tissue—carefully calculated purchases made to ensure that François would believe she had a reason to be in Bordeaux. Cherise selected a silk tie for François even though he mostly wore turtleneck sweaters or polo shirts. The tie was a merely a gesture to avoid suspicion. The idea of buying him a tender gift now appalled her.

Cherise requested that the merchant ship the kitchen fabric bolt to Sarlat to be picked up. The rest of the items she packed into her suitcase. Riding in the taxi over the Pont St. Pierre in Bordeaux, overlooking the Garonne River, she admired the pretty coach lights. Bordeaux was a bustling city, with large, stately stone buildings, dotted with small-paned windows and historic, classic French architecture. Three days in Bordeaux made Cherise realize how isolated she was at Roufillay and how simple and uncomplicated her life had seemed before she met François.

In retrospect, she wondered what she might have uncovered had she hired a detective to do a background check before their marriage. She now understood what *blind love* meant, needing François to be everything she wanted. Cherise was dismayed to think he could be so cruel, given what she had already endured with her failed marriage to Andy. Shaking her head and relinquishing an enormous sigh, she packed her bags, checked out of the hotel and took a taxi back to the train station. Storm clouds were gathering, along with intermittent gusts of wind. Cherise hoped it would not rain. Storms, thunder and lightning during a train ride made her nervous.

The weather subsided, and her train ride back to Sarlat was uneventful. Cherise felt a great deal better when she returned to the chateau than she had when she first arrived in Bordeaux. She did not know much about Brett, but she felt she could trust him, bolstered by Pierre's convincing professional recommendation. At this point, she had to trust Brett. She had no one else whom she could trust. How Brett would protect her from harm, she had no idea, but the idea of his presence in the chateau was more comforting than she could express, even to herself.

CHAPTER 23

Château Roufillay, Dordogne, France

François greeted Cherise at the door when she returned, kissing her on the lips. Revolted, she forced herself to kiss him back with pretend emotion, quickly requesting him to unload her packages. "How was your trip?" he asked.

"It was just what I needed," she commented. "I found the most adorable fabric for the kitchen, which is being shipped to Sarlat. I can't wait for it to arrive. Let me show you my new cashmere sweater and a pearl necklace I had to have, along with several other items. Oh, and I have a present for you." François looked surprised, but pleased. He opened the small box and pulled out the colorful silk tie. "Thank you, my dear. It's lovely." He thought to himself how naïve she was, purchasing him presents and loving him so unabashedly. Clearly she had been shopping and shopped well. He did not mind and was glad she had been away from the castle for a few days.

During Cherise's trip to Bordeaux, François determined Colette had been hostile and abnormally bitchy—screaming at him, demanding this charade to be over once and for all. She whined relentlessly, was not in the mood for sex and was tired of living in the cottage, constantly insisting on the life of wealth that he had promised her. Exasperated, she wanted to live in the chateau and demanded to be his wife, as he had promised her. François realized he had grown tired of Colette, and that he did not need her for his future plans. The current situation complicated matters and he did not know how he would get rid of her.

François concluded Colette was no longer of any use to him, nor did he desire to be with her physically. He enjoyed sex with women when they were new to him, exciting or useful. She was none of these things any more. Killing two people had not been his original plan, but the thought entered his mind and took root.

In the beginning when he'd met Diana, she had been exotic, exciting and daring. He recognized she was miserable in her concierge role, having to spend so much of her time alone in the cottage. It was callous on one hand, but it was something she had agreed to do. If she had not become such a bitch, François told himself, he would have considered marrying her once he inherited Roufillay. He would have provided her the money he'd promised her, after all, she had made him a wealthy man. François never considered how long he might stay married to her, but felt if he tired of her, he would ask her to leave and provide her with a substantial settlement. Money was something he knew she could not live without. Divorce was one thing—now he had to consider murder.

With François, it was not about what was right or wrong; it was simply about what he needed to do at the time. He acted without a conscience, a defense he had learned in childhood. He had devised different means of killing Cherise and planned what he would do with the money after Roufillay was sold, but he had not contemplated removing Colette. Now, it was a matter of which to eliminate first. He assessed various scenarios, weighing the pros and cons of killing Cherise first. However, he was worried that he could not trust Colette anymore. What if she had a meltdown and blew his cover in front of Cherise? Colette was insanely jealous, demanding and greedy—a pretty lady, but much too insolent and difficult to manage. As he evaluated his choices, Colette's recent behavior actually made the decision easy. François now knew what he had to do.

CHAPTER 24

Brett, at Pierre's suggestion and with his help, chartered a six-passenger plane to Sarlat. While in the air, he asked the pilot if he would fly over Chateau Roufillay. The pilot was glad to oblige him. Brett explained he would be staying there and was interested to see the chateau from the air. Since there were no other passengers on board, the pilot agreed to fly lower and took the plane down several thousand feet. As the pilot flew over the chateau, Brett was impressed with the enormous ochre-colored stone blocks, the massive size of the turrets and the way it was built into the side of the mountain overlooking the Dordogne River. He understood why Cherise had fallen in love with this property. It was magnificent.

The pilot started to bank the plane toward Sarlat when Brett spotted something he could hardly believe. He asked the pilot to make another turn over the chateau and, as the plane banked to the right, he clearly saw what he thought he'd glimpsed before. Parked in the driveway was a large, classic, black convertible car. He was willing to bet his life it was an *Invicta*. Heart thundering in his chest, he asked the pilot to quickly land at the airport.

Sarlat's small airport was under construction with only one operational runway. He paid the pilot and thanked him for his chartered service. Brett rented the only available car on the rental lot. It was a Smart Car—one of those little things barely holding two people and not much else. When Brett extended both arms, he chuckled to see the car was smaller than his wingspan. He plunked his luggage on the passenger seat and headed out to Roufillay.

The winding roads passed in and out of picturesque quaint villages and farms. Surprisingly, the car handled well for a stick shift, hugging the narrow gravel road without swaying excessively on the hairpin turns. The rocky cliffs towered above the tops of the trees in forests so thick he could not see the sky through the foliage. A familiar unpleasant odor assaulted his nostrils—a skunk, probably dead—one of God's odd creations, he mused, as he continued driving. Cascades of tiny waterfalls trickled across the road tumbling off the cliffs.

As he drove, he stretched out a kink knotted in the small of his back. Brett felt energetic and youthful, despite his fifty-five years. This case was now becoming a tense little game of cat and mouse. He could hardly wait to meet François. The deception had taken a new turn and Brett realized with a renewed sense of optimism this case could be solved. He knew he would not rest until justice was served and the death of his friend Raleigh was vindicated.

Knowing the undercover detective was due to arrive soon, Cherise explained to François that a travel agency had contacted her, hoping it would be possible to accommodate a guest with a special circumstance. She watched the expression on his face turn grim. "We're already closed!" he barked at her.

"I know," she pleaded, "but this guest had already booked a reservation to stay at Roufillay. He was unable to make it during the last week of our normal opening schedule due to a death in his family."

François glared at her, reluctantly agreeing to house one guest for the week, emphasizing that this would be a one-time exception. François was concerned that Colette, already at her wit's end, would create a scene. He also required additional time to craft his plan. An unwelcome guest was about to descend on them at the most inopportune time. François shook his head in frustration and indignantly went to the reception desk, opening the ledger.

Brett arrived, parking his little car in the courtyard. He glanced at the black convertible, parked next to the large walnut tree. He could see the wheel mounted on the side, the large headlights, considerable chrome detailing and the unmistakable *Invicta* insignia. The hunt was on. Like a bloodhound, all of his senses were acutely alert, signaling the cells in his body to energize and start the adrenaline flowing. If he accurately remembered his computer printouts of vintage cars, this was the exact car he was looking for. What were the odds? Could he be this lucky?

Cherise met Brett at the door, and welcomed him graciously, as she would any guest. He introduced himself as Brett Maxfield, just as François walked into the reception area. She blushed, feeling rattled, but was determined not to reveal any indication she had met Brett previously. She introduced him to her husband. Brett extended his right hand to François looking him dead straight in the eye, "It's my pleasure to meet you." François smiled urbanely and turned to the guest register. He pulled his pen from his pocket to write information in the ledger. Brett made a mental note of François' left-handedness. Images of the obelisk on Raleigh's console surfaced in his mind.

Relaxed, François played the perfect host, elegant in his black turtleneck and black slacks. Brett could see how Cherise had fallen for him. He was exceptionally good looking, his lithe muscular physique enhanced by the slight graying hair at his temples. François offered to help Brett with his luggage, escorting him to a room on the second floor. They went up the stairs, keeping their heads low to avoid the slanted beams, past the unoccupied guest bedrooms. Chateau Roufillay had been furnished with considerable charm and priceless antiques, which Brett openly admired to François as they walked the hallway.

Reaching the bedroom, François put down the luggage and turned to Brett. "How was your trip?"

"Fine, really nice."

"I'm sorry to hear about the death in your family," François mentioned, while opening the draperies.

Momentarily taken aback, Brett manufactured a stilted response. "Uh…yes. A favorite uncle who lived a long life." Jolted to his senses,

Brett remembered that his uncle's funeral, fabricated of course, was the reason Brett required this special post-season guest scheduling.

"Would you like a sandwich? You must be hungry," François offered, as he studied Brett for a moment, thinking he was a rather unusual man.

"Yes, a sandwich would be fine. Don't go to any trouble. Anything you have on hand is just fine."

"Roast beef?"

"Fine," he nodded affirmatively, scratching his head, hoping François would just leave the room.

"Wine or beer?"

"Uh…a beer would be great. Thanks."

François left the room and headed downstairs to the kitchen. Brett was not the least bit hungry, but he did not want to appear ungracious. He looked around the enormous room, the walls peculiar shades of salmon pink and sage green, with a floral bedspread and matching striped curtains. The ensuite bathroom displayed similar colors. He deduced, amused by the rabbits and ducks on the wallpaper, this must have been a child's room. Since Roufillay was officially closed for the season, perhaps this was one room the owners could accommodate.

Brett discovered the windows opened to the river and the courtyard on one side, and the driveway and an adjacent cottage on the other. Drinking in the view of billowing clouds streaked with sunlight reflecting off the Dordogne River and inhaling the scent of newly-cut grass, Brett was momentarily elated, feeling as though he was on a real vacation. Reality grounded him quickly. He was here to be responsible—to protect Cherise and avenge his friend Raleigh, not slip into a holiday mode. Brett reclined on the double bed, low to the floor, and wondered when or how he would meet Colette. He wanted to see the real Diana Aubrey in person.

François knocked at Brett's bedroom door, arriving with a ham sandwich, a hunk of local cheese and a cold beer. "Sorry, we were out of roast beef. I hope ham will do?"

"Yes, of course. It's fine. I really appreciate it. What time should I come down for breakfast?" He asked, rubbing the tip of his nose with his bent finger.

"Anytime you get up—say after 8 a.m. is just fine. Cherise will have something set out for you."

"Excellent." Wondering what a normal guest would say, Brett fumbled for words. "What tourist sights do you recommend during my stay?"

François answered Brett's questions by rote. He had provided this information, answers and details to guests who wanted to tour the region. François left and Brett turned the bolt on the door. It was late and already dark. He devoured the sandwich, tension making him hungrier than he thought. The cold beer was the best delight of the day and went down smoothly.

Brett had trouble sleeping. Perhaps it was because he had eaten before bedtime, but mostly because he ruminated about how to maximize his time productively during his short stay at Roufillay. It was evident, while he was there, François would not harm Cherise—Brett was certain. But it was the only thing he was sure of. He dreaded the thought of having to leave her in the chateau if he could not solve the puzzle during his week's stay. How would he protect her? With the cool evening breeze wafting through the windows, he finally succumbed to a deep sleep, unaware of the screeching of nocturnal bats flying into the proverbial belfry above the tower.

Cherise paced around their master bedroom and broached the subject that she knew annoyed François. She had talked to him several times previously about not retaining Colette as a concierge during the off-season. Cherise reasoned to herself that she'd be safer with one less person intent upon harming her. Without Colette on the premises, perhaps she could thwart François' plan. He had insisted Colette was needed to settle the entire season's books and reconcile all the accounts, a laborious task that would take at least several more weeks. Cherise knew she could not win this argument, nor did she want to further upset him, especially since she had already persuaded him to permit an additional guest in the chateau when it was closed for the season. She backed off and told François she understood, biting the inside of her lip till it bled, managing to produce a compliant smile.

Françoise escaped to the library to consider his original plan. He had known the castle would be closed for the winter but he had not anticipated that Cherise wouldn't permit Colette to remain in the guest cottage until spring. He pondered how his wife had miscalculated the necessity of a full-time role of the concierge. Certainly, he thought, she would be needed to help with menu planning, brochure updates, Internet advertising and a host of other administrative duties. François had assumed there would be year-round work for Colette. A small mistake, but a mistake nonetheless. He couldn't understand why Cherise was so determined against Colette remaining at Roufillay throughout the year. It didn't make sense to him.

Frustrated, he opened a lacquered rosewood box and searched for his favorite pipe. He gently tamped the tobacco, lighting it carefully while puffing slowly to ignite the leaves. Cradling the pipe with his hand, he inhaled slowly, trying to calm his rankled nerves. François was startled by a clamor outside the library window. He pressed his face against the stained glass, peering through a small clear pane to see what was causing the commotion. An unusual fog drifted across the valley below. It rolled like giant boulders up the hills, blotting out the scenery, but not so thick he couldn't catch a glimpse two cats posturing for dominance. François shut the window and drew the curtain, returning to his chair. He inhaled with a deeper draw, letting his lungs hold the taste of the tobacco, and then, with pursed lips, blew a smoke ring, drifting lazily into the room.

The number of leather-bound books in the library fascinated him. He ran his finger along the russet and gold-edged spines, venerating the signed first edition of Edgar Allen Poe's *Tales* containing his famous poem, *The Raven*. If only he had time to read—but it was not to be so, at least not now. He had to figure out how to placate Cherise. François knew Cherise had initially gotten along well with Colette and she had appreciated the concierge's assistance. François decided he needed to convince his wife that having Colette remain only a few weeks more would suffice to settle the books for the season. His primary concern was that Cherise might decide to speak to Colette directly and offer to close up the books herself.

Not anticipating the amount of stress or the ensuing complications of his plan made him uncharacteristically nervous. A stiff drink was in order and he was relieved the library had a liquor bar. He selected a Baccarat crystal decanter and inhaled the scent of aged whiskey. Regally seated in a tufted, nail studded leather chair, his drink in one hand, pipe in the other, François admired the library that would be his, all his and very, very soon.

While Cherise was napping, François walked to the caretaker's cottage, knocked on the door and, not waiting for an answer, strode into the kitchen. Colette turned to him, surprised. "Isn't this a little bold, you being here in the daylight?"

"Cherise is asleep and I need to talk to you."

"Oh, about what?" her mouth twisted in concern.

"I have to move you out of the cottage for a few months, just until spring. I'll put you up in a hotel."

"What! What for?" she wailed, hands on her hips, scowling, ready for battle. "I'm not going to a hotel. Absolutely not!"

"Don't argue with me. This is strictly a business decision. Cherise does not need the help of a concierge during the winter when the castle is closed for business."

"Well, that's not my fault. You should have thought of that! I refuse to go to a hotel."

He grabbed her wrist tightly. "I insist, dammit."

"I don't care," pulling her wrist away and slapping him in the face with her other hand so hard it left an inflamed impression on his cheek.

"You *will* do as I say," he yelled, enraged. François responded with his hand, striking hard across her face. Colette tumbled backwards into the hutch, hitting her head with a thud, sending plates and mugs shattering to the floor in a clatter.

Momentarily stunned, tears brimming with pain and anger, she glared at him, nostrils flaring. "Damn you," she said. "I didn't deserve that!"

"I'm sorry, but you did hit me first. I'm on edge. Your behavior provoked me to the point of losing control. You know I'm doing everything possible to make this work. Consider how far we've come and the amount of money you're going to have very soon. I didn't plan for an extra guest from God-knows-where to be here this week, which delays everything. With him in the chateau, there is no way I can get rid of Cherise."

Colette sniffled, wiping her wet eyes on the arm of her blouse. "Do you know how hard it's been for me to watch you with her, to put on this act of dutiful concierge? I'm so sick of it. "

"Please come here," he pleaded, extending his hand, his intense blue eyes searching hers, trying desperately to mend the rift between them. "You know I'm doing this for us. It's been difficult, but ultimately it will be worth it. You will have everything you have ever wanted."

Reluctantly, she edged toward him, head hung, seeking consolation. "I promise this will be over soon," he assured, pulling her to his chest, gently stroking the back of her neck. She sighed, letting her shoulders droop in compliance. François urged, "Let's sit down a minute, and I'll explain the new plan and why it's necessary to make these changes."

He emphasized that he required sufficient time and opportunity to kill Cherise. The situation meant Roufillay had to be closed for the season without a concierge. Rising, François said, "I need to get back. I'm sorry I struck you. Will you be all right?"

"Yes, of course."

Colette consoled herself, slumped at the kitchen table nursing a glass of Cahors, holding an ice pack on her head. A nasty bump had formed, throbbing painfully. This was not the first time she regretted agreeing to this charade. When François hit her, her reaction was more than physical pain. She now felt trapped in a relationship that made her distrustful. Colette had no money of her own and nowhere to go. Seething and crying, she sat in the kitchen uncertain if she was angrier with François or herself for agreeing to subjugate herself.

Colette bent to pick up the shattered pottery and disposed the pieces in the trash. Normalcy appeared to be restored, as though the angry

interaction with the undercover agent. They could covertly compare notes as she served him breakfast each morning. Second, Cherise had created a reason to escape the chateau. Shopping for groceries in the village would provide a mental break. Third, the many daily chores, including changing linens and folding fresh towels would keep her busy and away from François. Cherise knew she could not sit still—she would be too anxious and jittery during the daytime. And finally, Cherise had concealed a razor-sharp knife under her side of the bed, any notions of a fantasy marriage finally and absolutely shattered.

The bed moved and she held her breath. No he wasn't awake—he had just shifted positions. More time to think, she continued reviewing her situation.

Hosting a guest at the castle who was a professional detective provided Cherise assurance of much-needed, albeit fitful, sleep. François had never made threatening moves at night. His consistent pattern was to go to bed early, falling asleep immediately. Knowing Brett was one floor below her, she felt fairly safe, although she hated sleeping in the same bed with François. His body next to hers made her skin crawl. She despised him for his shallowness and Cherise considered his casual, deliberate deceit and nonchalance unforgivable evidence of his defective personality. She had married someone without scruples...again.

Looking at her life, she could not believe she had chosen two such different men, narcissists who cared more about themselves than they ever had about her or their marriage. Neither knew the meaning of commitment nor cared enough about their vows to remain faithful. Cherise promised herself, if she lived through this, she would never again provide implicit permission to any man to deceive her. Exhausted, she fell asleep with the covers pulled tightly around her head and shoulders, enveloping herself in a cocoon of safety.

Cherise awoke the next morning, her toes icy. The air blowing in through the windows was chilly, signaling time for a seasonal change in her wardrobe. She selected one of her new blue sweaters with a matching cardigan, accessorized with a printed silk scarf, and quickly glanced in the mirror. Make-up applied lightly—yes. Hair brushed, long shimmering strands, reflecting the light—yes. Earrings? Not there. Could not go anywhere without earrings. Cherise shook her head, knowing she was not concentrating on her usual fastidious dressing routine, she selected a pair of gold hoops which she fastened into her pierced ears. With a sigh, she straightened her skirt, attempting to bolster her courage to face the day and go downstairs.

Autumn was in the air and leaves were changing from pale gold to auburn red. As she passed a stairwell window, she watched a brown-speckled bird sitting on the window ledge wishing she, too, could just fly away. The flights of stairs were her daily exercise and she descended quietly, uncertain if Brett was awake. As she crossed the entrance lobby, she noticed François in the living room sipping coffee and reading a book.

"Good morning," she said, attempting a smile. "I'll prepare Mr. Maxfield's breakfast and set it out on the patio." He looked up at her, acknowledging her comment by nodding his head, but did not speak, presumably occupied with his book. Just as well, as she didn't have anything to say to him. She wanted to find Brett.

It was chilly but a clear and sunny day. The courtyard was enclosed on three sides with towering stone block walls, covered in ivy blocking out much of the wind, making dining outside possible. She desperately needed to talk with Brett. Perhaps he was already outside. Finding a serving platter, she piled several croissants, dabs of sweet-cream butter, boysenberry jam and chose a slightly ripe banana, wishing she had gone to the market to get more fresh fruit but this would have to do. Using her elbow, she pushed the latch, balancing the breakfast tray and opened the door to the courtyard, delighted to see Brett sipping coffee and flipping through a magazine. His back was toward her and, when the courtyard door slammed he turned around, providing Cherise an overall glimpse of his attire—a light blue oxford shirt, beige wool sweater hung over his shoulders, olive twill pants and sturdy dark cordovan leather walking shoes. Very much the preppy Englishman, sporting a style she found attractive.

"Oh, good morning, Brett. How did you sleep?"

"Very well, Mrs. Delacroix. Thank you," he winked. "This chateau, or do you call it a castle, is enormous."

"It's a matter of opinion. The French think it depends on size or historic significance. The largest is a castle; smaller impressive structures are called chateaux and castles too, and large homes are named maisons. We tend to use the words interchangeably here. Roufillay is large enough to qualify as castle, but the word can imply to the public something medieval and lacking plumbing or good heating. To avoid confusion, we use the word *chateau*, which sounds warmer and more personable, especially to bed and breakfast patrons. Does that make any sense?"

Brett nodded, setting down his coffee cup. "When was this castle, I mean chateau, built?"

"Roufillay was built in the late 1700's and completed in early 1800. Isabelle Brosande, the previous owner of Roufillay before I bought it, grew up here. Her father was a zoology professor and wrote encyclopedias for the Sorbonne, where he taught in Paris. His publications had been shelved on the second floor of the enormous library. However, his books were returned to the Sorbonne before his daughter sold the property to me."

"What became of her?" Brett asked, sincerely interested, enjoying watching her talk.

"I am not really sure, Brett. Isabelle mentioned moving to the South of France, maybe to Cap Ferrat on the Mediterranean, or Seville. She has a daughter in Spain."

"Interesting. The scale of this place is daunting. I could put my own English cottage in here many times over. I cannot imagine growing up as a child in such a home. It must have been magical. My room here, by the way, has wallpaper covered with rabbits and ducks. Did you think I had a juvenile sense of humor?"

"Oh yes, sorry about that," she giggled. "Indeed, it was a child's room at one time. I agree about the magic. There is always a sense of fantasy about living in a castle. The history alone makes you feel honored to walk the same floors as the royalty did in past centuries, imagining the women in flowing dresses and men in armor suited up for a war, or attired in ornate silk embroidered coats embellished with fur, ruffled shirts and leggings with leather boots and that famous French cavalier hat, accented with a feather or two."

"I imagine one so attired could rescue a damsel in distress," he smiled warmly. "I can see men with long curled locks, swashbuckling musketeers. All that's missing is the horse."

She laughed, "Well, we have those too. They are not mine, but are boarded here. I get a nice stipend for boarding them on the property where they can run freely. The property is fenced and the horses stay near the corral. The barn is down the road, on the other side of the caretaker's cottage. Occasionally I ride or just let the horse amble through the woods. I like the sense of peace, riding on a horse."

"You sound like you were brought up in Kentucky."

Laughing, she said, "Oh gosh, no. I was brought up in Woodside, California, a suburb of San Francisco. Woodside residents are sometimes referred to as 'The Mink and Manure Set' because of the number of wealthy residents who own horse properties."

"I see," he said, enjoying listening to her as she described her background. "What kind of home did you grow up in?" he asked, stirring another lump of sugar into his coffee.

"Well, that's an interesting question," she replied. "There are many older homes in Woodside and also many new, expansive trophy residences. The dot-com and high tech venture capital success stories created the context for conspicuous ownership. My family had money, but I grew up in a modest ranch-style home, enjoying a casual lifestyle, hanging around in jeans and t-shirts. We owned several acres, and we always had horses. I learned to ride when I was eight years old, and it was every child's dream to have her own horse. Mine was an Arabian named *Shiloh*."

"Do you ride here?" he asked, buttering half a croissant.

"Not as often as I would like," she sighed. "There are two horses I ride at Roufillay—*Dartanian*, a black stallion, and *La Femme*, a white mare who is gentle, but can be unpredictably skittish about squirrels and forest critters. Both are boarded here and provide a helpful source of income for us. La Femme can bolt unexpectedly if you aren't paying attention." Caught up in her previous riding memories, she continued, "Dartanian's name is not spelled the way it was in the novel, *The Three Musketeers*, and I never had a chance to ask Isabelle why the owner decided to change the spelling. He's a stallion, powerful, smart and a good horse if you are an experienced rider."

Brett nodded, fingering the rim of his empty coffee cup. "I've never been on a horse. It would scare me to death."

"Do you like animals?"

"Oh don't get me wrong, I love animals, however I'm afraid a basset hound is more my speed. My wife, Vivian, had one we raised as a pup. Called him Baskerville. Not very original, I'm afraid, and too long a name to pronounce, so we nicknamed him *Villy*. I adored that dog. When he was a pup, he tore up my good leather slippers and gnawed a hole in the toe. Did much of nothing, followed me around, slept at my feet while I ate or read the paper—never asked for anything more than me to be there to pat him on the head. He died a month after Vivian did, probably of a broken heart. They were very close because we didn't have children. I've been meaning to get another dog, but haven't gotten around to it. You get so attached to your pet they become human, like a person in a dog-suit. When they die, the bond is so strong they cannot be replaced with another dog. I miss him."

"Oh I am so sorry."

"No, don't be. I shouldn't have brought it up. Someday I will get another dog when the time is right."

"Did you get new slippers?"

"Naw. I never got around to getting new ones. I'm embarrassed to admit I still have the ones with chewed holes so my toes can stick out."

She laughed at his easy humor and enjoyed their conversation, not thinking once about François or the real reason Brett was a guest at the chateau.

François left the living room heading upstairs to his third floor bedroom to do some work. The windows were open, making concentration difficult as he listened to the giggling and chatter going on in the courtyard. Distance hindered his ability to hear the words. The muffled sounds of levity annoyed him and he was disgruntled to have to host this unwelcome guest. François rose to close the windows.

As he glanced down at the two of them, he observed Cherise closely, narrowing his eyes. His wife appeared to be enjoying herself more than merely serving as hostess. Her joviality could be construed as somewhat flirtatious. He had not seen her so animated and lighthearted for weeks. Suddenly, the conversation went quiet. He continued watching them surreptitiously through the window opening, disconcerted to see Brett reach across the table and squeeze Cherise's hand. François could not hear every word Brett said to her, but when the wind died down, he did hear Brett assure Cherise, "Don't worry, it will be okay."

François stalked away from the window and cursed out loud, throwing his morning paper on the floor. "Dammit!" Who was this person? *What* was going to be okay? He was suddenly suspicious and wary. Mentally re-winding, François wondered if Cherise had really gone to Bordeaux to go shopping. He went to his computer, booted it up, accessing the Internet search engine. He typed *Brett Maxfield, England*. Information appearing on the screen was vague. The first *Brett Maxfield* turned out to be a young Welsh writer. Another click revealed a *Brett Maxfield* veterinarian, followed by twenty minutes of unproductive searches. The second to the last line on the 12th page looked interesting. He clicked, it opened…giving him a shock. François read a clip from a local paper, *Brett Maxfield, retired Scotland Yard inspector attends the funeral of his loving wife, Vivian, in Chippenham.* Apparently there was a large service held for her, also attended by various colleagues from Scotland Yard. The press noted that large contributions had been donated in her behalf to her selected cancer charity.

Stunned, François stared at the computer, the screen-saver swirling around in colors, making his head spin. Brett was a detective. *Shit!* His heart began thumping, blood pulsing through his temples, skipping beats in his chest. "I'm so fucked," he snarled aloud.

Slamming down the computer screen, he sat on his artist stool, selected a pallet knife from a canister of art tools and slashed each canvas he'd painted of Cherise. One slash across her back—another deeper cut across her face, systematically ripping the canvas to shreds. Furious, François stood shaking, sweat dripping from his forehead. He muttered under his breath, trying to calm down. "I'm overreacting. Brett *could* be a guest and that's all. Because he was formerly with Scotland Yard does not mean he was looking for me or that he has any idea who I am. Yes, that must be it. It's probably a weird coincidence."

He paced back and forth, trying to gather his wits, palms sweaty. No one had ever gotten in the way of his well-crafted plans. And now some fuck from Scotland Yard shows up the week he plans to kill his wife? Ridiculous. Incredible. Ludicrous. Yet, there was Brett casually sitting in *his* courtyard. But what if his intuition was right and his visit was not a coincidence? François realized he needed to change his plans. He could not take a chance on a botched perfect plan. What problem would one more "accidental" death be, anyway? If he could plan two murders, why not three?

Brett finished his breakfast and suggested he and Cherise go back to the kitchen together. Colette had arrived on the premises and Brett could clearly see she was Diana Aubrey, but good lord, what had happened to the gorgeous woman in the photo? Brett was dumbstruck, seeing her in person as compared with the picture he had of her. Forgetting her manners, Colette asked Cherise in a snippy tone, "Did he pay by credit card?"

Cherise said yes, wondering why Colette was acting so rudely. Colette pursed her lips, indicating she would process the necessary paperwork required to set up his account. Motioning with his hand for Cherise to remain in the kitchen, Brett deliberately followed Colette into the reception area.

"Hello…Miss?"

"Armond," she said, continuing to write and not looking up.

"Mr. Maxfield, I presume" she uttered, looking blandly at him, sorting papers with an appearance of annoyance, strands of her red hair trailing down her neck from the bun loosely assembled at the back of her head.

"Yes. Is something wrong Ms. Armond?"

"No. Everything's fine. I just have a dreadful headache. If you will excuse me, I need to leave. Please, have a good day, Mr. Maxfield."

"Yes, I will. Merci." He watched her scurry out of the castle, rapidly walk down the short gravel road to the cottage and slam the door.

Brett figured she was a feisty woman, obviously upset about something. He was astonished at the difference between the image of the woman he had been searching for and the reality he had seen. Once a gorgeous model, Colette's face was drawn and her demeanor dowdy. Brett wondered what François saw in her. In her present incarnation, she did not seem his type. If they were as conspiratorial as Cherise had described, it was difficult for Brett to imagine François and this woman in the role of Colette, entangled in an affair. With someone as attractive as Cherise, why would anyone choose this unattractive concierge over Cherise? He believed Cherise's apprehension about a nefarious scheme to harm her so the motivation had to be money. Nothing else would make any sense, Brett concluded.

CHAPTER 25

Brett spent the day lounging on a comfortable patio chair resting on finely crushed gravel strategically spread to the edge of the veranda's vantage point. He absently glanced through a coffee table book he had borrowed from the entry table while watching unobtrusively, keeping an eye on both the cottage and the castle. He did not notice anything unusual. The wind gusts were starting to nip the back of his neck and ominous dark grey clouds rolled in toward the castle.

He was getting hungry and realized with dismay that no food, other than breakfast, would be served at the chateau. Brett left the windy veranda, headed back to the kitchen entrance and walked over to the refrigerator. Glancing around, making sure the owners would not catch him, Brett opened the door. Pickings were slim—a pitcher of orange juice, a bin of fresh vegetables lacking appeal, several wrapped unrecognizable items, and a chunk of slightly smelly cheese—definitely not appealing. François strolled into the kitchen, his hair uncharacteristically ruffled and askew, as if he had been standing in front of a fan. He surveyed Brett rummaging through the refrigerator. "Can I help you?" he asked coolly, with a bare modicum of civility and an unpleasant smile.

Brett, startled, pulled his head out of the refrigerator and mumbled he was hungry. François stiffly apologized but emphasized it would be best for Brett to drive into Sarlat for dinner. He recommended several good restaurants. Brett thanked him, and considered pocketing the cheese from the refrigerator, then decided against it. His dilemma was he did not want to leave Cherise alone, but on the other hand, he was starving. Brett decided it would be feasible to take the short drive to Sarlat. He could eat dinner and be back in an hour or two, at the most.

The clouds had broken, and lightning flittered across the sky in the distance, far down the Dordogne River. The wind was picking up and rain started to pour in pounding sheets, splattering against the window glass. Brett shrugged, went to his room, grabbed his tweed jacket, trench coat, and umbrella, and started downstairs. He ran into Cherise in the vestibule and she looked petrified, so he explained to her he was going to Sarlat for dinner and would be back as soon as he could. She nervously offered to make him something, but he told her François had suggested he go out and he did not want to behave any differently than any other guest. Reluctantly, Cherise closed her eyes, nodded her head, and agreed. It was best not to create suspicion and for Brett to act like any other visitor to the region.

Brett pushed the castle's heavy entrance door open, leaning his full weight against it, managing to step through the opening before it before it crashed back into its vast doorframe. Out into the wild weather, he struggled, fumbling with the umbrella latch until it sprang open. The umbrella immediately flipped inside out in the wind, nearly making him lose his balance. Cursing, he got into his car, his trench coat and shoes already soaked. Fiddling with the ignition, he searched for the windshield wiper lever. Where were the damn things in these compact toy cars? He tried one set of buttons and the hood popped up. He had to get out and slam the hood, getting even more drenched. His driving glasses were spotted with raindrops, visibility was difficult and he hadn't yet started driving.

He got back in the car and tried several other levers and buttons, finally getting the wipers to work. Finding the headlight lever was another ridiculous challenge and once on, they did not emit a great deal of light, barely sufficient to see the road ahead. Brett cautiously headed down the driveway's switchback, creeping along until he reached the main road. All in all, he wished he had pocketed the smelly cheese, stayed in and gone to his room, he thought to himself, as he drove toward Sarlat.

As Brett cautiously navigated the narrow road, he noticed a car approaching closely behind him, pressing fast and tailgating. The headlights of the car behind him were bright, creating a blinding glare in his rear view mirror. He adjusted the mirror upwards but the intense glare reflected into his side view mirrors in the small car. He could hardly see but was forced to increase his speed. The car continued to gain on him aggressively, approaching within a few feet of his rear bumper, so Brett pushed down on the gas pedal rounding turns faster than he wanted to, the rock walls steep on one side of the road, leaving barely enough room for one car. The car behind him pressed faster and closer. "Dammit," Brett swore as he looked frantically for any slim space to pull off the road.

Instantly, without warning, he saw a deer standing in the road. Brett slammed on the brakes but they did not hold in the muddy slickness. He skidded into the deer, instinctively crossing his arms in front of his face, feeling the impact of the deer, hearing the shattering of glass and sensing in split seconds the complete loss of control of the car as it went off the embankment, rolling through the trees, down the deep slope, flipping over and over until it crashed into a large boulder, propelling the car into the side of a tree where in finally landed. His vision went black—and then everything was silent.

François got out of his car, putting his hand over his eyebrows to shield the downpour, and peered over the embankment. He could not see much of Brett's car. Far below, the wheels were spinning upside down against a tree and, in the crux of shrubs, the deer's hindquarters protruded from the window. During a flash of lightning, François saw Brett's arm dangling out of the car's window. No movement. No sound except the rain. He was sure Brett was dead.

Climbing into his *Invicta*, shaking the icy rain off his hands, he warmed his fingers together, pleased with himself. This was much easier than he'd planned. François thought he would need to run Brett off the road, damaging his *Invicta*, which would have pissed him off. He had not counted on the deer. Some days were better than others. He no longer had to worry about Brett, nor did he need to make up a story to Cherise about a dented car. François intended to create a plausible story about Brett's disappearance since he wouldn't be returning from dinner in Sarlat. All was well. Yes, all was very well indeed.

Françoise returned to Roufillay with two bottles of milk from the local village shop, several bottles of wine, baguettes and an assortment of cheese, providing an alibi for being out on the road. Cherise had not noticed François had left the castle. Anxiously, she'd kept herself occupied, washing towels and folding sheets, waiting for Brett to return. François startled her in the laundry room adjacent to the kitchen.

"Oh, there you are my dear. Endless laundry, I assume."

"Yes. Just some items I needed," she glanced at him, fluffing a towel. Have you seen Brett? It's been over an hour and he hasn't returned. I'm concerned."

"No, I've not seen him. Dinner undoubtedly took longer than expected, and he's probably enjoying a couple of drinks."

She glared at him and started to pick the corner of her cuticle on her thumb. "I suppose," she considered. She continued folding and sorting laundry without looking up at him. "Well," she said, "the storm is heavy but not violent, and the power has remained on. You know how nervous I get during lightning storms." Cherise was perpetually concerned, during a violent storm, the lightning rod in the top turret tower would be struck, blowing out all the power in the castle.

"These storms don't last very long, and I think this one is letting up. Try to stop worrying. I'm going to read awhile. I'll be in the library," he said.

"Fine," she echoed, as he wandered down the hall, out of sight. Cherise uncertain, her fear mounting, continued folding the same towels, over and over. Aloud she voiced shakily, "Maybe it's the rain. That's what's taking Brett so long." Her stomach was knotted and her thumb raw, bleeding on the towels, requiring a bandage she was reluctant to find. She whispered aloud, "How could Brett leave me here alone?"

François needed time alone to think. Although this could be the opportune time to eliminate Cherise with Brett lying dead in the forest, François decided to focus next on Colette, who had become a conspicuous liability. She was annoyingly in the way and had stopped being fun and exciting to him months ago. Why should he share the wealth with her? With Cherise gone as well, he would become the sole owner of Roufillay, planning to sell a year or two after her death—the same plan as he had devised successfully with Diana and Brightingham.

François was experienced. He had cleverly planned and accomplished other deaths—from a stroke caused by untraceable drugs—to car accidents where the brake fluid had been drained in advance—to a plugged-in hand-held hair dryer tossed into the bathtub, causing a nasty electrocution. That last one was messier than he bargained for, and he quickly swiped the memory. Good reason for a cognac. The ice clinked into the glass and the liquor swirled in his mouth as he thought about his past.

With masterfully devised plans, François had been married three times, acquiring wealth by manipulating trusting women. Naively, they'd named him the beneficiary in their wills or married him, deeding their property to him upon their demise. He never sold the properties immediately; rather he enjoyed living luxuriously off the inherited wealth while he planned his next asset acquisition cruise, disappearing before anyone could follow his pattern of deceit and murder.

François enjoyed the strategic planning that included identifying his next gullible victim. They were easy to find. Widowed or divorced—all lonesome, often traveling on luxury cruise ships or vacationing at jet-setter resorts like St. Tropez and Cannes, they identified themselves, flaunting dazzling jewelry, the latest designer clothing, and toting expensive Valentino Noir calfskin handbags. He'd met all his wives this way—watching them, stalking them until he was certain he could charm them into bed. The heated passionate sex he provided for these emotionally and physically starved lonely women caused them to lose all common sense and financial responsibility. François' good looks and undeniable charm mesmerized women. He found he could name his fee and women of means were glad to pay the price.

Sipping the last drop in his glass, François felt a renewed sense of confidence. Unexpected situations required modifications but, at this point, he had adjusted and perfected every detail. Starting tomorrow morning, his first step would be to send Cherise off to a designated bookstore in Bergerac to purchase books that he had specifically ordered to create a diversion. With Cherise off the premises, he would have time to take care of Colette, including disposing her body. When Cherise returned, he would deal with her.

François set the glass down. Spotting a letter opener lying atop a pile of bills, he smiled as he picked it up. Fingering the blade, he stroked it slowly, enjoying the sharp pointed edge, visualizing the damage it could do.

CHAPTER 26

Cherise felt and looked ragged the next morning when Brett did not return. She had sat awake in the living room the night before, watching for him out of the windows. She was increasingly concerned about what may have happened and why he did not return to Roufillay. She repeatedly asked François if he had heard from Brett.

François, toying cruelly with her, remarked Brett was behaving as most single male adult guests would. He taunted her, "He can stay in town if he wants. Perhaps he met an attractive woman and decided to spend the night with her."

Cherise paled at the thought, but in her heart, she knew Brett would not leave her. It was a matter of professionalism and he was certainly not about to engage in a tryst when it was his job to protect her and follow the leads in his own case.

Frightened and dismayed, she got into her car and headed to Bergerac at the request of François. The rain had ceased and the roads were only slightly damp and relatively safe for driving. She wanted to go to Sarlat, but Bergerac was the opposite direction. She knew she should be back by noon. Hopefully Brett would have returned to the chateau. At least, she considered, while she was on the road she was safe. She realized that she felt safer away from François than with him. As she drove, she bit her fingernail to the skin. She had a growing uneasy suspicion something had happened to Brett.

Brett slowly regained consciousness, his brain as foggy and thick as the mud he was stuck in. He'd blacked out after the accident. He reached out to rub his forehead and felt something fuzzy and warm wrapped around his head. Blinking, he opened one eye, blood dripping past the eyelid and let out a scream. *Holy crap!* He groaned in agonizing pain. The deer's head and dead body were against his head and the deer was gazing straight at him with glazed eyes. He tried to get his bearings and realized he was suspended upside down, looking at the ground and not the sky. Brett was disoriented, not knowing if the dripping blood was from the deer or himself. Dazed, fading in and out of consciousness, he shook his head, fighting to remain awake and alert. Every bone in his body ached.

His memory returned in flashing snippets, like an old movie reel spinning backwards. He recalled he had hit the deer in the storm. Was that last night? How long had he been here? He winced, remembering the impact of the buck and the shattering glass. Touching his forehead with his hand, he could not feel an open wound. The blood running down his face was not from his head but he was not sure where it was coming from. He tried to move but the searing pain was excruciating. Upside down, dangling from his seatbelt, his head nestled in the dead body of a deer was surreal. He felt like a Salvador Dali painting, except this *was* real.

He reached for the seat belt buckle with his right hand, clicked to release it and immediately fell deeper into the neck of the dead animal. Dizzy, rolling over on his side, he managed to turn himself and used his leg to push a large section of the shattered glass out of the window frame. Touching the inside of his shoulder, he found the wound and realized the buck's antler had punctured his shoulder. The wound was bleeding profusely, but not in spurts, so he doubted the antler had punctured an artery; if it had, he'd be as dead as the deer. If he had not actually experienced surviving this crash, he would not have believed it possible.

The car probably looked like a rolled-up sardine can, dented on all sides. Had he taken out car insurance? He couldn't remember. No time to think about it now. Brett assessed the size of the car had saved his life that, being so small, it had rolled like a ball without actually flying in a trajectory over the cliff. The car had rolled until it finally slowed in the ravine filled with shrubs, and ended up stuck against a tree surrounded by boulders. The deer crashing in through the car's window was undoubtedly a miracle as its upper body had provided a cushion for his head and chest as the car bounced and rolled down the embankment like a giant rubber ball. No airbags had exploded—none were included on the cheap rental model he'd selected.

Finally fully awake, Brett shoved the deer out of the window with immense effort. It was like pushing a heavy sack of grain, a dead weight. With the deer out of the way, he crawled out the front window, splattering glass everywhere as he eased out, and he managed to stand up. He gingerly tested the strength of his legs, wobbly as a newborn colt. No bones seemed to be broken, although every muscle and bone in his body ached. Reaching for the cell phone in his pocket, he hoped to call Cherise. His mobile phone was not there. He went back to the car, knelt on the ground and crawled in through the broken front window and discovered the phone lying on the roof next to his mangled driving glasses. Brett had no idea how far he was from Sarlat. He tried to get a dial tone, blood dripping close to the phone's keypad. The cell phone battery was low, but that was not the problem. There was no signal.

Brett clawed his way up the hillside, using his good right arm, blood oozing from his left shoulder. Momentarily resting, he took off a shoe and a cotton sock, wadded the sock toe into a twist and jammed it into the wound. Pain shot through his shoulder and he thought he would pass out. Very slowly he removed his trench coat, and wool jacket, which had prevented the puncture wound from piercing an artery or worse—perhaps his heart. He pulled the belt from the loops of his trench coat, wrapping the belt around his shoulder. Biting the end, forming a loop to create a tourniquet, he secured his shirt and wadded sock against his wounded shoulder. Shaking clammy sweat off his forehead and listening to his own labored breathing, Brett realized he was in shock. He forced his bare foot back into his shoe and began the agonizing climb over the boulders, up the hillside to find the spot where the car had rolled off the road.

The rain had stopped but water from the storm gushed down the ravine in rivulets and waterfalls. He leaned back and let the streaming water wash over him, drinking thirstily while trying to focus, thankful his smashed nighttime driving glasses were unnecessary in the daylight.

The cold water quenched his thirst and parched mouth. Struggling for what felt like hours, Brett finally reached the top of the ravine. When he saw the roadway, he recognized that, even though it seemed the middle of nowhere, he actually was not too far from Roufillay. He recalled he had not been on the road more than ten or fifteen minutes before hitting the deer. When he saw the skid marks on the road, he felt sick, knowing how close he had come to death. Brett recollected the car that had forced him to drive so recklessly and wondered what kind of idiot would drive that way during a storm, and why the hell he hadn't stopped.

Wondering when someone would drive by, stop and offer assistance, Brett looked at the road, head turning left and right. Weak, confused and starving from the many hours he'd not eaten, Brett slumped on the edge of the roadside in a patch of gravel with his back against the jagged rock wall. He knew he urgently needed to get back to Roufillay. Feeling weaker and less coherent, he thought of Cherise. What if she wasn't alive? He'd never forgive himself. The thought she might be dead was overwhelming. It occurred to Brett that he could possibly die of exposure. His heart began to beat irregularly—and then he passed out.

CHAPTER 27

François knew he had a very short time to carry out his plan and this day the groundskeeper would not be on the property. He went to the cottage and banged on the door. Colette, dismayed by the noise, let him in. She did not hide her irritation, a scowl darkening her eyes with suspicion. "Well, what's so urgent?" she demanded. He explained he had sent Cherise to Bergerac and now Brett was dead. He informed Colette of Brett's Scotland Yard identity, asserting he could not afford to have anyone upset their plans.

Colette shrieked at him, "*You killed him? Are you a fucking idiot?*"

"Stop screaming at me. I didn't *have* to kill him. Yes, I planned to run him off the road in the storm, but he hit a deer on the road and he slammed his breaks. His car flipped off the road and rolled down the steep embankment. Could not have planned it better."

Squeezing her fingers into a tight-fisted knot, Collette pounded the kitchen table demanding, "When will you get rid of Cherise?"

François answered, "Today, as soon as she is back from Bergerac. That will be it. She will have a little riding accident."

Her face smirked with satisfaction. Collette's drawn-out agony would end that day.

Turning her back to François to make herself a cup of tea, Colette was finally happy.

She never felt the knife that, quickly and efficiently, slit her throat. Collette dropped to the floor, blood spilling from her neck onto the

207

counter, splattering the kitchen rug. Her lovely green eyes were open, staring vacantly at the ceiling. Once a very pretty lady…now a dowdy, dead shrew. François dispassionately looked down at her body. Too bad it had to end this way.

Blood raced through his throbbing temples. François wrapped a towel around her oozing neck, and rolled up the body and knife using the rug on the kitchen floor. He carried her out through the kitchen door toward the old dry well behind the property. Her inert body was heavy and the dragging went slowly. Sweat poured down his face onto his bloody shirt.

François dumped her unceremoniously into the well, head first, and tossed in the rug, knife, and bloody towel as well. He returned to the cottage, retrieved her small suitcase from the armoire, and tossed it into the well. Every bit of evidence was removed, including her toiletries and damp undergarments, hanging on the bathroom curtain rod. François closed her laptop on the kitchen table, and regretfully disposed the expensive electronic into the abandoned well.

Lighting the wood in the stone kitchen fireplace, François collected Colette's clothing and shoes, emptied her dresser drawers, and tossed everything into the blazing fire. François watched the flames incinerate her personal effects. He retrieved the shovel he had left by the garage outbuilding next to the cottage and shoveled the cooling ashes into an empty metal garbage container and dumped the ashes into the well. His final task was to heap piles of muddy silt and leaves into the well, camouflaging his actions. Satisfied, François mopped the sweat off his face.

François ran back from the well to the cottage. He stoked the fire, tossing in magazines and papers, anything associated with Colette's period of residence in the cottage. With so many hectares of land surrounding the castle, smoke rising through a cottage chimney in autumn would not be noticed.

Using a kitchen towel, he scrubbed the bloody floor and cleaned the kitchen counter. When every surface was spotless, he pitched the towel and his muddy blood-stained gloves into the fire. Realizing his shoes were mud-caked, he removed them, hosed them clean, and set them on the outside steps to drain.

There was no evidence Colette had met with foul play. Other than several boxes of cereal in the cabinets and soda in the refrigerator, the cottage was clean and tidy. François was not concerned that anyone would think it odd she had left. If asked, he would say he had released the concierge for the season, and Roufillay would not reopen for guests until spring. If questions continued, he could indicate Colette needed another job and had moved on. It did not matter if her fingerprints were all over the cottage—or his. After all, the cottage was his property and her domicile during her employment at Roufillay. Cherise's fingerprints were also in the cottage, as were Sandrina's who had entered regularly to clean and change linens.

When the fire had burned to embers, François wrapped his handkerchief around the handle of the iron poker and probed through the ashes to be certain nothing of Colette's belongings remained. He swept the area where he had dragged the body, eliminating all mud drag marks. A quick hose rinse over the broom, he set it out to dry on the back porch. Tugging wet boots over his dirty socks was uncomfortable but necessary.

His tasks complete, François walked to the well and looked down, making a final check. He placed the metal lattice grate over the top and stood a moment, tired but exhilarated. Every vestige of Diana/Colette was gone. What a load off his mind. He felt like a lion that had just devoured its prey. He looked down at himself, realizing he had to quickly get rid of his bloody, soot-filled clothes.

Furtively glancing right and left to be certain no one had witnessed his actions, François scurried to the castle and removed his muddy boots at the door. He noticed several bloody stains on his boots and used a garden hose to wash them off. Stripping off his dirty socks, François ran upstairs with the energy of a ten-year old, anxious for a hot shower. He washed off all traces of blood, mud and soot. Changing into equestrian attire, François pulled on his riding boots and then bundled his stained clothes into a towel. He laughed with the realization that a fortuitous benefit of running a hotel included an abundance of fresh towels. François hurried down to the kitchen, grabbed the trash and hastened down to the basement. Igniting the incinerator, the towels along with his incriminating clothing flamed and disappeared with the garbage.

François calmly walked into the living room, poured himself a brandy and carried the snifter to the courtyard, waiting for Cherise to come home. Settling comfortably in a chaise longue, brandy snifter in hand, Cherise would not find it odd he was in his riding clothes or that his other boots were drying on the doorstep. François rode often and it was customary to leave dirty boots outside. Flawless thinking—flawless behavior. François had already loosened the cinch on La Femme and would insist Cherise go riding with him.

CHAPTER 28

Cherise returned to Roufillay, cornering the long driveway turns in a state of agitation. With no sign of Brett's car, she bit her lip in dismay until it bled, turning off the ignition. Walking into the kitchen, she looked for François and found him in the courtyard, attired in his riding clothes.

"Oh, you're back," he said calmly. "Any trouble getting my books?" he eyed the cloth sack she was carrying.

"No trouble. I have your books," she shrugged, handing him the sack. He grabbed the cloth sack with the investment books he had ordered and nonchalantly flipped through the pages, feigning interest.

"My dear, I appreciate you went to Bergerac for me. How about if we go for a ride? We have not ridden together in a long time and the horses need the exercise."

Suddenly alert and afraid but unable to fabricate a good reason to decline, she pleaded, "François, I am really tired. It's been a long day and don't feel up to it."

"Yes you do my dear. I insist! Now please get changed," he demanded, indicating he would not accept no for an answer.

Irritated, she barked at him, "Don't order me around," and then regretted her acerbic tone, fearful she might anger him. Attempting to change the subject, she asked, "Have you seen Brett?"

"He called while I was here. Said he had car trouble, apparently. He remained the night in Sarlat and said he would be on his way as soon as the car was repaired." It was an easy lie, without any hint in his voice for her to think otherwise.

Hearing that Brett was all right, she felt an enormous sense of relief she dared not reveal. Cherise did not want to ride, but had never seen François this demanding, his eyes ablaze. She was frightened by his controlling intimidation. To resist riding with him was futile. He already had both horses saddled and tied to the iron pillar next to the courtyard. La Femme and Dartanian were pacing, kicking up dirt anxiously and ready to go. Cherise felt trapped into riding. With a deep breath, she acquiesced, confident in her skills, knowing she was an excellent rider.

Cherise asked about Colette. François told her she had already left for Sarlat, had packed her bags and was gone for the season. Surprised, but grateful the concierge had departed, Cherise changed into her riding jodhpurs, pulled on her leather boots and buckled the strap of her black velvet helmet under her chin. Brett was on his way, and Colette was gone. Odd, she thought, Colette had not said goodbye.

She walked into the courtyard and started to mount Dartanian. François shook his head, insisting Dartanian was his choice. They argued and Cherise demanded that, if he would not permit her to ride the horse she preferred, then she would not ride. Frustrated, François finally agreed, covertly readjusting the purposely loosened cinch on La Femme.

They rode side-by-side down the winding path away from the Roufillay to the open field. Digging his heels into her flanks, François startled La Femme, her pace increased from walking to trotting and finally into a full gallop. Not wanting to run behind, Dartanian increased his stride. François turned toward the woods where the path was narrow. Cherise was surprised he did not guide his horse in front of her as was customary, instead, he remained side-by-side on his horse. François abruptly yanked Le Femme's reins and his horse's head jerked, strongly resisting, and she lost her footing. La Femme unwillingly slid into Dartanian, inches from the towering stone cliffs. Cherise yelled, *"Move over, dammit!"* François edged Cherise and Dartanian closer to the wall, rocks ripping Cherise's elbow raw through her blouse. She screamed at François, as she realized he was trying to hurt her.

Blood trickling down her elbow, she kicked Dartanian hard on the left flank, galloping faster, edging away. La Femme was no match for Dartanian and, at seventeen hands high, he was a powerful stallion, adept at responding to Cherise's firm hand and bit in his mouth. Recklessly galloping through the forest, Cherise was forced to nimbly duck under low tree limbs to avoid catastrophe. Her heart was thundering in her chest in rhythm with the thudding hooves slamming into the ground. François viciously kicked La Femme and, rebelling against his whip she bucked her hind legs, but kept running. Pale with alarm and holding on for her life, Cherise rammed Dartanian into La Femme.

A raccoon in the path startled La Femme. The horse reared, slamming François backwards into a large tree branch. His head struck on impact knocking him off his horse. His foot was caught in the stirrup and François was limply dragged along the ground for several meters until his boot came loose, flipping him over a boulder, onto the ground. François lay motionless.

Cherise tightened Dartanian's reins as the horse continued to gallop, nostrils flared. Using her equestrian skills and strength, she controlled Dartanian to a walk, returning to the site where François had fallen. Mounted on perspiring Dartanian, Cherise was horrified to see François' body, lying motionless on the ground, face down, helmet torn off, blood dripping out of his ear. She considered dismounting to check François's pulse, but he did not seem to be breathing. François appeared to be dead.

Panicked, Cherise needed to return to Roufillay as quickly as possible. Cautiously trotting over to La Femme, she saw the horse was trembling, her dark eyes darting frantically. Cherise stroked the horse's muzzle, calming her. Carefully she looped La Femme's reins in her hand and, riding Dartanian with La Femme in tow alongside, she galloped smoothly back to the castle. She prayed Brett would be at Roufillay.

Cherise tied the horses to the post at the courtyard entrance, and looked desperately for Brett's car. With no sign of his car, Cherise hurried into the castle, dashing upstairs to her room. Sitting on the edge of the bed, sweating and shaking profusely, she pulled off her riding boots. Her knees were wobbly and her anxiety intensified. If

François was dead, what should she do? She needed to talk to Brett. She considered calling Inspector Pierre, but what could he do to help her from his office in Bordeaux?

It was getting dark and starting to rain again. A storm was brewing. Although the brutal Mistral wind was not a feature of southwest France, the storms that roared through the Dordogne could be just as fierce and cold. Startled, Cherise heard the splitting crackle of lightning, and watched bolts from the sky hitting the ground astonishingly close, followed by loud thunderclaps, deafening her ears. It was imperative she close up the castle windows or everything within would get drenched and ruined.

She slammed the windows in Brett's room first, fastening the interior shutters. Thankfully with no other guests, the other bedroom windows were already closed. Another lightning bolt flashed, thunder crashed and an enormous wind gust snapped a tree nearby. The wind roared with hurricane force, blowing the patio furniture out of the courtyard over the stone wall, down the hill. Fumbling in the dark, Cherise flipped the light switch on the wall. The storm was affecting the circuitry, the lights flickering with an intermittent faint amber glow. She carefully made her way through the hallway, her intent to close windows in their bedroom. "*Damn, damn, dammit!* Where is he?" she called out in agony. How could Brett leave her here under these circumstances?

A bolt of lightning struck the castle turret lightning rod with such force it sounded as if the entire castle's walls had blown out. Cherise screamed shrilly when the power, including every light, blinked off. Thunder exploded in regular bursts, interspersed with lightning crackling and torrents of rain hammering sideways, the wind tilting and bending the trees. She needed to find a flashlight. Where did she leave one? She crawled on the floor of her bedroom, careful to avoid the low slanted wood beams on the ceiling or the stairway banisters, invisible in the dark. She remembered she had stored a flashlight near the breaker box in the small reception room on the main floor and she fervently hoped it was still there. Shaking, Cherise felt her way, crawling backwards, step by step, down the stairs until she reached the bottom step. Standing, she groped along slowly, placing one hand after the other, along the stone hall wall for support. The dark was absolute. Cherise screamed in terror as her hand touched cold, wet flesh instead of stone.

François grabbed her shoulder and turned her around. She could feel the warmth of his blood, dripping from his head onto her shoulder, and she twisted away from the stench of his foul breath. Panicked, she could not breathe but she wrenched away to free herself. She tried to kick him in the groin but couldn't see his location in the dim light and, instead, slammed her foot into a wooden bench, nearly breaking her toes. He grabbed her around the waist, pushed her to the floor, and roughly dragged her toward him.

"You, my dear are going to have a little accident by the pool." Cherise futilely groped for any item to use as a weapon as he as he dragged her along the slate floor. Kicking at him frantically, she slammed his shin with her free leg and managed to stand, stumbling towards him. Cherise bit down hard on François' arm and he responded with a roar, striking her head brutally. Dazed, Cherise feared for her life. Never in her wildest imaginings did she think François could do this to her—so violent, so intent on murder.

He wrestled her towards the kitchen door, dragging her by one leg while she kicked at him with the other. François tripped over the seat bench, momentarily losing control of her. Cherise crawled crablike, groping for the table, catching the tablecloth, pulling it to the floor, sending dishes and pewter mugs sailing through the air, and crashing to the floor. François scrambled along the slate floor, lunged for her waist, pulled her up, arms flailing and dragged her out the kitchen door to the courtyard into the torrential rain.

"*Stop it!*" Cherise screamed and managed to kick him in the ankle. François stumbled, slipped in the mud but managed to maintain his tight grip, as she struggled to stand. They both went down in the mud. As Cherise got to her knees and started to crawl, he grabbed her ankle, pulling her down again. François bent her left arm painfully behind her back and held his right arm firmly across her throat, while forcing her to take one slate stone step at a time, down to the pool. Cherise gasped for air, crying out with no one to hear her. The wind was howling, and lightning flashing in the distance over the castle. Cherise prayed for a miracle.

François forced her to the outer edge of the deep end of the pool. She shrieked at him above the rage of the storm, "What are you going to do, drown me? Do you think anyone would believe I'd be out here on a night like this swimming in the pool in the pouring rain?"

"No, Cherise," he shouted back. "They will have assumed you slipped and fell earlier in the day, cracking your head against the slate."

"You are a murdering asshole, François. You planned this from the beginning."

"Yes my dear, I had a lot of time to think about it," he bellowed at her.

"Why?" she screamed at him. "Why kill me?"

"For the money! With you dead, this castle is completely mine."

Cherise struggled, twisting in his arms to escape his hold, but she knew her arm would break if she tried to wrench herself free. François shoved her into the pool face down under the frigid water. She held her breath. François jumped in after her, diving down, he grabbed at her ankles, attempting to pull her under. Cherise choked, gulping water, and managed to knee him in the face. Surprised, bellowing in pain, François momentarily released his grasp. Cherise swam, arms flailing and gasping for air, managing to touch the pool's ladder. François lunged forward, grabbed both her legs, and flipped her backwards to the center of the pool. She swallowed enormous gulps of water, choking. François pulled her up against the side of the pool; his hands firmly gripped her head. He prepared to crack her skull against the ragged slate coping that surrounded the edge of the pool. Cherise knew she was going to die.

She cried out hysterically, "François don't do this! I'll give you the damn castle."

He screamed back at her above the roar of the storm, "No my dear, unless you are dead, you can only give me half. I want it all!"

An explosion blasted the air. François slumped forward and Cherise wriggled away from his loosened grip. The second shot struck directly through the back of his head, as did the third. Shocked, Cherise watched François's body plummet into the water, blood seeping around him as he floated away from her. Intermittent lightning flashes revealed the blood-red water. Barely treading water Cherise froze, unable to move as if lightning had struck her.

Cherise turned and saw Brett, gun in his right hand, his left shoulder bandaged. She screamed during the next ragged streak of lightning followed by the boom of thunder. The ghastly sight of François, floating in the pool face down, jolted her to her core. Miraculously she realized she was alive. Horrified and relieved, Cherise could not stop staring at his body now lifeless with blood from the gunshot wounds, eddying around the pool. Cherise weakly gripped the edge of the pool without the strength to swim to the ladder to pull herself out of the water. Kneeling, Brett stretched his hand toward her, wrenching her up and out of the bloody, cold water. His wounded shoulder throbbed in pain. Brett enfolded Cherise with his good arm, supporting her back to the chateau. Inside the hallway it was dark but thankfully dry.

She turned to him in agitation. "What happened to you, Brett?" Cherise glowered. She was equal parts grateful to see him and upset he had left her alone.

"It's a long story."

"I thought you left me here knowing I was in danger. How could you?"

"I would never abandon you, Cherise. I hit a deer on the way to Sarlat in the storm. It crashed through my car window and I lost control. The car tumbled off the embankment and rolled over the rocky cliff until the car wedged between boulders and the trees. I was probably unconscious. For how long, I don't know."

"Oh my God! I'm so sorry, I feel horrible accusing you."

"It's okay. After I pulled the deer's antler out of my shoulder, I crawled out of the car and up the hillside. I sat on the side of the road for what seemed like hours, waiting for anyone to drive by. I knew which way to walk, but was weak from loss of blood. I must have passed out."

"How did you get here?" she asked, dismayed.

"A local farmer finally came along in a pickup truck, with ducks in cages, probably on the way to their death as well. He saw me lying on the side of the road with my shoulder wrapped and realized I was hurt.

He stopped and took me back to his cottage. When I came to, his wife cleaned the wound and bandaged me up. She gave me several shots of Calvados, and offered some hot homemade soup. I was starving but could hardly hold myself up, so she spoon fed me until I just collapsed for the night."

"Don't you need to go to the hospital? Are you all right?"

"It's a puncture wound. My compassionate farmers disinfected, padded and bandaged it. It will heal cleanly. I had a tetanus shot a year ago. Anyway, the next morning when I woke, I told them where I was staying and the farmer drove me back to the castle. They did not understand much English, but he knew Roufillay. When I saw the castle had no electricity and the horses were tied out front, I knew something was terribly wrong. I yelled for you, but you did not answer. I ran up to your room and looked out the window. A flash of lightning lit up the grounds and I could see you both struggling by the pool. I knew he was going to kill you and I had to stop him. I ran to my room to get the gun Pierre had given me."

The combination of shock and hypothermia overwhelmed Cherise. She sobbed uncontrollably, gasping for air. Her skin was clammy and her lips were blue. Entering the kitchen, Brett grabbed the first thing he could find in the dark, wrapping her in the cotton kitchen tablecloth.

Without electricity, power and phone service, Brett asked Cherise about a flashlight. She directed him to the vestibule and he inched his way in the dark by touch, discovering the flashlight in the reception desk drawer. The small beam of filtered light cheered them. Brett guided Cherise, his good arm around her waist, past the entrance lobby, into the living room, where he wrapped her in a plaid throw that he pulled from the back of the sofa. Cherise was still shivering, with fright, exhaustion and cold. Teeth chattering, she told him where to find the matches and he lit two large candles enclosed in glass sconces, and ignited a blaze in the fireplace. The soft amber glow warmed the room, the orange and blue flames greedily gobbled the paper and small pieces of kindling.

"What do I do about François?" she asked Brett, horrified by the day's events.

"We'll call the police in the morning and explain what happened.

They will come to Roufillay and proceed with a full investigation. Inspector Pierre will confirm your story to the police, explaining your visit with him in Bordeaux."

Brett tried his cell phone and found he could access service. He considered calling Pierre but it was very late and the situation had been resolved. With the storm still gusting full force, there was nothing that could be done about François, floating dead in the pool.

Cherise implored him to put the horses in the garage since the barn was too far away. Still tied to the pillar, Dartanian and La Femme were tugging and pawing, quite terrified and agitated in the storm.

"Animals don't like storms any more than people do," she snuffled, unable to deal with any more stress.

Not a horseman, Brett was concerned about controlling them, managing their reins with only one good arm. He asked if he could instead bring the horses into the castle's vaulted stone entrance vestibule. She agreed and helped Brett lead Dartanian and La Femme's inside, tying their reins to the ancient wrought-iron ring door-knocker. Brett held the flashlight, comforting the horses, while Cherise felt along the walls in the dark, toward the direction of the laundry. In darkness, she fumbled for fresh towels on the shelves.

When she returned to Brett and the weak light of the flashlight, Cherise soothed and dried each horse, wiping each down thoroughly using several soft clean towels. She visited the refrigerator and returned with a bunch of carrots. Both horses were calmed, unaware of the intensity of the wind, now muffled by the massive castle walls. The storm had subsided to intermittent gusts of rain, thunder and lightning, finally abating.

"I think they will be okay," she said, relieved.

"I agree, he nodded, "let's sit down before we fall down."

Brett helped Cherise to the sofa, tucking the blanket around her to stay warm. She was subdued and tearful but not hysterical, sounding more like a wounded animal, whimpering in pain and grief. Despite her disgust and fear of her husband François, his death was an emotional blow.

Sitting next to her on the sofa, Brett wrapped his arm around her, pulling the blanket up over both of them. Neither had ever been more exhausted in their lives. They could see the horses from where they huddled on the sofa and the horses were watching them back, ears flicking, nickering contentedly. Brett reflected that horses had been within this castle's walls in earlier centuries and he smiled at the thought.

"Do you mind if I lie down?" Cherise yawned, unable to sit up any longer.

"No, of course not. Let me shift over a bit so you can rest your head on my lap," he offered without any awkwardness.

His head bobbed forward as he fought sleep. Absently, he stroked her damp blonde hair. A feeling greater than compassion stirred in Brett as he looked down at Cherise, finally sleeping peacefully. He wanted to lean over and kiss her but he resisted the impulse.

Cherise woke, startled and wiped her swollen eyes, aware the nightmare she had lived through had not been a dream. Brett had not slept. Rehashing all that had happened to both of them he realized he had been the one who had killed Cherise's husband. It had been necessary, but awful and he felt deeply troubled.

"Brett, I don't know how to thank you. You saved my life."

"I nearly didn't. Another few minutes and he would have drowned you."

They talked until dawn. Cherise shared everything about her life with Andy including the mistakes she had made in her marriage. Brett told Cherise about Vivian and his memories conveyed his cherished love and respect for his beloved wife. Cherise could see the loss of his wife had deeply affected Brett, and yet he was full of compassion.

She talked about what it was like when François first arrived at Roufillay and how giddy and stupid she had been. He assured her that her feelings were normal. At the time, she was recovering from a marriage that ended badly in California, and needed to feel valued and cared for. Brett could not imagine how Andy could have left someone as special as Cherise for anyone else.

Neither Brett nor Cherise had slept much. Faint morning light filtered through the stained glass windows. "Hungry?" he asked, smiling at her, hearing his stomach growl.

"A little," she smiled back at him. "I think I could down something."

He shifted her gently off his lap and fluffed a pillow under her head. In the kitchen, Brett surprised himself that he could prepare breakfast with one hand, selecting bread, cheese and orange juice from the refrigerator. The castle's three-foot thick stone walls maintained a cool environment, insuring produce and juice remained cool and fresh even during a power outage.

After devouring breakfast, Brett asked Cherise if she wanted to take a hot shower, forgetting the electricity was still out. Instead, Cherise borrowed Brett's cell phone and she called her groundskeeper at the local village, explaining the castle's lack of power. She nodded, relieved, hearing affirmation on the other end that help would arrive soon to restore electricity. Cherise handed his phone back to him and Brett called the police in Sarlat, explaining who he was and that a shooting had occurred the night before. Officials indicated they would be on their way to Roufillay immediately. Brett untied the horses, opened the castle door, and watched them gallop to the corral.

Brett looked out the window and was appalled at the horrific mess in the pool. François' corpse, floating face down, drifted from one side of the pool to the other like a buoy in the choppy windblown bloody water. Brett requested Cherise not to look in that direction, in an effort to protect her from the traumatic sight.

Cherise huddled on the sofa, nibbling the bread and sipping juice, not hungry but acknowledging that she needed sustenance. Bluish-purple bruises had emerged on her neck and arms and deep blood-dried scratches crisscrossed her swollen legs and ankles, souvenirs of her struggle. Her elbow was raw and bloodied; the scrapes evidence of her impact with the stone cliff wall during the raging horse ride. Every bone and muscle in Cherise's body ached. She would need to disinfect her wounds and apply bandages but she decided to tend to herself after the police visit.

The chief inspector and three policemen arrived with fanfare—four cars, lights blinking and horns blaring. Brett went outside to meet them.

He introduced the inspector to Cherise and she explained the entire saga, which had all of the gendarmeries shaking their heads, taking copious notes and asking a myriad of endless questions over and over again. Did Brett have a permit to carry a gun? Yes. Was François her boyfriend? No, her husband. How long had they been married? And on and on. Was Brett her lover? No, he was a guest staying at Roufillay at the suggestion of Inspector Pierre Molyneaux. Agonizingly long, confusing questions continued until they finally had the story correct. Satisfied they understood Brett's role in all of this, they needed to investigate the corpse of François Delacroix.

Two policemen cordoned off the crime scene with yellow tape. They removed François's body from the pool, placing it in a black bag to convey to the coroner in Sarlat. Brett submitted Pierre's registered gun, minus three bullets, to the authorities. The chief inspector asked to see the cottage where the concierge resided. Brett and Cherise led them to the small outbuilding. Inside the cottage, Cherise remembered the sight of François making love to Colette that stormy night—and it was painful to look at the kitchen table. Standing in the cottage was eerie. She wondered what Colette would do once she learned François was dead. It was evident their plan had failed. Wrapping her arms around her elbows, Cherise wondered how much more time the investigation would take.

"Mr. Maxfield?"

"Yes, inspector."

"Where is Ms. Armond now?"

"I have no idea," Brett said, trying not to sound flippant.

"I believe she is somewhere in Sarlat," Cherise volunteered. "My husband dismissed her as we were closing for the season and there was no reason to keep her on here as a salaried concierge."

"I see," said the inspector, jotting notes in his small notebook.

"She was part of his plan," Cherise said, convinced. "I'm sure of it. They both planned to kill me."

"Oui, oui, Madame." The inspector nodded, his tight lip and face concealing emotion. "We will check into it." Taking out his cell phone, the inspector sat on the sofa in the cottage and called hotels in Sarlat inquiring if Colette Armond was registered there. She was not. This was suspicious. "There are only a few hotels in Sarlat. If she is staying in the city, we will find her," he said confidently. The inspector pondered. If the two of them were plotting to murder Cherise, why would François send Colette away? And if he had, why would she not be waiting for him? "I think we should check the train stations and flights, as well. Perhaps, she went on a trip?"

"Maybe," Cherise said.

The inspector glanced around the cottage more closely, looking for clues and evidence. Nothing looked disturbed. There were no clothes or suitcase in the armoire, the place where Cherise had indicated the concierge stored her personal effects. The inspector moved systematically throughout the cottage. No toiletries or drugs in the bathroom medicine cabinet. He opened the kitchen cabinets furnished with plates, cups, pots and pans, silverware, but found nothing personal. After checking the bedroom, he returned to the group in the kitchen and sighed. Other than a pile of ashes in the living room fireplace, there was no evidence—not even a hint that the concierge lived in the cottage. "Strange," he thought aloud. "No one is this tidy. If she was planning to return the next season, why wouldn't she have left any belongings in the cottage?"

Flummoxed, he opened the back kitchen door, noticing a dirt path leading to the old unused well. As the inspector stepped onto the threshold, his boot crunched something between the wood and stone floor. He bent over and his fingers plucked up a small ruby necklace lodged between the boards. He called to Brett and Cherise who were talking in the cottage's living room. Cherise approached the inspector, intent upon what he had found. She bent to look closely at the necklace. Hands rose to her face and, shaking her head back and forth, new tears slipped down her cheeks. This was the necklace François had given to her at their wedding. Cherise was revolted to conceive François would have taken the necklace from her jewelry box, heartlessly bribing Colette with her treasured bridal gift. Brett put his hand on Cherise's shoulder and offered his handkerchief, attempting to console her. The inspector looked at Brett with a raised eyebrow.

"Well," Brett considered, "maybe Colette stole it." Cherise asserted, "I don't care. It really doesn't matter anymore."

The inspector stood in the kitchen, pondering. Opening the kitchen door for some outside fresh air, Brett gazed at the vine-covered abandoned well in the distance and noticed a dog barking frantically, pawing at the metal grate on top of the well. Brett stiffened and, whether by instinct or training, headed purposefully toward the well to check on the commotion.

Brett had a bad feeling about the well. The inspector and several other police followed him. Together, Brett and the police officials removed the cover and peered down the well. The violent rains had disturbed the mud and dirt that had covered the body, hidden deep within. Shining a flashlight into the depths, the men could see the murky water revealing a filthy rug, lodged sideways. A small foot, sticking up out of the debris, provided macabre evidence of a dead body. A small tool shed on the property contained some rope which they used to haul the body out.

The corpse was ghastly. It barely resembled Colette. The sunken eyes, the jagged slit across her throat, where the necklace had been under her blouse—even though each man was a seasoned professional, the horrific sight disgusted and sickened each witness to such a gristly murder.

Brett's knees weakened in response to the stench. He knew he had to tell Cherise, and, even though his instinct was to protect her, she needed to know the entire truth. François had never loved her. He was a methodical sociopath without scruples or conscience. It was evident François apparently had an affair with Colette, but something had gone wrong with their plan.

Brett walked reluctantly over to Cherise, who was sitting on the living room sofa in the cottage. Stressed, she was breathing in fitful gasps and didn't look well. Putting his hand gently on her shoulder Brett said, "I wouldn't tell you this if there was anything I could do to prevent causing you any further pain, but I think François killed Colette and threw her into the well."

"Oh, no, no," she moaned. Her face was ashen, feeling as though the blood was draining out of her head, "I don't know how much more of this I can take." She struggled to stand up, legs like rubber and managed to walk to the kitchen door with Brett. Looking out, seeing the body being dredged out of the well, Cherise collapsed, her body limp.

Brett caught her with his right arm before she hit the floor. He let her lie undisturbed until she opened her eyes. Disorientated, she sat up and, still feeling shaky, she remained on the floor, her face pale with shock and exhaustion. Tulare, the caretaker's dog stopped barking at the well. He scampered through the door, tracking muddy paw prints across the floor, anxious to find someone to calm him. Cherise reached out to scratch Tulare behind the ears and he sat by her, content someone was paying attention to him.

Brett looked at her with concern. "Are you all right?" he asked Cherise. "Can I get you some water?"

"No," she thanked him, rubbing her arms as if to bring life back into them. "I'm ok, just feeling overwhelmed. What happened?"

"You fainted but you were only out a few minutes." Brett informed her the police had taken Colette's body to the coroner. Cherise looked at Brett, appreciative of the compassion in his eyes. "Why did this have to happen?" she asked aloud, rhetorically, Brett hoped.

"None of this was your fault, Cherise. It's who he was."

She considered his words, trying to assimilate François' death and Colette's demise, thinking she should feel pain or relief, but she couldn't feel anything. "I just feel numb, angry and miserable," she uttered. "I can't even cry. There are no more tears left." Brett patted her on the back. "I'm sorry you had to be onsite when you learned about Colette's murder. I would have spared you this pain, if I could have."

"Is it your belief François killed her?" she asked, blue eyes pleading in anguish.

"I don't know, but it doesn't look good," Brett muttered.

The inspector and his team loaded Colette's body into a black bag. Before he left, the inspector admonished both to remain available. "I'll be in touch," he coughed from the stench, rolling down the window as he drove off the property.

Brett assisted Cherise back to the castle. Exhausted, she wanted to go upstairs and lie down on her bed. Tulare followed them partway up the path before dashing off to the caretaker's property. Cherise felt sick to her stomach and was aching in every bone and muscle. Brett helped her stagger up the stairs and he carefully supported her back while she stretched out on the bed. Tendrils of blonde hair curled over her arm and glistening lashes surrounded her closed eyes. Cherise looked young and vulnerable and Brett's felt his heart beating. He wanted to take care of her. Before she fell asleep, he asked Cherise if it would be acceptable if he took a look in François's studio at the end of the hall. Cherise murmured to him the location of the keys and, before dropping off to doze, she pointed to the correct key and winced, remembering where it had started…the studio that held the first of many revelations.

Perhaps living a lie would have been easier. Questions crowded her unquiet mind. Did François hate her or was he incapable of love or both? He told her at the end it had always been about the money. How could someone pretend to love so deeply and not really care at all? What kind of human being was he? A monster? How could she have married a cold-blooded murderer yet loved him so much? What was wrong with her lack of insight that she never suspected anything about François' character during their marriage? She sighed deeply. Mentally fatigued, there were no more tears, just numb disbelief and exhaustion.

Suddenly the lights went on in the castle and electronics hummed and phones beeped. Power had been restored. With the afternoon sun streaming into her window, Cherise turned off her bedroom lamp. Cocooned in bed, she finally felt safer than she had in a long time. She fell asleep reassured, knowing Brett was in the castle.

Brett walked rapidly to the end of the hall, banged his head on one of the slanted beams, and cursed. He rotated the keys on the ring until he found the studio key that Cherise had identified. From several rooms away, he heard a phone ring, but it was not his cell phone. He heard Cherise's answer, but her voice was muffled. François' door had to be shoved open—the wood swollen from humidity. François's laptop was on the desk, unplugged from the wall, which was a good thing since it could have been fried by the electrical storm and power outage. Brett looked around the room at the many canvas paintings, and spotted the portrait of Cherise, slashed numerous times across her face and the curve of her back, the painting entirely shredded and destroyed. Appalled, Brett realized evil had resided in this room. He chose not to dwell on the intensity of rage that had motivated François.

He plugged in the laptop, attempting to guess François' password. A blinking blank space said *Enter Password*. He typed F-*r-a-n-c-o-i-s*. Too obvious. He typed in *C-h-e-r-i-s-e* which didn't work. He tried *Colette*, *Diana*, and even *Aubrey* and nothing worked. He typed in *m-o-n-e-y*, and even *m-u-r-d-e-r*, thinking it was clever on his part, but that did not work either. The last word he typed, *I-n-v-i-c-t-a*, lit up the screen, causing a frisson of satisfaction. He was in. Brett stared at the emails in disbelief. What he discovered was overwhelming—emails back and forth between Colette and François—very recent communications between them and emails going back over a year.

He read about the entire plot and the unconscionable promises François had made to Colette and how he had coaxed her into believing she would have a fabulous life of shared wealth at Roufillay. Brett discovered the proof he'd only deduced now seeing François' email to Colette reminding her that a one-year wait after Raleigh's death would be financially lucrative. Brett was disgusted with the volume of email promises François had made to Diana, now in character as Colette. Brett stood up, rubbing his wounded shoulder. François disgusted him. It never failed. Follow the money. Greed was often the motive and excessive greed made people careless. He read on, seeing that Colette had demanded proof that he would fulfill the plan. François had bribed Diana with Cherise's wedding necklace because, in his own words, it was a damned expensive gift.

The emails provided clear evidence François had not only killed Sir Raleigh Aubrey, but this had been premeditated murder, planned by both. He wondered how despicable people lived with themselves, but reminded himself these monsters have no conscience or sense of remorse or guilt. Their sole motivation was greed. Brett removed a blank diskette from a pile, burned a copy of all the emails and inserted it into a plastic case which he put into his pocket.

Brett debated with himself. How much to tell Cherise? He realized he owed her a full explanation of how François had murdered Raleigh and Colette, who was really Diana Aubrey. She had been his willing accomplice. Cherise had been correct. They were both in on the plan to kill her. Brett concluded he could spare her the details of every single email and, instead, provide Cherise a less painful summary. He hoped, after her initial shock, knowing the full truth would help her move on with her life.

CHAPTER 29

When Cherise woke in the morning, Brett was sitting asleep in the chaise in her room, wrapped in a blanket. She got up and gave him a nudge, wanting to talk. She also needed to tell him about the call she had received last night.

"Are you awake, Brett?"

"I am now. What time is it?"

"It's about 10 a.m. We both slept like dead people. Oh God, I am sorry, I said that," she winced, rubbing her eyes.

He smiled at her, realizing she looked very enticing in her nightgown, despite the cuts and bruises on her arms and legs. She raised her eyebrow at him as she slipped on a robe. The robe did not conceal the curves of her body, stirring Brett's imagination.

"What was the call about last night?"

"Oh, Brett," she said shaking her head, "it was my mother-in-law, of all people and especially now. I have not heard from her since the divorce. Karen never liked me very much. She blamed me for focusing on my career more than her son, which was true."

"Why did she call now?" Brett asked, smoothing his disheveled hair, trying to shift his sore shoulder to a more comfortable position.

"Andy had a stroke. She tracked me down through a private investigator here in France, knowing I'd bought a bed and breakfast castle here in the Dordogne. She told me Andy had been flying transatlantic flights and apparently had been experiencing double vision

229

and blinding headaches. Turns out, he has an inoperable brain tumor, and is not expected to live."

"What does she want from you, Cherise?" Brett asked, wincing. His insides tensed, knowing what was coming.

"She asked me to come home. Andy has been asking for me and, fearing he probably won't live much longer, she asked me to do this for him."

"Will you go?"

"I thought about it all this morning. I am not "in love" with Andy, but I still love him in a way. There were many good years in our marriage."

"Yes, I know what you mean," Brett said, his voice cracked. What will you do with Roufillay?"

"I've decided to sell it. I cannot live here any longer. There are just too many awful memories and, despite how much I love France, I could never handle the violent storms here in the Perigord. Running a castle bed and breakfast was a way for me to reinvent myself after a painful divorce. The experience gave me strength to go forward and find a sense of fulfillment and accomplishment. I discovered new skills for the business side of running this castle and I really enjoyed meeting new people. However, I have been humbled, realizing my gullibility. I tend to avoid seeing the bad in people, because I just don't want to acknowledge evidence otherwise. I'd rather focus on the good. And, God knows, I am overly trusting."

"That's not something to be ashamed of, Cherise."

"I know. But whatever I do next, I think it will be on a smaller scale. I need to figure out how to live and take care of myself."

Brett hid his chagrin and disappointment. He so much wanted to tell her he cared for her and he wondered if she felt the same way. The timing was rotten. There was no way he could tell her now. She had obligations and needed to be with her terminally ill ex-husband.

Cherise contacted Prestige Properties, a company specializing in French castle and chateaux real estate. Her plan was to put it on the market immediately, fully furnished. Except for a few lovely personal items, there was nothing she wanted from this place anymore. She quickly made calls and arranged for an agent to list the property. It would probably take months, possibly a year or more, to sell Chateau Roufillay. Once word got out about the murder and the shooting, it might not even sell at all. However, she had enough money saved to pay the castle's expenses for at least a couple of years. Cherise called the local travel agency and booked a flight out of Sarlat, to Bordeaux, and directly to Paris. From Paris she would fly to San Francisco to see Andy.

While Cherise was reviewing arrangements with the real estate listing agent, Brett contacted Pierre and explained the entire story to him. Next, he called Kent Olson, repeating the saga. Both Pierre and Kent were flabbergasted with the details of such a gruesome account. Pierre was gratified he had the opportunity to meet Cherise and connect her with his detective friend, Brett, resulting in a positive outcome. Kent had asked if Brett would be finally coming home.

"Yes, I plan to return to England soon and I'll give you a call as soon as I'm back in London. We'll swig a few pints and toast solving this case."

Brett unenthusiastically drove Cherise to the airport and walked her to the departure gate. People were starting to board. Feeling awkward, not knowing what to do, she gently held him by the shoulders and looked into his eyes, seeing more than just a friend. "Is there anything I could do to repay you? You saved my life."

He said jokingly that he really needed a car now that his rental was a piece of crushed metal rubble on the hillside. Cherise smiled at his quip. She considered giving him her car, but realized he deserved better. She provided him the location of the keys to the *Invicta*, telling him it was his. He laughed and said it was hardly his style of car. Reminding Brett the *Invicta* was very valuable, Cherise encouraged him to accept her gift. Brett decided he could sell the vintage convertible and use the proceeds to select a car that would suit him better. In fact, a long, leisurely drive back to Paris and a short ferryboat journey, transporting the *Invicta* to England, would provide a welcome distraction from murder and... missing Cherise.

Cherise inquired once again if there was anything else she could do to repay him, pleading for some sensible answer.

"Buy me a new pair of slippers," Brett, humorously winked.

She laughed, looking into his melancholy blue eyes and suddenly felt terribly alone.

"You have a funny sense of humor for a Brit."

"It would be if I was British, but I'm from Wisconsin. My wife was the Brit."

"I'm shocked. There's obviously a lot I don't know about you."

"I know everything I need to know about you," he looked deeply into her blue eyes.

They stood, looking at each other, neither knowing what to say. "Last call for flight 4421," the desk attendant announced into the microphone. The back of the plane was already full and her seat was in the middle. Cherise knew she did not have much time left with Brett.

"Goodbye Cherise…I will miss you. I know the emotional journey of going back to see Andy won't be easy but it is something you have to do."

She looked at him, feeling a sudden urge to kiss him, but stopped. Instead, she held him close for a few seconds, putting her head on his chest. Feeling his strong steady heartbeat, Cherise was comforted by his presence and solidity. Wishing she could stay wrapped in his arms, she reluctantly pulled herself away, turning toward the open door to board. With a deep sigh, she tremulously smiled at Brett once more, then dragged her suitcase down the ramp to the plane, shoulders slumped, trying not to cry.

Brett watched her board at the entrance of the plane and she briefly turned and waved goodbye. Just like that, she was gone.

CHAPTER 30

San Francisco, California

It seemed strange to be back in California. Nothing much had changed, but instead of feeling at home, Cherise felt like a visitor. Two Ambien, chased with a glass of white wine, she'd slept most of the flight. When she woke, still in flight, she attempted reading magazines but was unable to concentrate. Cherise did not want to think about what had happened in France nor did she look forward to what was bound to be a difficult visit with her ex-husband. She thought it odd she was at a point in her life where neither the past nor the present was a desirable emotional landing place. Each contained regret and pain. Unable to imagine the future, she could think only about the present. Someone she once loved was dying.

Cherise went straight to Mills Peninsula Hospital, dreading her first encounter with Andy since she'd stormed out of his apartment. She asked the nurse at the floor desk the location of his room, and walked hesitantly down the long corridor of polished linoleum floors and pale green walls, searching for number 202. Apprehensive, she wondered what she would say to Andy and how she would feel.

Passing dismal rooms of sick patients, hooked up to wires and tubes, staring at televisions or staring into space, the song *Mad World* repeated in her mind. Elderly patients, feeble, with wrinkled spotted skin translucently pale, lay immobile—death seemingly imminent. Hospitals were such awful, depressing places. The smell of the antiseptic made Cherise gag. Where was room 202, anyway? She located a directory on the wall indicating a range of room numbers could be reached through the double doors in front of her. Squaring her shoulders, she increased the pace of her stride.

Andy's room in the hospice wing had a small window, facing north. Standing by the window, the patient or visitor could see the San Francisco Bay. Cherise gingerly tiptoed around the white curtain surrounding his bed and seeing him, put her hand over her mouth, stifling her gasp. She barely recognized her ex-husband. Andy's head had been shaved and was wrapped in large, white bandages. Tubes were in both arms attached to drip bags and another tube was attached to the nib of his nose permitting oxygen to flow into his lungs to help him breathe. A nurse came in and said hello and adjusted his morphine so he would not be in pain. Cherise sat down in the chair, waiting for him to open his eyes. Andy was sleeping peacefully, but he was so terribly thin and frail. She could see, watching the laborious rise and fall of his chest that it was hard for him to breathe. Pity and love overwhelmed her. Cherise put her hand in his and was surprised by her unexpected tears. With gratitude and sorrow, she recalled the good times they had shared together.

She remembered a special Christmas, skiing at Squaw Valley near Lake Tahoe. Cherise reminisced about their wedding and honeymoon in Hawaii...how rumpled he'd looked in the morning, standing at the bathroom sink, unshaven, hair fluffy, happily brushing his teeth. These memories were gems she'd kept tucked away in a treasure box in her mind, too painful to recall during the divorce, they now made her smile. Andy slowly opened his eyes and blinked at Cherise, sitting next him, holding his hand. He shifted in bed and tried to speak, but his words were weak and inaudible. She shushed him not to talk if it hurt. It was troubling to Cherise to comprehend his pain, to see his life ending so pitifully.

In a raspy voice, Andy whispered, "Thanks for coming. I...uh... am so very sorry for leaving you. I was selfish and confused, but I never stopped loving you." Tears glistened in his eyes, difficult for Cherise to bear. Squeezing his hand tightly, she said softly, "It's okay, Andy. I forgave you a long time ago. Just rest now. Don't try to talk. Everything is all right." His chest rose and fell, in a deep sigh. Watching him suffer, she spared him the details of her life during the past year. He drifted in and out of consciousness while she sat patiently with him. When she finally left the hospital, she felt as if the air had been sucked out of her body.

Throughout the following week, Cherise visited Andy often. He became weaker, and finally, completely unable to speak. The tumor affected his vision and his speech. She asked the doctor how much time remained and the doctor said it would not be long—maybe a few days. Andy died the following Sunday, his mother, Karen Eden, at his side.

Karen was grateful Cherise had returned to San Francisco to spend time with Andy. Reconciling their past differences, Cherise helped Karen organize the funeral. Cherise was surprised by the number of friends Andy had made over his years as a commercial pilot. Talking with Andy's friends and family, Cherise mentioned only that she lived in France and ran a small business. She didn't want to elaborate about her life in the Dordogne and everything she had gone through. She was grateful that Andy's friends didn't pry or push for details.

After the funeral, Cherise helped Karen settle Andy's estate and during the process with the attorneys, Cherise was dumbfounded to learn Andy had left his assets to her. Perhaps it was guilt and a last act of contrition, or perhaps it was because he had always loved her, and wanted to prove that divorcing her was the mistake of his life. It did not matter now. His condo needed to be sold, and he had close to one hundred thousand dollars in savings.

Recognizing Karen, Andy's mother, was not well off, in a gesture of good will, Cherise split her inheritance. Karen was quite pleased to accept the windfall, especially as her husband had not left her with much when he died. At one point during their many meetings, Karen glanced, at Cherise, discomfited. "I'm so sorry about how I treated you. It wasn't right of me. I should not have acted so rudely toward you during your marriage to Andy." Karen sighed, folding her hands in her lap like a child about to be punished, "I never even bothered to contact you after the divorce."

Cherise stopped her, putting her fingers to Karen's lips, "What's past is past and forgiven." Karen reached out her hand, and Cherise took it in hers, looking into the eyes of a woman filled with years of guilt and sorrow. They hugged each other and promised to stay in touch.

Cherise remained in Andy's condo until it was sold, taking only three weeks. Furnished South of Market Street properties were hot San Francisco real estate and it was easy to find eager buyers who would benefit from the quick commute to the financial district. Cherise arranged for Andy's clothes to be donated to charity. She packed his books, CD's and belongings and had them delivered to Karen. She wrapped one silver framed photo of the two of them smiling on a bench on the shores of Lake Tahoe and held it briefly next to her heart. She decided to keep the frame and put the picture into a scrapbook.

Cherise rented a room at the Residence Inn where she could have a kitchenette and cook for herself. It was fully furnished and seemed to be the sensible thing to do since she did not have the slightest idea where she wanted to live. She did not need money, and she certainly did not feel like working. The idea of going back to a high-tech job seemed pointless and ridiculous.

Even so, she searched Internet job websites and pored through the papers looking for jobs with the title of *Marketing Director* or other executive marketing positions. She reluctantly prepared a résumé, thankful she had resigned her last position, easy to explain with a conglomerate merger. She sent her résumé to prospective companies, hoping not to get a reply.

The idea of sitting at a desk, working to promote a new product line, seemed bizarre to Cherise, especially after running a bed and breakfast chateau. No more freshly baked, melt-in-the-mouth croissants with a steaming café au lait. No more mornings, waking to the sight of dew settling on the sweet-smelling grass with just enough sunlight to glisten like scattered diamonds. No more conversations with interesting people from different cultures, discussing their vacation plans. No more duvets stuffed with thick Hungarian down feathers. Cherise shook her head at these pleasant memories and, taking a deep breath, remembered also there would be no more crashing thunder, bolts of lightning and no more dead bodies either.

Cherise received a call on a Tuesday, asking her to interview for a marketing position with a privately held bio-tech company. She had nothing better to do, so she decided to test the waters. Maybe she should work. She needed to be busy. Work would be therapeutic. Work would keep her from wandering around aimlessly, surprisingly missing Brett. Why was she missing Brett? What was that all about? She dared not think about it. Brett had saved her life and had gone home to his sane world in the Cotswolds.

Cherise drove to Palo Alto, California located on the mid-peninsula of the San Francisco Bay Area, for an initial interview with the human resources vice president, who was recruiting for the marketing position. She greeted the woman, coiffed in a trendy short hair, wearing stylish glasses and casual clothes. The V.P. had to be half her age and suddenly Cherise felt much older than her years. She tried to be enthusiastic, explaining the duties and responsibilities of her previous job, answering the questions about the absent year on her résumé. Mentioning she had purchased a castle in France as a bed and breakfast business caused sighs of overt jealousy. *"Oh wow! That must have been so incredible,"* was the reaction from the interview team. She chose not to share during the interview anything of the horror she had experienced at Roufillay.

Throughout the interview, Cherise withheld answers to specific questions, giving as her reason to return to the States, that she felt she did not really fit in to the French lifestyle. A lie of course, but it was necessary to provide a plausible explanation for her return to San Francisco. She stated convincingly she'd missed the excitement of working in a high tech environment.

Questions made her uneasy. Inwardly cringing at the evasion, she recognized the importance of brief, uncomplicated answers.

Cherise apparently passed the initial interview. The interview team indicated she would receive a call within two weeks and that there were other candidates for the position.

She recognized this was a good company. It was a small startup with substantial seed money, strong investors, representing cutting-edge bio-technology. Travel would not be required and she would report directly to the Chief Executive Officer. Her job would require expansion of the marketing department with a mission to create a new market for the company's innovative technology. Cherise was confident she could succeed, but, digging deep down she acknowledged to herself she didn't feel enthusiastic. The recruitment department called her a few days later with news that she had been selected to meet and interview with Barton Rexford, the CEO.

Cherise shopped at Neiman Marcus and purchased a navy business suit, a tailored white blouse, a pair of professional pumps and a leather briefcase bag, hoping to make a positive impression. She persuaded herself it might be fun to work in the business world again, even if her staff would be thirty-something whiz kids competing for her job.

Walking down University Avenue near the Stanford campus, she grabbed a pastry and a black coffee from *Il Fornio*. Comparing the crusty croissants and steaming café au lait she'd enjoyed in France, breakfast on the run in the States was a disappointment. Cherise sat on a sidewalk bench and pored over the prospectus and Internet information about the company that she had researched in advance of her upcoming final interview. Memorizing the key points about the company, Cherise honed her presentation. Nonchalant about the final outcome, she considered the final interview as a challenge, a game with the prospective job offer as the 'win."

Edgy, Cherise sat in the reception area, smiling at the people buzzing around self-importantly. They were so young and energetic, laughing and bustling through the lobby. A young and, as yet, modestly financially endowed company in the start-up stage, the building's lobby was not impressive. Standard chrome chairs with generic grey and black print fabric. A fake orchid sat on the coffee table, surrounded with magazines appealing to Millennials. The receptionist informed Cherise Mr. Rexford would be with her momentarily.

Expecting a seasoned professional, instead she was greeted by a young man with gel-spiked hair wearing jeans and a navy blue t-shirt, Birkenstocks without socks, his footwear of choice. Cherise felt foolish in her suit. The young man ushered her into his corner-windowed office furnished with a black leather sofa, a round glass table and four club chairs, file cabinets, a glass desk with several computer screens, dangling cords dripping over the frayed beige Berber carpet.

Distracted in conversation on his cell phone, Barton extended his hand, holding up an index finger, motioning to her to sit. Affronted, Cherise sat and crossed her legs tightly waiting for Mr. Rexford to look up at her. While Barton Rexford continued his phone conversation, Cherise looked out the window. There was nothing interesting to look at either outside or in the office. No artwork, no personal photos, indicative perhaps that he had no family or time for one, or maybe he was divorced or gay. Cherise fidgeted with her hair, curling it around her finger.

His phone conversation finally concluded, Rexford rapidly scanned her résumé dragging a pencil across areas of interest. It was clear he'd not read it before the interview. Once again, Cherise found herself in interview mode, describing her employment experience and skills. "What are your major achievements and perceived shortcomings?" She hated that question. Didn't everyone lie about what they did not do well? Why would anyone want to talk about weaknesses?

Cherise dredged up her old standby answer. Her 'weakness' was working too many long hours, a statement of commitment which always satisfied interviewers. He continued to drone on, "Where did you go to college?" "Why did you take a year off?" "What can you do to give us a competitive brand-marketing edge in the industry?"

Answering the questions mechanically, Cherise felt throughout the interview as though she was having an out-of-body experience. She could hear herself talking, but it was as if she were on remote control, observing the interview like a fly on the wall watching herself. The words were not coming from her heart, but from her head and out of her mouth like a robot. The interview continued for nearly a half hour. More than once, Barton noticed Cherise was staring out the window distractedly as he described new products and the competition. Finally, he startled her back to awareness, "Look, Ms. Delacroix, do you really want this job? You don't seem to be all that interested."

Embarrassed, but relieved, Cherise picked up her briefcase and said without hesitation, "No, Mr. Rexford, I really don't want this job."

Glowering at her, he frowned that she had wasted his time. His cell rang and he turned his back to her, waving her off like an insect crawling on his desk. Cherise unobtrusively left the building complaining silently to herself that Barton was an annoying, arrogant twit.

Cherise drove back to her room at the Residence Inn, kicked off her new, too-tight shoes and collapsed on the bed in her business suit resolute, knowing the new clothes, shoes and briefcase would be donated to a girlfriend or worthy charity. She tossed the company prospectus into the trash. Reheating the day-old pizza in the microwave, she ate and watched mindless television, propped up in bed. Bored with trivial 'reality' shows, she shut it off, removed her clothing and crawled into bed. She could hear cars entering and leaving the hotel parking lot and people chattering on the way to their rooms, making sleep difficult.

Lying awake in bed, she ruminated all that had happened in her life which now seemed like several lifetimes. So many thoughts of her marriage to Andy, the divorce and his recent death were hard to deal with, but she was at peace knowing at the end, Andy did love her. She faced the last tumultuous year in the Dordogne, including François' painful deception. He had so masterfully convinced her to fall in love with him. She winced. That was something for which peace and forgiveness would never come.

Cherise realized that despite, or even as a result of, the pain and deception, she had gained new strength. She had lost two men in two years—one who loved her but not enough to stay with her and one who claimed to love her, but who did not love her at all. Her thoughts flittered to Brett Maxfield. She closed her eyes, remembering Brett's arms around her on the sofa at Roufillay and the look in his eyes when he had said goodbye at the airport.

Suddenly, Cherise knew exactly what she was going to do. But first she needed to call Cindy. She could trust her friend and it was time to tell her about François. Although it would be difficult to acknowledge to Cindy that she had been correct about him, the full story of François' scheme to murder her would be a devastating revelation. Cherise needed to unburden herself by discussing the pain of Andy's death and her plans for the future. Her dear friend Cindy friend would provide solace and perspective.

CHAPTER 31

Chippenham, England

Brett had settled into his former routine of taking long walks on sunny days and cultivating his garden in anticipation of the snowdrops and foxgloves that would bloom in the spring. The library provided a retreat where he could browse the classics, but his taste ran more often to cloak-and-dagger suspense, and he often selected a good spy novel to bring home. He had dragged his heels about returning the obelisk to Brightingham.

Brett finally mustered up his courage to return to Brightingham. Mr. Weatherly opened the door, inviting him inside. Brett explained the reason he had borrowed it without permission and the results of his investigation. He had been concerned, when the Mr. and Mrs. Weatherly learned that Sir Raleigh Aubrey had been murdered in their home, they might not want to continue to live at Brightingham. Brett's conscience asserted that he owed them the truth.

Mr. and Mrs. Weatherly were dismayed, expectedly. Fortunately, after their initial shock and distress, Mrs. Weatherly determined any ghosts of Raleigh's past were now at peace. Grateful for their good sense and composure, Brett departed and promised to stay in touch... something he resolved he would do.

Returning to the Cotswolds, and the comforts of his home in Chippenham, Brett felt re-energized. He made a plan, starting with catching up on news—many magazines and newspapers had piled up unread for a year. If it weren't for the television, he wondered if he would be connected to the rest of the world. When he felt restless, he would drive out of Chippenham in his beloved MG. Having sold the *Invicta* for a handsome price, he made some repairs on the twiggy thatched roof on the house, and invested the rest in several emerging stocks.

Brett enjoyed visiting the quaint English villages like Bibury or Stratford-upon-Avon, indulging in an amble around Shakespeare's birthplace and the satisfaction of sitting in a pub, savoring a cool stout. Enjoyable as these were, Brett could not forget about Cherise—how she would twist a strand of her long honey-colored hair as she talked; how her eyes had sparkled with fondness as she groomed her beloved horses. Brett could not get her out of his mind. In his cottage, confined by a daily routine, he realized how much he missed Cherise. He considered calling her, but he did not have her contact information. It was arrogant to think she would be interested in him, he told himself.

Needing a diversion one sunny day, he opted to walk to town. He strolled along, reflecting he was quite pleased he had sold the *Invicta* for a very handsome price. The *Invicta's* infamous "Black Prince" image remained horridly sinister and it conjured up images of François sitting in that car. There was no way Brett was going keep the *Invicta* in his driveway. Watching the new owner drive the car away, it gave him as much satisfaction as dumping the garbage in the waste bin. Brett's car, a green MG with tan convertible top, seemed happy in his garage. It was an older model, but it fit his personality—comfortable, dependable, and familiar, with just a hint of adventurous spirit.

Wandering the charming cobbled streets of Chippenham, he stopped for a hot chocolate and a raspberry pastry, fresh out of the oven, at the local pastry shop. Brett relaxed on a bench outside at the café courtyard, appreciating the beauty of the countryside and the familiar faces of townsfolk he recognized. Barnacle geese waddled in the courtyard next to the church, their black and white heads bobbing for insects in the grass. Sounds of children laughing and kicking a rugby ball filled the air. Chippenham was a lovely and vibrant town. Brett was relatively content yet something was missing.

Without Cherise, Brett felt empty...a different kind of emptiness than when he'd lost his wife Vivian, but now a hollowness inside that he wished he could fill. He knew Cherise had felt gratitude he'd saved her life, but there was no reason to assume she would be interested in a relationship leading to love. They had met under extraordinary circumstances. Had he not been in Bordeaux at precisely the same time she had arrived to plead for assistance from Pierre, their paths would never have crossed. He sighed as he sipped his hot chocolate, wishing for the thousandth time she was here. He also wondered how Cherise was coping with Andy's terminal illness. What a terrible year for her, filled with unspeakable suffering.

Waving at a neighbor, he managed, "Hi, how are you doing?" The neighbor tilted his cap, in pleased acknowledgment. "Nice to see you back," the man said. "It's good to be back," Brett commented, listening to his words and then thought it wasn't *good* at all.

The clouds rolled quickly by and Brett watched them form different patterns and shapes. The air had turned chilly and he wished he'd brought a wool scarf for his neck. Pulling up his jacket collar, he stretched his legs out in front of him. He fondly remembered holding Cherise on the sofa the night he'd shot François, how awful that night must have been for her. François had been her husband and although she had made a very bad choice, Brett did not fault her gullibility. How could she have realized someone so handsome and charming could be so deceptive and such a diabolically cold-hearted killer? If the horrific vision of François floating lifelessly in the chateau swimming pool was not enough to quell all emotional possibility of a new future with her, the impending death of her first husband, Andy, would only add to her heavy burden of grief.

Brett empathized with Cherise's emotionally distressing experiences. He remembered the hollow finality of his wife's coffin being lowered into the ground at the cemetery. Loving Vivian as he had, he felt a sympathetic pain for Cherise. She had experienced the anguish of a failed marriage as well as marriage to a murderous sociopath. Two devastating events…how could she move beyond that amount of trauma? Brett wondered.

How long would she need to feel whole again, to be able to trust and love? And what could he offer her? Brett's life was simple. Some might even say dull. Brett headed home, dejected, ruminating over the losses in his life. He munched his pastry as he walked the narrow streets, careful to avoid oncoming cars and couples on bicycles. Brett concluded that, although his home was comfortable, it was an absolute mess. What woman would want to be with a guy who forgot to shave, strewed his clothes all over the floor, who stacked piles of papers and magazines everywhere in every corner, and had not dusted in a year? Shrugging his shoulders, Brett shook his head in disgust.

Taking a shortcut through the park, he remembered the soft smile on Cherise's face, as she'd slept in his lap the night they stayed awake, talking until dawn. He wanted her then and he wanted her now, but decidedly, he acknowledged, she deserved better. Brett yearned for Cherise, recalling the image of the soft cotton nightgown clinging to her sinuous body, illuminated by candlelight. He ached with longing, as he wearily trudged home.

Darkening grey clouds rolled across the sky. Brett increased his pace, hurrying to reach his cottage. He arrived just as the clouds burst.

CHAPTER 32

London, England, en route to Chippenham

Cherise arrived at Heathrow feeling ebullient and optimistic. During the red-eye flight, she'd slept well on the plane, enjoying the movies and the novel she had removed from her carry-on. The weather was pleasantly cool but sunny, filling the sky with high stratus clouds. She styled her long hair into a ponytail with wispy bangs, and was pleased she had chosen a pale yellow turtle neck, comfortable jeans and flats. She refreshed herself in the restroom, applying minimal makeup with just a touch of blush and a peach lip tint. She was set for the journey and was thankful she did not look like she had lived through a year from hell.

Renting a modest car, Cherise asked for directions to Chippenham. But first, she had to make a special stop. She had perused the newspapers, made calls and found exactly what she had been looking for. She paid 100 pounds, stowing the crate into the car. Cherise enjoyed her drive through the Cotswolds and on to Chippenham, with its thatched roofs, half-timbered and stone houses. She was surprised Chippenham was a dynamic market town, located between Bath and Swindon on the River Avon. Only a few kilometers south of the M4 motorway, Chippenham had easy access to London.

Charmed with the quaint towns and pastoral landscape, Cherise arrived at her destination fiddling with a pencil in her mouth, searching for a certain address. Finding it, she drove up the winding narrow street, lined with hand-laid cobblestones edged with lavender, periwinkle and gardenias. Wooly sheep meandering along the roadside interrupted her journey but Cherise was amused and enchanted.

Excited and nervous, Cherise did not know exactly what he would do when he saw her. What if he didn't want her? If Brett's response to her sudden appearance was lukewarm or disinterested, then she would treat the visit as only that—a visit to a friend who had saved her life.

After her life-changing experiences, Cherise discovered she felt the need and solace of prayer. Having invoked divine assistance in Cathédrale Saint-André in Bordeaux, she believed Brett had been the answer to her prayer at that time...and now.

As she turned up his street, her heart fluttered, spotting him. He was digging in the garden in front of his house. Brett was wearing a green plaid flannel shirt, tan slacks, and rubber gardening boots standing knee-deep in dirt, intently planting bedding annuals. Cherise parked the car at the end of his driveway. Smiling, she cradled the brown, white and black basset hound puppy, lifting him gently out of the boxed crate. The dog was difficult to hold, squirming and wiggling as he licked her face enthusiastically.

Brett raised his head and stared incredulously. He walked...then ran...and she ran to him, nearly dropping the puppy. Brett laughed aloud and seized Cherise, kissing her hesitantly, questioningly. Whole-heartedly, Cherise kissed him back, laughing while the puppy licked his face, then hers.... then they kissed each other again.

"What in the world?" he asked, shaking the dirt off his clothes.

"I just could not stay away."

"I missed you terribly." He held her tightly, squeezing the puppy between them.

"I missed you too, Brett."

"I didn't think you cared," staring at her in disbelief.

"I do. I did, but so much was happening. I needed to sort out my feelings."

With the puppy between them, Brett looked down, laughing. "And who is this?"

"Well, this is either Baskerville or Villy the second. You can choose the right name for him."

"I see!" he smiled. Cherise passed him the energetic puppy with its absurdly long floppy ears and huge paws he would grow into. Brett carefully set him on the sidewalk and the puppy immediately made himself at home, peeing on the freshly dug flowerbed. They both laughed.

"And I brought you something else." Cherise ran back to the car and pulled out a long, gift-wrapped box with dark green paper and a gold bow.

He looked at her inquiringly, one eyebrow slightly raised, tore off the paper and opened the box to discover a pair of new, fine calfskin leather slippers.

"You remembered!"

"Yes, I did. It was the least I could do. It was the one thing you said you needed."

"Well, I lied. I needed you." Leaning over, his arms wrapped around her in a crushing embrace, Brett passionately kissed Cherise and she held him tight. When they finally pulled apart, Brett led her up the cobblestone walkway, past the garden to the front door of his half-timbered, thatched roof cottage.

Before entering his home, Brett turned to her and, caressing the side of her face, asked without hesitation, "Cherise, would you marry me now, today, tomorrow? I fell in love with you that terrible night when we were huddled in the dark on the sofa in Roufillay. I didn't want to say goodbye to you at the airport. The timing was wrong, but I should have told you I loved you then."

"I know, Brett. I think that's when I fell in love with you, too."

He opened the door of his charming cottage and she was smitten immediately with the fairy tale diamond shaped leaded windows, despite the dust motes floating between the window frame and the rough-hewn beamed ceiling. It was lovely, but oh what a mess. The unkempt interior did not worry her. She had a lifetime to clean it up.

"Would you like some English tea?" he asked.

"Oh, I'd love some. It was a long drive, but so delightful."

Brett bustled into the kitchen to prepare tea and Cherise relaxed on his green sofa, playing with the puppy. She called to Brett in the kitchen, "Let's call him Baskerville. I love that name."

"Sounds good to me," he yelled back, as he poured hot water over the tea strainer filled with Earl Grey tea leaves. He bore the tray into the living room arranged with a steaming pot and china teacup, and he'd included two warm scones and a cold beer for himself. Baskerville turned over and stretched out on the wood floor.

"It's chilly in here," he said solicitously. "Mind if I start a fire going?"

"Not at all," she smiled at him, while curling her toes under her legs on the sofa.

They talked about the funeral and Brett was relieved to hear that Cherise had reconciled with her past. Cherise was pleased to share that, as a result of Andy's death, the rift between her former mother-in-law and herself had healed. Cherise explained to Brett how comforting it was that, in the end, they had become friends.

He inquired if Roufillay had been purchased yet. It had not. They both agreed that, at some point in the future, it would certainly sell. Its beauty and its new-found morbid reputation would appeal to two kinds of buyers. As many people wanted to buy castles in France with a tabloid history as were prospective purchasers who would cherish a residence with historic value. Cherise looked forward to the time when they could travel the world together with the proceeds from the sale.

"You know, he said, "when I was with Scotland Yard, I did not travel much beyond England. Business was too pressing, too full of long hours and hectic weekends. Vivian and I rarely had a chance to travel outside Chippenham, except for occasional brief excursions to and from London. There were so many places I longed to see, especially Ireland. Vivian had talked about the Baltic countries and visiting Russia. There were many things we'd wanted to do together but she just didn't get the chance. We weren't given time," he said, eyes downcast, momentarily saddened.

As Cherise listened, shared and laughed with him, she felt more secure than she had during the last ten years of her life. Here was a man who truly and thoroughly loved her, faults and all. No questions. No analysis. No trying to change her habits and behaviors. And she did not want to change anything about him. Certain Brett would bring out the best in her, she was wholly content to be by his side. The peace and simplicity of his life, was exactly what Cherise craved.

"Do you think you can adjust to the slower pace of life here," he asked anxiously, watching her face.

"Are you kidding? After all I've been through? Of course I will enjoy living here" she chuckled while adding another lump of sugar to her tea. "I'm good with words. Maybe I might try writing a novel. I've certainly lived the life that would fit a romantic thriller gone bad—unbelievable, yet real! It could be a best seller," she chuckled and smiled, flicking her ponytail off her shoulder.

"I think you should try writing," he said. "You've got a great audience with me and I'd love to read anything you write. Would you like some more tea?" he asked, grinning happily.

"Yes, a refill would be nice. It's helping me keep warm."

"You can grab a sweater from the closet," he said, heading back to the kitchen.

Cherise sighed contentedly. She knew Brett would never leave or harm her. He was so easy to be with, whether engaged in conversation or sitting quietly together, sharing contented moments. His finances were not important. Although they had not yet slept together, Cherise felt the deep, unspoken connection. She knew that, when she gave herself to him fully, it would be from the depth of her soul, as it would be with him.

Glancing around the room, she discovered a warm woolen blanket folded on a shelf…just what she needed. Cozy and content, she curled up on the sofa with her feet under her, observing a chaffinch sporting a blue-grey crown and orange-colored breast, perched outside on the windowsill, pecking at the window glass.

Brett returned from the kitchen with his favorite beer and more tea for her.

"Oh, by the way, where's the bathroom?" she asked. "I can't drink another drop without a potty stop."

"We don't have one," he said, straight-faced.

"What! Oh, you're not serious, are you?"

"No," he said laughing. "It's down the hall."

"Don't think for a minute," She said, "I'm marrying someone without a bathroom," giggling as she headed down the hall.

When Cherise returned, Brett set the platter down on the coffee table and snuggled next to her on the sofa, arm draped around her shoulder. The puppy was already nosing around the slipper box. They both started laughing and Brett got up, retrieved the new slippers and put them on the leather ottoman, out of the dog's reach. Cherise chuckled, "I expect these slippers to last you at least a week."

"Good luck with that," Brett snickered, knowing it was only a matter of time before he'd have a chewed hole to poke his toe through. He plunked back down onto the sofa, watching Cherise nibble her scone, thinking her the most beautiful woman he had ever seen. Brett felt overwhelmed by the unexpected gift of this lovely woman to share his life. A future to savor, overflowing with moments to anticipate and discover together.

"So, pretty lady, after the wedding, where would you like to go to honeymoon?"

"Oh, so you do want to marry me?" she teased.

"Yes." Brett continued earnestly, "You are the second woman I have ever loved. I commit to you, right now in my home and in my arms that I will love, honor and protect you for the rest of your life."

Realizing the depth of his feeling, Cherise assured, "Perhaps that's more than I deserve, but of course I will marry you."

Brett embraced her tightly and then drew back, taking both of her hands in his, he smiled at her. "So I'm asking again, where would you like to go on a honeymoon?"

"Well, I will have to think about it, but certainly not back to California and anywhere but the Dordogne!" He rolled his eyes in agreement.

"How about Ireland?"

"That could be a possibility," she smiled. "I was thinking about your friend Raleigh and, as awful as it is to think about what happened to him, if you had not investigated his death, we never would have met."

"Isn't it incredible how Pierre happened to call me and I ended up going to Bordeaux? I think we were meant to find each other," he mused, draping his arm tightly around her shoulder.

"I've never seen the Lake District. Would it be okay if you took me on a honeymoon there?" she asked hopefully. She brushed his tousled hair to the side of his forehead. "I've read about Cumbria. Beatrix Potter lived there—I think she purchased Troutbeck Farm. I've always wanted to visit the author's home," she said excitedly.

"Okay," he agreed with a grin. "Cumbria it is. You know, however, they have black sheep. Everyone there has a black sheep in the family. Should we get one?"

"Oh, very funny," she said, poking him playfully. Brett considered. "The more I think about your idea, I really like it. It would honor my friend Raleigh. He would have liked that. There are some lovely towns, like Ambleside. Idyllic, peaceful and very picturesque. Nothing exciting ever happens there."

"'Nothing exciting' is exactly what I'm hoping for. Except in love," Cherise kissed him ardently. Brett returned her kisses with passion long repressed. Neither noticed Baskerville had managed to pull one slipper off the ottoman, trotting purposefully from the room, tail wagging.

THE END

A new Romantic Suspense writer breaks through with insightful writing about love and loss. A well-crafted plot with characters that remain in your head long after the last page is finished. Plan to stay up all night reading...

Cindy Sample, *Author of Dying for a Date* and *Dying for a Dance*, a 2012 LEFTY AWARD Finalist

With her eye for detail and description of interiors and European landscapes, Sherry Joyce transports the reader from San Francisco to a bed and breakfast castle in the South of France. The plot twists and turns along its turbulent journey of romance, mystery and nail-biting suspense. **The Dordogne Deception** *would make a great movie!*

Lisa Dane, Film Producer, Senior Vice President, Dane & Associates

The Dordogne Deception *is an entertaining mix of passion and deceit among characters rife with self-absorbed motives that take us on a journey through murder and mayhem before landing us squarely among the stoic and strong. Cleverly plotted amid richly depicted scenery, Sherry Joyce makes us feel as if there, in the castle sipping tea and eating croissants while reading about romance and recompense.*

Kathryn Mattingly, author of the literary suspense novel *Benjamin* with Winter Goose Publishing